# THE MUSIC MAKERS

## and other Jewish stories

To Andrea,
Best wishes,
Mark

Mark Harris

# THE MUSIC MAKERS

and other Jewish stories

Matador
9 Priory Business Park,
Wistow Road
Kibworth Beauchamp
Leicester LE8 0RX, UK
Tel: (+44) 116 279 2299 / 2277
Email: books@troubador.co.uk
Web: www.troubador.co.uk/matador

Apart from historical figures, all the characters, including the narrators, participating or
mentioned, named or anonymous, in these stories are entirely fictitious; and any resemblance
they may bear to any person, living or deceased, is purely coincidental and unintentional.

ISBN 978 1780884 059

British Library Cataloguing in Publication Data.
A catalogue record for this book is available from the British Library.

Typeset in 11pt Bembo by Troubador Publishing Ltd, Leicester, UK

**Matador** is an imprint of Troubador Publishing Ltd

Printed and bound in the UK by TJ International, Padstow, Cornwall

*"Imagination is the beginning of creation. You will imagine what you desire, you will what you imagine and at last you create what you will."*

George Bernard Shaw

*"Logic will get you from A to Z; imagination will get you everywhere."*

*"Imagination is more important than knowledge. For knowledge is limited to all we know and understand, while imagination embraces the entire world, and all there ever will be to know and understand. Imagination encircles the world."*

Albert Einstein

*In memory of my parents*

# Contents

# Foreword

When I was a little boy in the late 1940s, I thought that our wireless (or radio, as the apparatus has now long been known) was the family's most treasured physical possession. I could have been seriously wrong about that, though somehow I do not think so.

We lived in a cramped, two-room flat with a tiny scullery and a miniscule lavatory (bathing meant, of necessity, a trip to the nearby public bath house) in a dank and decaying Victorian era tenement close to Petticoat Lane in London's East End. I suppose we were quite poor really; but, of course, my tender age and an all-pervading narrowness of perspective, ensuring a lack of comparison, dictated an almost complete and happy ignorance of that condition. In any event, I came to live more comfortably inside rather than outside my head.

I do believe that my mother had a diamond engagement ring,

which doubtless had some value, aside naturally from the sentimental aspect. But the concept of worth in the sense of monetary terms held little meaning for me. And it was not an occasional peek at the small sparkly jewel which captured my childhood imagination. That was down to the old arched wooden wireless, with its dully glowing yellowish dial. The, at least to me, quite magical contrivance stood prominently on top of a quaint but incongruous, black-lacquered and curvy-legged Chinese cabinet in a corner of the compact living room.

It may have been the darkest corner of the dimly lit room but it was a puzzling and mysterious yet, at the same time, an amazing if not startling focus for me … like a gun must have been to a Native American when the Spaniards first swashed, or swash-buckled, ashore onto their ancestral lands. Astoundingly, to my embryonic mind, sounds of music and the spoken word issued forth from the big brown box. I guess it was a sort of equivalent to me of the discharge of noise and smoke from the conquistadors' muskets and cannons. The wireless was not so deadly of course, but I was nevertheless transfixed.

In the evenings, and for a short while before being sent to my little bed in the room I shared with my parents, I was allowed to sit cross-legged on the linoleum-covered floor to gaze up and point my ears at the wonderful machine. When I got a bit older, the duration of my listening experience was permitted to increase; and so did my understanding of the verbal utterances that cascaded from the equipment's oddly meshed, round speakers. As you would expect, I did not think in these terms at the time. I tended to accept somewhat ludicrously, though I was only about six years old, that the fantastic and tantalising sound-box was inhabited by a number of really tiny people, Lilliputian types if you like. This rather added to the mystique, intrigue and appeal of the exotic wireless. But it was not too long afterwards that reason trumped my gullibility. Talk about *Gullible's* … sorry, I mean *Gulliver's Travels*.

And thus my imagination was ignited by the mind-blowing wireless; and particularly by the broadcast plays, drama serials and short stories variously performed or related by some great contemporary character actors, or rather their disembodied voices. I had been taken to see Hollywood movies at the local fleapit cinema or occasionally at a more distant picture palace. They were mostly Technicolor musicals and Westerns, but also black-and-white films featuring Chicago gangsters of the 1930s or the war in the Pacific in the 1940s, and suchlike. My favourite Tinsel-town stars were Doris Day and John Wayne. Then there were the marvellously eccentric Ealing comedies. We did not acquire a television, a fourteen-inch table-top *Vidor*, until the 1953 Coronation of Queen Elizabeth. Serendipitously, my father had just won sixty-five pounds on the football pools! And he swiftly purchased our first TV.

In a way, what I had seen goggle-eyed on the cinema's silver screen helped evolve my mental process of scene visualisation when listening to dramas on the wireless. I really enjoyed the science fiction series because my imagination could run riot, creating all sorts of alien creatures and bizarre worlds in my buzzing head. At the picture house I had also watched some silent films; maybe strangely for a kid, I was only mildly amused by the slapstick antics of Charlie Chaplin and Buster Keaton. But what struck me in this connection, and even at the time, was that a screen could project meaningful visuals without spoken dialogue and other sounds; whilst a wireless could project meaningful dialogue without visuals. It seemed very peculiar and perplexing to me; but it was something that evidently encouraged, maybe even inspired my imagination to fill the visual void.

But inevitably, like other children, I soon discovered books and the public lending library in Whitechapel where you could borrow them. And I realised that it was not only the wireless that could motivate and stimulate the imagination. After moving to a council housing estate in the early 1950s, my performance of small and meagrely paid local jobs after school meant that I could save something called money. One of my little earners involved knocking on doors and collecting old newspapers to sell as wrapping material to the butchers and fishmongers in "The Lane" for one (old) penny a pound weight. Another employment concerned the use of a large red-coloured magnet, which I needed to grip with both hands, in order to attract hundreds if not thousands of fallen pins from the floor of the noisy workroom where my mother strained her tired eyes as a meticulous fur machinist over many years.

At the age of seven I was recruited as a choir member, and later was promoted to be a boy soloist, at the now long-gone Great Synagogue in Duke's Place (I have been a chorister ever since). This choral engagement paid the princely sum of nine shillings a month (about forty-five pence now, but worth much more then). With this magnificent increase in income, I managed eventually to save sufficient capital to purchase a portable typewriter. At last, I now possessed the wherewithal to write my own little tales, with what became for me the virtual sanctity of the printed word.

However, I found the writing of dialogue extraordinarily difficult compared to paragraphs of descriptive narrative. And I wondered whether my earlier years of creating, imaginatively, many and varied environments for the one-off drama productions, serials and story-telling on the wireless had somehow impinged adversely on my absorption of dialogue formulation; and also of the techniques relating to verbal interaction between characters in, say, a play.

The writing of short stories became my literary passion as a teenager (the French author Guy de Maupassant was my principal idol in the genre), even though I was not a confident writer. That is until I won my first writing prize (when a member of Brady Boys' Club, under the inspirational leadership of Paul Yogi Mayer, and just before taking up my place at London University to read Law). The National Association of Boys' Clubs "Writer of the Year Award 1961" was for a fictional though semi-autobiographical short story I had penned about a shy lad growing up in the heart of the "Jewish" East End. And I was presented, excitingly and somewhat surrealistically, with a silver-coloured trophy on a plinth by famous songsters Frankie Vaughan and Vera Lynn at the Royal Festival Hall. It so happened that the well-known athlete, Olympic gold-medallist, sports journalist and co-founder of the London Marathon Chris Brasher, who was a guest at the RFH event, had read my modest but winning tale of adventure and misadventure around "The Lane". As a result, he asked me to provide him with two specially written stories for publication in an anthology of the best in contemporary youth writing that he was then preparing.

I cannot recall ever having read a short, or indeed a long story that has been comprised entirely of dialogue (except my own). Such a literary piece would more usually constitute perhaps a theatre drama, a screenplay or a script of some sort. This does not mean necessarily that no such *dialogue only* short stories exist in the literary sphere anywhere in the world of fiction publications. The law of chance, if not of probability, suggests there may well be some around. But if they do exist somewhere, I wonder about their raison d'être. The stories in this my third anthology of Jewish-themed short stories are designed to fuel and fire up the imagination, to prompt the creation of unique environments, urban and rural and even extra-terrestrial, in the mind's eye of the reader.

Educationalists, psychologists and others frequently express serious concerns about the growing lack of imagination in our modern generation of children. There can be no doubt that huge numbers of young boys and girls read many books, prompted by some really enthralling fiction material. Nonetheless, maybe there is some justification for the anxieties voiced by the experts. Today, millions of youngsters are besieged by a galaxy of electronically and digitally sourced visuals that threaten to deprive them of an inherent, but increasingly dormant or even suppressed, ability to allow the mind to wander freely and … to imagine. Television, cinema, computers, DVD and games platforms, smart phones and various other enticing items of electronic paraphernalia purvey constantly to vast swathes of young people (and indeed adults also) spectacular images, real and computer-generated, that can negate any need for imaginative creativity.

In reality, and paradoxically, everything derives from imagination. Imagination is a miraculous power; and it *is* a power. All of us possess a potentially vivid imagination; I am grateful that my imagination, such as it may be, was untrammelled or undiluted by a lengthy career as a lawyer. In this *dialogue only* compendium, you will not be fed detailed narrative descriptions which would form precise images in your mind. But you will be able to deduce and visualise scenarios from the words spoken by the variety of characters; and consequently, you will be participating in the creation of the stories. In a real sense, you the reader will complete the picture … and in your own individualistic way.

"Everything you can imagine is real." The great artist Pablo Picasso made that statement; and, in a sense, it rings true. Ursula K Le Guin, the famous American fantasy and science fiction writer, once wrote: "It is above all by the imagination that we can achieve perception, compassion and hope." Coincidentally, these are attributes or elements that are not unfamiliar to the Jewish people.

Mark Harris
*Cambridge*, 2012

## The Music Makers

"I BEG of you, Ephraim … don't go. It's far too dangerous. They'll find you and kill you! We're safe here … we've been safe here for three years. So please don't leave, Ephraim. Stay here with me … until the end of this horrible war."

"I know you don't want me to leave you alone, Shlomo. I know that, I really do. But I can't remain down here in this cellar any longer … it's like being buried alive in a grave. And with all those bombs dropping from the sky and exploding around us, it's a wonder we *haven't* been buried alive! I'm sorry, Shlomo … I can't take this unpredictable existence any longer. If you don't come with me, I'll have to leave without you, may the Almighty forgive me. Look what we've become … troglodytes! We don't breathe the fresh air. We don't see the blue sky, the trees and the birds. Down here we don't witness Hashem's Creation. We wouldn't have survived at all, spiritually and physically, had it not been for the books we'd salvaged and the vital help of …"

"I know, I know, but please don't go Ephraim! The Holy

One, blessed be His Name, intends this underground room to be our sanctuary till peace comes to us ... and we pray for that time at Shacharis, Minchah and Ma'ariv."

"Yes, we do. We pray every day even though we're the only two bochas from our yeshivah left hiding in Berlin now ... like Daniels in the Lion's den. We now know that all the others, and our dear Rosh Yeshivah, are niddah."

"We've been fortunate, albeit that's a relative term Ephraim. But don't ask me why ... why we've been chosen to survive, at least so far."

"Only the Almighty knows, Shlomo. And only He knows the reason for all this, a reason beyond our mortal comprehension. But look at us! We're only nearing our mid-twenties, though we look like old krenkers ... and we've thrown ourselves into this hole in the earth. I know Joseph was hurled into a pit by his brothers, but he didn't jump into it himself."

"He was there for a purpose, Ephraim ..."

"We should be married by now, and starting our own families. I've got this feeling, and it's not a good one. I know it's a risky thing I'm planning to do, but I've got to take the chance ... it may be my last. I know you're scared out of your wits, Shlomo ... terrified that, if you leave the tentative security of this parlous place that's served as our home for three years like some prison cell or dungeon, you'll be picked up by the Gestapo. But I've got to attempt it ... before I go completely mad, do you understand me?"

"You must already be completely mad ... to take what amounts to the slimmest of chances."

"Slimmest? Well, if I stay here any longer I'll be even

slimmer than the virtual skeleton I am now! Ducks would throw bread at *me*!"

"That isn't at all amusing. And starvation isn't entirely the case. Our food supplies are humble but adequate. Anyway, if you decide to go Ephraim, rest assured ... I'm not coming with you."

"Believe me, Shlomo, I'm *going* ... and tomorrow, before dawn."

"Listen to me ... *please*. I'm not going to beg, implore or plead with you any longer. But peace may be just around the corner. Freedom can arrive sooner than you think. The snippets of news we've been given recently tell us that the Russians are closing in on the German capital from the east ... and that the Americans and British are now somewhere on this side of the Rhine. It's only a matter of time, Ephraim my dearest friend."

"Take hope from that if you will, Shlomo ... my dearest friend. But remember this ... our clandestine subterranean cocoon has been filled with hopeful rumours from time to time over the last one thousand days. But what's the authentic truth?"

"Of course, I can't tell you that. Only the Almighty knows the absolute truth ..."

"Yes Shlomo, but do you recall a time when the rumours seeping into this cellar niche beneath an ordinary suburban Berlin house were telling of death camps in Poland, where thousands upon thousands of Jews were being gassed and their bodies cremated to ashes ... hundreds of thousands, perhaps even millions of Jews ... Jews like us, and Jews perhaps not quite like us. Where are our families, our beloved parents, our siblings and our many other relatives now? Sadly, I *do* know the answer to that question, Shlomo. The world to come is their world *today* ..."

"But where will you seek to go, Ephraim? And how will

you escape detection? There must be soldiers, security police and Gestapo informers everywhere!"

"I'll head west towards the Allied lines, moving at night and relying on the chaos that apparently exists up there in this ruined and evil country. Even though the candles are burning low I can see you shaking your head, Shlomo. I'm absorbing what I perceive in your dark sunken eyes, my dearest friend. I really don't underestimate the difficulties … the obstacles in my path that I'll need to overcome. And above all, I realise that I could be signing my own death warrant. But with Hashem's help, as my shield and salvation, I'll make it. I *have* to make it. You know what Shlomo, and this may surprise you, I want to pick up where I left off learning to play the piano. Ha, ha, just what I prophesied, Shlomo … Your beautifully perplexed, bearded and haggard grey bony face tells me all. Yes, I know we wanted to take semichah and become rabbis … though that hasn't proved possible of course, at least not yet. But this doesn't mean …"

"I don't know what you're talking about, Ephraim. And I doubt whether you do, either. Perhaps, may the Almighty forbid it … you *are* losing your mind."

"Listen, Shlomo … it's almost the middle of April 1945. We've just finished celebrating our third Pesach down here … as best we could, of course. Now I want to taste the fresh air. We've been confined and concealed in this pit successfully, if not miraculously, since 1942. We know there are still other traumatised and desperate Jews hiding away in their secret bunkers and boltholes in this wicked Nazi city. We're also aware that they're called 'U-boats' and for quite obvious reasons … though submarines do break surface when necessary. And don't forget, Shlomo, you play the flute. In fact, you're an exceptionally talented flautist. It's a great pity you've mislaid the instrument. Though, on the other hand, we do have to keep sounds to a minimum … just in case."

"I don't understand what you're saying, Ephraim."

"Then please allow me to explain further, my dearest friend."

"I'm sorry."

"No need to be. You see, we've once again marked the Jewish festival of freedom, and now I want to gain my own liberty. It's that simple, and it's not that simple. But I do have to break out of this dark place, rise to the surface and find the scarce commodity that so many long oppressed, persecuted and subjugated peoples now seek. I want … no, I need to be a good Jew but also a free one, free to follow my own chosen path in life. And I would like to play the piano. This aspiration I *will* achieve, I just know it."

"Quite a little drosha, Ephraim … but I have to admire your fearless confidence. I do, honestly. But if the dreaded Gestapo get their hands on … on your hands, you'll not be playing any piano. Perhaps you'll be playing a harp."

"Very funny, Shlomo, though in somewhat bad taste all round … remind me when to laugh. You say that I'm *fearless*. You're quite wrong, Shlomo. I'm not courageous in any way. I'm filled with trepidation, if not terror. But I know that Hashem will assist me to survive and guide me in attaining my objectives."

"I wish you all the mazel and gezunt. I really do sincerely mean that, Ephraim."

"And I know you really do mean it. I'm truly sorry to break this upsetting news of my imminent departure, though I'm sure you may've sensed something in the wind. Particularly, I suspect, when I intoned the final words of the Haggadah on the second night of our Pesach seders ... those ringing redemptive words, *Next year in Jerusalem!*"

"Yes, you could say ... but that provides no comfort to me. Your deep frustration, certainly more profound than my own, has definitely come through our long and intense studies together o-over r-recent m-months. I-It's j-just that I-I d-don't w-want to l-lose the c-closest, d-dearest and o-only f-friend I p-possess in the w-whole w-wide w-world ..."

"Please don't weep Shlomo, my dearest friend, companion and fellow student of our glorious Torah. Continue to put your trust and faith in the Almighty, as I know you do ... precisely like me. You should be safe here until freedom arrives, as it does eventually in the gloomiest and direst of places. Good will always triumph over evil and wickedness. And please don't worry. I'll be protected by Hashem as I travel westwards on my own quest. When you wake up tomorrow morning, I'll be gone. Take care, my very good friend. I wish you well ... and perhaps one day, with Hashem's assistance, we'll find each other again. Don't cry Shlomo and please mention me daily in your prayers, as I will you. I hope you haven't forgotten what our spiritual leader, our beloved Rebbe of blessed memory, would say that good friends should do on parting before a long journey. Yes ... I can see your eyes glistening in poignant and respectful remembrance, Shlomo. So now let's give each other a long warm hug ..."

★ ★ ★

"Who's there? I said ... *Who's there*? I can see you ... just about. I can see your leg sticking out of that pile of stinking straw up here. You're hiding in this hay loft, I know you're hiding ... but not very carefully if you ask me, which you didn't. And I know you're not dead. I just saw the straw move, and there's no breeze up here. Come on out now ... please. I've been walking for days, mostly nights really. I'm exhausted and hungry, and my food supplies are running out. But above all, I really need someone to converse with ... I can tell you're a fugitive, just like me. Why else would you be trying to conceal yourself, though not wholly efficiently if I may say so, in this freezing barn? If you don't respond soon, I'll ..."

"Please don't hurt me ... I'm coming out now."

"It's about time, too. Come here, let me brush you down ... you look like a scarecrow with the stuffing knocked out of it!"

"Thanks, though you hardly look any tidier than me ... if *I* may say so. Who are you? How did you find me here?"

"Please excuse me, but I wasn't particularly looking for *you*. I was merely searching for somewhere to rest up for a while and grab some much-needed shut-eye. I've been crawling, almost literally, through the forest all night. When I emerged finally from the tree cover I spotted this stone building ... this old thatched cow barn, silhouetted against the rising daylight. I'm supposed to be travelling westwards, but I've now lost much of my sense of direction."

"Why were you crawling?"

"What?"

"Why were you crawling through the forest?"

"Maybe you're Rip Van Winkle and you've been in the Land of Nod for the last six years, but actually there's a war going on don't you know. Not surprisingly I guess, I've been hearing explosions and sounds of military activity in the last hour or so … I've been endeavouring to keep as low a profile as possible. And my knees are killing me!"

"I'm sorry … I know that lots of troops have been moving through this farm … German soldiers. I've been very lucky they haven't discovered me."

"They were *German* soldiers?"

"Yes."

"So clearly I haven't reached the Allied lines yet …"

"Who are you?"

"My name's Ephraim. What's yours?"

"*Ephraim* …"

"That's a strange coincidence."

"No, no … you misunderstand me. Ephraim is not my name. I'm just pondering yours."

"Why?"

"Are you … are you … are you Jewish by any chance?"

"Why do you want to know?"

"Do you always answer questions with more questions? Now I know for sure, and without your confirmation. You *are* Jewish, aren't you?"

"Are you one of those Gestapo informers? If so, I'll …"

"Don't be stupid, whoever you are … just take a close peek at me. I'm Jewish, too. Looks like we're two petrified fleeing Jews who've found each other in extraordinary circumstances …"

"First, I'm not *stupid* but I take no offence from a fellow … I understand the pressures. Yes, you're right of course. I *am* Jewish … from my ancient battered forage cap to my muddy old boots. I've been moving at night from the Berlin suburbs for the last week, though it seems like months since I began this journey."

"Very pleased to meet with you, Ephraim, but as they say …

only on simchas. By the way, my name's Paul. I've also come from Berlin. I'm sure we don't need to tell each other about the awful history and situation of the Jews in Nazi Germany. I thought so … I can see you nodding."

"Where's your family?"

"I don't know … I really don't know. My darling wife, our two teenage sons, identical twins as it happens, and I were rounded up for deportation to what they said are resettlement or work camps in the east … must be more than a year ago now. To this day, I don't know how … you see I was separated from them on the transport. Somehow, I managed to escape and disappeared into the countryside. I hope my family is alive and well; though like you I'm sure, I've heard unbelievable stories of mass shootings of Jews, and much worse, in Poland and other countries under Nazi domination in Eastern Europe. I've been tramping around quite mindlessly, stunned you could say, ever since my miraculous getaway. I've been avoiding towns and villages, and just generally trying to survive by living off the land. Looking at my somewhat dishevelled appearance right now, you might find it hard to believe that I was once a professional person … a dentist, in fact. We had a good middle class life with a lovely home but now I'm reduced to this filthy wreck you see before you, thieving food and whatever else I've required to carry on … to survive."

"Pikuach Nefesh!"

"Sorry?"

"The commandment not to steal doesn't apply if it's necessary to preserve human life. Just like infringing the dietary obligations of our faith … and even contravening the laws of Shabbos is permissible on that basis."

"Okay … Look, we're both sporting beards. But whilst I haven't shaved for ages for good logistical reasons, I suspect you're a pious Jew. Am I right?"

"You are, my friend. I was a yeshivah bocha … a student at a religion academy. As I mentioned I've been on, or rather more sensibly off, the road for about a week or so; though the shock wave of my experience has left me without an accurate sense of time. But with sun-up, which I can just about espy through that very dirty little oval window over there, I need to do something."

"What's that? And what are those black things that you're taking from your knapsack?"

"This is a prayer book … a Siddur, and these are my tephilin. Please excuse me, Paul. Once satisfied that I'm facing east, I'll be davening Shacharis. And then I'll have something to eat from my remaining meagre rations."

"You really *are* a religious Jew, aren't you Ephraim. I've never actually spoken to anyone like you before."

"Yes, I am … and I hope that I don't seem to you like some alien from another planet. I come from a long line of very orthodox Jews. Several of my ancestors were rabbis in Germany and, before that, in Poland."

"I'm afraid we're not so religiously inclined. I reckon you could say that we're more what you would call Reform Jews. We would go to our synagogue on Rosh Hashanah and Yom Kippur. And, if possible, we would participate in some of the community events on the traditional festivals, like Purim and Chanucah. We're more cultural than religious Jews, I suppose. Apart from the occasional barmitzvah, you wouldn't find us in the synagogue too often on a Shabbos. But we did attend from time to time. Our synagogue was architecturally beautiful. You may've seen it in passing. And we were fortunate to have had a wonderfully sympathetic and supportive minister, and a cantor with a tremendous tenor voice. Together with our excellent choir … it was a mixed choir with male and female choristers … the music produced was really inspiring. Oh yes, we also had an organ in the building. We do believe in the Almighty of course, just like you; though personally, I think you can still be Jewish even if you don't believe, if you know what I mean. I suppose we've followed adherents of the so-called Enlightenment and become more German and less Jewish. My sister-in-law isn't Jewish you know … actually, she's a Lutheran. N-Not that all this assimilation has d-done us J-Jews any g-good in the e-end … and I-I s-should mention that our l-lovely s-synagogue was b-burned to the g-ground by a screaming and d-destructive N-Nazi r-rabble on K-Kristallnacht."

"Please don't upset yourself, Paul. Nothing that's happened can be changed. I'll recite some prayers for the wellbeing of yourself and your family. And may they be fulfilled, with Hashem's help."

"I-I t-thank you, E-Ephraim … And I do appreciate that I should be more philosophical, though I find that very difficult right now."

"You're very welcome, and I understand. And please don't be *afraid* that you and your family aren't too religious. As you've told me, you're a believer in the Almighty. It's not for me to be judgemental in any way. And I'm sure you strive to do the best you can to maintain your faith in all the circumstances of *your* life. You seem to be interested in liturgical music and even enthused by it, as I gather from you."

"Yes I'm very interested in music, whether performed in

the synagogue or in the concert hall. In fact, I play a musical instrument myself. Look what I've got here in my bag ..."

"Oh my, it's a violin. That's marvellous!"

"Indeed. And I've managed to keep it and the bow safely together all this time I've been trundling around or lying low."

"What do you like playing, Paul?"

"The music of Ger ... of Central Europe's great classical composers, but especially Mozart ..."

"What's your favourite piece?"

"It's Mozart's Violin Sonata in F, K Three Seven Seven. I would play it for you now, but you know how it is here."

"Yes, I understand. I play an instrument, too."

"Is that right? Amazing ...!"

"Yes, I play the piano a little ... not as well as I would like. But I haven't played for more than three years. After the war's over and I've reached my ultimate destination, I want to learn how to play properly and seriously."

"You should, Ephraim. Music is so important. It transcends ..."

"Yes, I agree. And my dearest friend Shlomo is also a musician. You know, I left him in a cellar in Berlin and I'll probably never see him again. I can't stop thinking about what I've done. I do hope he'll be safe. There's going to be one appalling final battle in the German capital, I'm sure of it ... Shlomo plays the flute marvellously ... he makes such soul-soothing sounds. You say that music is so important, and I've concurred wholeheartedly. But it reminds me of what's so important right now ... at this very moment in time. We're not schmoozing at a Kiddush, you know. We're in a highly dangerous position and surrounded by the enemy. How long did you say you've been holed up alone in this barn?"

"I didn't. But I've been hiding in here for about a fortnight. I've managed to organise enough stuff to eat, and to get sufficient water. There are still people living in the farm house. I don't know exactly how many, but there does seem to be a reasonable amount of food around. I've been very careful in scrounging bits and pieces. A lot of luck has also made the difference to my survival. It's sad and unknowable how and why some people fall to be in the wrong place at the wrong time. Just a moment or two can make the difference between life and death. Walk around one corner and you're safe, turn another and you've had it! But I appreciate that I can't stay here for much longer … else my agricultural neighbours may begin to get a trifle suspicious about the missing sausages, eh Ephraim?"

"Yes … er, absolutely. I never stay more than a single day in the same place. Like me you've been very fortunate so far, Paul. Hashem has been good to us. But you must realise that German infantry or SS troops could burst in here and find us at any second. I really do think it's time for you to leave this decrepit structure …"

"I can't be too fussy about my accommodation. But where shall I go now?"

"Come with me, Paul. We'll help each other to survive until peace comes … and I just know that freedom isn't that far off. Maybe I'm destined one day to piano accompany your violin playing."

"That would be truly admirable. So my answer is … yes. I will come with you, Ephraim."

"Very good, we'll leave when it gets dark. And Paul, don't forget to bring along your fiddle. But now I must put on my tephilin and daven Shacharis …"

★ ★ ★

"Get down … quick, behind this undergrowth … and keep your voice low!"

"What is it, Ephraim?"

"Just get down now, Paul … right away!"

"Ouch! That really hurt!"

"Better a bruised arm than a bullet-smashed face, eh?"

"No real contest there, I suppose. Sorry, I should've flattened myself more promptly. But what have you seen? Whisper if you must."

"Over there, about fifty metres to our right. There's something moving at the base of the tree …"

"Where exactly are you looking Ephraim? I can't see anything but trees, and still more trees. We *are* in the middle of a wood, after all."

"Follow the thick line of beeches towards the right until you spot a dark object against the greenery …"

"Yes, I can see it now. What do you think it is, Ephraim?"

"I wish I knew exactly. It could be a wounded soldier … maybe a German, possibly American or British. It might even be a civilian who has been hit in the crossfire. Needless to say, I don't know. But listen, Paul. Can you hear the rat-a-tat-tat of a machine gun? We must certainly be close to the front line. But I'm not sure from which direction …"

"It sounds like the gunfire's coming from further to our right flank."

"I'm going to get a bit nearer. Maybe someone requires our help …"

"Are you out of your pious little mind, Ephraim? It could

be a trap. Perhaps a sniper has got his beady eyes on the object of your desire. If you approach it, *you* could be the one needing help … like for an oozing brain!"

"That gives me a charming picture, Paul … and I don't think. Anyway, I'm going … are you coming?"

"Some idiot has got to watch your back."

"Okay now, hug the ground and propel yourself forward with your elbows. Like this. Follow me …"

\* \* \*

"It doesn't appear to be a soldier, Ephraim … See, I'm right. The man's propped against the tree trunk and dressed in ragamuffin clothes, just like you and me. I bet he's a fugitive, too. But it does appear that he's got some kind of problem. Catch that grimace on his face?"

"Pssst … pssst!"

"What the hell are you doing, Ephraim?"

"I'm trying to attract his attention … and look, I've succeeded. He's peering in this direction. I think he can see us, Paul. Look, he's waving now. I believe he *does* need our assistance. I'm going over to him. Come on, if you want …"

\* \* \*

"Who are you? What are doing here? Can you assist me, please? I think I've twisted my ankle."

"So many questions my dear fellow German civilian, but I think we need to prioritise our responses. Paul, please lend me a hand to haul our new-found acquaintance gently to the shadowy cover of that rocky outcrop ... and do try to keep a low profile."

"Okay Ephraim, I've got him. Let's go ...."

★ ★ ★

"Put him down here for now, Paul."

"Right ..."

"Thank you so much for your kindness ... Ephraim and Paul. Obviously, I've just overheard your names. Mine is Martin. Thanks again ... Aaagh!"

"Let me have a look at that ankle of yours. I've had some first aid training."

"Thank you, Paul."

"No problem. Ephraim, lift up his left leg while I take off his boot ... yes, you've diagnosed your little physical difficulty quite correctly, Martin. There's not a lot we can do for it at the moment. You'll have to keep off the foot for a while, and hop or crawl maybe wherever you want to go at present ..."

"What are you saying, Paul? We've got to stay with Martin until he can stand on his own two feet again ..."

"What are *you* saying, Ephraim?"

"Paul, we have to ..."

"Gentleman, gentlemen ... please don't argue on my account. I can take care of myself. I've been doing that for a long time now. Listen, I know that you're Jews on the run ..."

"What? How do you ...?"

"Don't run away from me ... Paul, Ephraim, come back! I'm Jewish, too ... I'm *Jewish*! That's right, come back ... I'm sorry, don't be alarmed. I regret having startled you. Sit down next to me, please."

"How do you know we're Jewish, Martin?"

"Well, I wasn't sure about you Paul, and I don't want to be like the Nazis with their racist stereotypes … but Ephraim, you *do* look Jewish to me. So I just assumed that Paul is Jewish, too. Besides, who else these days might be wandering around in a bloody forest in rubbishy civilian clothes … and at dusk?"

"I take your points, Martin. Yes, you're completely correct. Paul and I are on the run … we're seeking peace, freedom and salvation just as you are no doubt. Both of us hail from Berlin. Paul's been trekking around the countryside for quite a long period now. His wife and children were transported to the east. I've only been on the road, so to speak, since earlier this month. I met up with my loyal companion by a chance encounter only recently. What's your story, Martin? Excuse me, but just look at that red glow in the darkening sky over there …"

"It would seem that something big is on fire, Ephraim."

"You could be right, Martin … Excuse me, but I think your story will have to keep for now. We need to get ourselves inside some substantial protection for the night. Remember Paul, we passed some abandoned workmen's huts a short while back … let's try to find them again. Okay?"

"Yes I recall them too, Paul. They're not too far away. Help me get Martin up. Thankfully, the masking blanket of fading light will enable us to hold our new friend safely upright between us …"

"Thanks, Paul … Ephraim … Aaargh!"

* * *

"It's really quite cosy in this little hut. Makes a pleasant change from some of the hideouts I've inhabited in my peripatetic existence. And thanks for sharing your food with me … I've got a little in my own bundle, and I'll be more than delighted to divide it with you for breakfast tomorrow morning."

"Don't concern yourself with that, Martin. More critically, how's the ankle now?"

"Not too bad thanks, Ephraim … it certainly feels a trifle easier. I'm so grateful for the kindness and support you've given to me. I don't know what …"

"Look, if we can't help a fellow Jew …"

"Thank you, Paul. I *am* Jewish by birth, as I told you. But … I'm an atheist now."

"You're a Jewish *atheist*?"

"Yes, Paul. I know it sounds like a contradiction in terms. I'm Jewish because, of course, my mother was Jewish. My father was Jewish too, incidentally. I've got no siblings. I'm an only child. I don't know where my parents are now. Like your family Paul and probably yours also Ephraim, they were transported to somewhere in the east, possibly Poland, a few years ago. We lived in Bremen. I'm a science graduate of the city's university. Of course I received my Chemistry degree before Jews were denied the possibility by the Nazis' racist Nuremberg Laws. I was sent to a slave labour camp in Austria. But after a few months, and a couple of failed but mercifully undetected attempts, I succeeded in escaping. I did harbour the somewhat vague idea of heading for Switzerland …"

"You've been on the run ever since?"

"Yes, Ephraim."

"We've heard terrible rumours about what's happening to our people deported to countries occupied by the Nazis …"

"I've heard them too, Paul. You might ask how a supposedly civilised and apparently cultured Christian nation could perpetrate such crimes against innocent human beings … men, women and children. But I've not only *heard* about gas chambers and crematoria burning Jewish bodies all day and all night … I myself have witnessed some horrific incidents. In our camp, men were starved to death when they were unable to work any more through sickness, weakness and utter exhaustion. Others were shot summarily or hanged from a gallows, for the least infringement of the rules … or randomly, for no reason whatsoever. It was a waking nightmare … oblivion was always a mere icy breath away!"

"M-My God …!"

"Yes Paul, but not mine."

"Sorry? Oh, of course … you're a Jewish atheist. Look, I'm not the most observant Jew in the world, but I do have faith in the existence of a Supreme Being. I accept, however, that not everyone has such a belief. Is your atheism anything to do with your science background?"

"Maybe … I'm not entirely convinced that *is* my exclusive and entire motivation. I find it very complicated to explain. I try hard to be a good person. But as you would know, Paul, there are all kinds and degrees of Jews with all sorts of views and notions. In fact, I don't think that I'm a rarity. Perhaps the emancipation of Jewish thought in the last century opened the gates of the ghetto mentality to some free thinking about being Jewish, about being religiously Jewish or otherwise. When I was in the camp, I saw Jews praying fervently to their Almighty for mercy, for life … only to be stood up against a wall a moment later and shot to death. And I'm thinking of maybe hundreds of thousands of other Jews who've perished in Hitler's inhuman racial crusade against the Jewish people. Why weren't their prayers received and answered?"

"We haven't heard much from you, Ephraim. What do you say to all this?"

"What do you want me to say, Paul?"

"Well, as a religious Jew, you must have some comments on the subject."

"Please leave him alone, Paul. You don't have to say anything, Ephraim."

"All I can say to both of you is this … that I have a deep and constant faith in Hashem, the Creator of the universe, to whom my eternal soul will return one day. Being a mere mortal, I'm unable to comprehend the reason why bad things happen to good and innocent people. Nor why the Jews are suffering now as they've suffered anguish, torment, pain, suffering and martyrdom many times during their long history. Man has been given the free will to choose to do good or evil. So my reaction to the question '*Where is Hashem?*' is '*Where is Man?*'."

"Well said, Ephraim. I'm sure that Martin respects your views, even though he may not be swayed by them. And in turn, I suspect that you Ephraim would yet think that Martin, whatever his opinions, remains a fellow Jew. Certainly, his atheism makes no difference to the Nazis' attitude towards him …"

"There was one thing, however, that helped me to hold onto my sanity in the camp …"

"What was that, Martin?"

"I'll tell you, Paul. When I was young, my parents took me to the synagogue every Sabbath. I had a sweet soprano voice, so the chazan told me, and I was invited to join the choir. I was a boy chorister for quite some time, until a couple of years after my barmitzvah. I began to read works of philosophy, and then books containing arguments for and against the existence of God ..."

"But what was the thing that prevented you from going mad, in that hellish place you described?"

"I'm coming to that straightaway, Paul. I would sing in the camp. Not aloud you understand, but in my head. I would sing all the songs, the liturgical music that I'd learned and performed in the synagogue. Strange, you might think ...an atheist singing religious music, albeit silently so to say. But doing this gave me great comfort and helped me to get through the dreadful days, and also the long wakeful nights in our wintry barracks. I'm a baritone now ... and I've continued singing, sometimes audibly if safe to do so, on my enforced solitary march around rural Germany. I have a passion for singing. To me, singing *is* a kind of self-administered freedom."

"Really, that's quite a phenomenal coincidence."

"Why's that, Ephraim?"

"Well, you see ... I'm a musician. And so is Paul. He plays the violin, and tells me he adores the instrument. And I'm reasonably proficient at the piano, though I'm determined to improve considerably if I can after the end of the war. Sadly, I left behind in Berlin my dearest friend Shlomo who's a wonderful flautist. He was too frightened, or maybe too sensible, to venture with me into the unknown."

"Yes, this is all quite an astonishing twist of fate. I mean us meeting up like this ... and also our mutual love of music. Never in a million years could I have thought, twenty-four hours ago as I lay in agony on the forest floor, that I would be sharing philosophical thoughts tonight with two other Jewish musicians."

"Could be we're your redemption, Martin … Sorry, that's terribly arrogant and very wrong of me to suggest. But it occurred to me that you've been a Hebrew slave who has escaped captivity, who has made his very own Exodus and who is now heading hopefully for a Promised Land, whatever that might mean for you. Does this remind you of anything?"

"I went to our synagogue for long enough, Ephraim, to know that Passover would be celebrated around this time of the year. I do follow your allusion … and that's a truly charming smile, Ephraim."

"Yes, well I think we should try to get some sleep now. Paul and I normally travel during the hours of darkness, but I consider that we need to make an exception for tonight. We'll see how your ankle is tomorrow evening, Martin … before we leave you."

"What are you saying, Ephraim? Perhaps Martin would like to join us on our epic journey …"

"Would you, Martin? We would make quite a trio … a pianist, a fiddler and a singer!"

"Why would you want me to accompany you, Ephraim? I know that I'm Jewish, but I'm also an atheist … I don't have any faith in the existence of God. You're an orthodox Jew and Paul's …"

"… Not an orthodox Jew. Like Ephraim, and as I mentioned just before, I *do* believe in the Almighty though I'm not that observant you know. I might also say that I can't get my head around a literal interpretation of the opening chapter of Genesis. Personally and with the greatest of respect, I think that it's all allegory."

"Come with us, Martin. We all have a unifying passion for music, which I believe comes from the soul. And we're all made in Hashem's Image."

"Let me think about it, Ephraim …"

★ ★ ★

"Paul and I are delighted you made the decision to come along with us, Martin."

"Thank you, Ephraim. It wasn't really that difficult to reach in the end. I've been on my own for so long, I'd almost lost touch with the idea of companionship. I'm very happy to be accompanying the both of you."

"And maybe one day we'll be accompanying you …"

"Eh?"

"On the piano and violin …"

"Ha, ha … that's very good, Paul."

"Glad you appreciated my jest … finally."

"I'm afraid I've got some work to do on redeveloping my sense of humour."

"Sorry, Martin … I was only joking."

"I know, so don't concern yourself. Is anyone half aware of our whereabouts at this precise instant?"

"According to my calculations, we should be somewhere near …"

"Admit it, Ephraim … apart from knowing we're somewhere in western Germany to the east of the Rhine, you haven't got a clue about our precise location. That's correct, isn't it?"

"I take no pleasure in telling you this, Paul. But, yes … you're absolutely right."

"It's odd we haven't seen much military activity, though I think we've acquired a sort of subconscious knack at successfully giving the war a wide berth."

"That does appear to be the case, Martin. We've neither heard nor seen any gunfire or explosions for a couple of days now … since we left the hut, in fact."

"And in addition to that Ephraim, it seems so eerily and emphatically quiet."

"Yes, Paul. There's something out of the ordinary going on … I've got a peculiar feeling in my gut."

"Look over there … it's a house, standing by itself not far from that pathway."

"Shall we investigate? What do you say, Paul … Martin?"

"Yes."

"I agree."

"Okay both of you, but please tread warily. You never know …"

★ ★ ★

"The place seems deserted. And it's pretty isolated here. I can't see another building, let alone a village, anywhere nearby. I'm going over the back garden fence to look into the window of that low-rise annexe … it appears to be a garden room of some sort. Paul, Martin … you two go round to the front of the house. Be careful, and meet me back here in ten minutes. We'll report on our respective findings …"

"Well it's a large detached house, probably with four bedrooms. I looked through the conservatory window, and guess what I saw."

"What did you see, Ephraim?"

"I saw a piano, Paul!"

"What?"

"Yes, an upright piano … it's wonderful!"

"What do you mean *wonderful*? It's not *your* piano."

"I know that, Paul. But I haven't seen one for years. What did you two spot from the front, Martin?"

"Well, this might shock you. Anyway, we peered in through the window … into the main living room, as it would appear to be. Above the fireplace is a huge oil painting, or maybe a reproduction of a portrait, of Adolf Hitler in military uniform. And on either side of its imposing gilt frame is the black, red and white swastika flag beloved of the Nazis."

"What?"

"Yes, Ephraim … and I noticed a copy of *Mein Kampf*, that evil monster's book, on a shelf close to the window. But in any event, the front door was ajar. It seems like there's nobody at home. We went inside, but only for a minute or two. We didn't go upstairs. There's stuff strewn all over the place … it's a terrible mess in there. It does look as if the residents left in quite a hurry … doubtless fearful of reprisals, now that Germany's evidently losing the war."

"Is that right, Paul?"

"Yes it is, Ephraim. It seems that we've come upon the residence of a really dedicated Nazi family. I think it's unlikely that they'll ever be returning here. Therefore, I think we should liberate and take possession of this house in the name of, in the name of … Freedom!"

"How can we do that, Paul? It's not *our* house. And in any case, how can we stay inside it openly? There's a war on and we may be encircled by the enemy at any minute, whether the military enemy or the civilian enemy."

"Perhaps we could at least remain here for the time being, possibly in the attic or the cellar if there is one … just until we know the true situation."

"Good thinking, Martin. Bet you knew that your science degree would come in useful some time."

"If that's supposed to be funny, Paul … well then, there's really quite a way yet before I regain my sense of humour."

"Enough said … let's go inside, clean up the place, remove all the Nazi rubbish and see if we can find some food that may've been abandoned. After you Paul, Martin …"

★ ★ ★

"I'm dying to play that piano out in the back room. I tinkled a couple of the keys, and it seems fairly well tuned."

"Why don't you wait, Ephraim … we don't want to make any unnecessary noise right now, if we can help it."

"You're quite right, Paul. I'm sorry. Well, I'm going upstairs to daven Ma'ariv. See you both soon. I know it's night time now … but please don't switch on any lights. And keep a close watch at the front and rear. We can't take any foolish chances at this stage. Okay?"

"Okay, Ephraim."

"Good, Paul …"

"O-Oh my God …! W-Who's that knocking at the front door, Ephraim?"

"How should I know? Get down! And try not to speak louder than a whisper, Paul. We don't want to give ourselves away."

"Martin, can you see anything through the window?"

"No, Paul. It's dark in here, but it looks as black as hell out there. Who can it be? Do they expect the Nazis to be still living here? Hear that? It's the knocking again."

"What shall we do, Ephraim? I'm afraid. I don't want to die …"

"Nor do I, but I don't know what to do Martin … and we'll not be killed if we keep our heads and stay still and silent. Let's just pray or hope, as the case may be, that whoever it is will go away … and very soon."

"What's that sound, Paul?"

"What sound, Ephraim?"

"Listen carefully… it sounds something like a … No, it can't be!"

"Can't be what?"

"I'm going to open the front door."

"Please don't do that, Ephraim."

"Sorry Martin, but …"

"O-Oh my God, he's going to open the door!"

★ ★ ★

"I-In h-heaven's n-name, h-how …?"

"Hello, Ephraim … well, it's a longish story. I'll tell you all about it later. But in the meantime, aren't you going to be welcoming and say you're pleased to see me? Incidentally … I thought my flute, which I'd located at last, would serve to attract your kind attention."

"S-Shlomo? *S-Shlomo*! *S-Shlomo*! H-How did you find …?"

"Please close your gaping mouth, and allow me to enter

your lovely house here. Oh, and do introduce me to your equally startled companions."

"S-Shlomo! *Shlomo!*"

"Stop repeating my name in that shrieking way, Ephraim. Make your eyes smaller, get them back further inside their sockets ... and, once again, do please shut your mouth. You look as if you've seen a dybbuk or a golem. My appearance may leave much to be desired, but I hope that I look rather more human. Oh, and by the way ... Hitler's dead, Germany has surrendered to the Allies unconditionally and the war's over! Now remind me Ephraim, what did our dear Rosh Yeshivah of blessed memory say that friends should do when they meet again after a long separation ...?"

# A Dream

"PLEASE TELL cook, Greschen, there'll be eight of us for dinner tonight."

"Yes I will, Ma'am."

"I've told you, Greschen, you don't have to call me Ma'am. Frau Rosensweig will do very nicely. We don't stand on ceremony in this household, as I've mentioned before."

"Sorry, Ma' … I mean, Frau Rosensweig."

"I know our name is a bit of a mouthful, but I'm sure you'll manage."

"Yes, I will."

"Good. I know you've been with us for only two weeks, Greschen. But I can see already you're a very bright and obedient girl. And our dear cook-housekeeper, Frau Midden, who has been with us rather longer, around ten years as I recall, advises me that you've assisted her very competently in the kitchen. So tell me, how have you been settling in?"

"Frau Midden has been very kind to me … and I'm settling in nicely, thank you."

"You don't have to inform me, but how do we compare to your previous employers? We knew the Morgensteins a little … My husband and I sometimes chatted to them during intervals at the Opera or the Philharmonia. They knew we needed a new maid, and recommended you before they immigrated to the United States. I think I understand their motives in leaving Germany at this time. Herr Morgenstein didn't deserve the beating he got from those Brown-shirt thugs. Mind you, he was very unlucky to have been in the wrong place at the wrong time. How did you get on with the Morgensteins, my dear?"

"I don't want to gossip or speak out of turn, Frau Rosensweig …"

"Don't worry, Greschen. Your comments will not go beyond the four walls of this study."

"The Morgensteins were quite strict with me. As you probably know, they had a very big apartment close by the Unter den Linden."

"Yes, I did know. They invited us back for coffee one evening after Die Zauberflote … that's a Mozart opera you know."

"Well, it was my first post … and I wasn't always sure about how to do things properly. Their cook thought I was a pipsqueak upstart! But I wasn't. I'm a really hard worker and I think you know that now, Frau Rosensweig. I was on my feet at the Morgensteins from dawn until dusk, practically every day. I was so tired that I almost fell asleep before my head hit the pillow."

"I hope you'll feel more comfortable and at home here, Greschen."

"Thank you, Frau Rosensweig. I do appreciate the kindness

everyone has shown to me. Frau Morgenstein always insisted I call her Ma'am …"

"As I've explained, that's not my style. Well, this is what I'd like you to do this morning. I'm sure cook will need you to help her later, but for now could you please clean and dust the dining room. I'll ask Marleine to help you lay the table when she gets home from school this afternoon."

"Your daughter is very pretty, if I may say so. Can I ask how old she is?"

"She was fourteen a couple of months ago. She loves singing, you know …"

"Yes, I do as it happens. She's very talented, if I may say so. I've heard her singing in her bedroom and accompanying herself on the piano in the music room. She has a very sweet voice. May I mention that I sang with the choir in our church for a short while."

"Yes, your intonation is very clear and confident. Marleine's a chorister in the choir at our synagogue. Albert Einstein, the famous scientist, has played the organ there a few times though I don't believe he's at all religious. On the other hand, our son Freddie … Frederick … is tone deaf. That seems strange, really. Anyhow, he'll be going to university to study Law next year."

"May I ask who will be coming to dinner tonight?"

"Of course you may, Greschen. Ask me any questions you like. It's the only way for you to learn about our family and friends, my husband's business partners and their wives and other people you might see here on a fairly regular basis."

"Thank you, Frau Rosensweig."

"Well, apart from Max and me there'll be Frederick and Marleine, my parents Herr Alex and Frau Freda Mendelsohn and, as I think you know, our very good friends Herr Karl and Frau Stella Wartburg. They live out by the lakes at Wannsee. You should see the size of *their* house and garden!"

"You have a lovely home, too, if I may say so. I've never been inside anything quite like it. It's very tasteful … and so many rooms! I almost got lost when I first arrived. The Morgensteins had a large apartment, but it was cluttered with antique furniture. I think the view of the Tiergarten from your drawing room is wonderful. I'm just able to see the Spree from your study window here. And I can even see the tops of some trees in the parkland from the tiny window of my little attic chamber."

"We love it here in this house. It's like residing in the countryside, where I lived as a young girl. Yet it's not that far from the centre of Berlin with its shops, department stores, furriers, culture and coffee with cream cake at Krantzler's. I do hope it's comfortable for you up there in the roof space, Greschen."

"Yes thank you, Frau Rosensweig. It's small but I'm really delighted with my accommodation, and there's plenty of room for my few possessions. I've never been to that café in the Ku'Dam, though I've seen people sitting at tables outside in the summer sunshine. As I think you know, I'm an orphan."

"Yes, how sad. Frau Morgenstein mentioned it to me. She said your father had been killed in the war and that your mother was pregnant with you at the time. Let's see … it's now February thirty three, and I know you were seventeen at the beginning of last month. So your father must've died in 1915. Is that right, Greschen?"

"Yes, it is. My father never saw me, his only child. And my

mother died from influenza in 1919, a year after the war ended. I was brought up by my aunt, my Mutti's sister, and her husband."

"You poor thing …"

"We lived just east of the Alexander Platz. Not a very pleasant area. Quite down at heel in fact, as I'm sure you know … or maybe not. Lots of loutish SA men hang about the street corners now, with nothing better to do than look to pick a fight with communists or seek out defenceless Jews to beat up. I suppose my guardians did the best they could for me. They were very restrictive Lutherans, for ever going to church and quite stringent with me as I grew up. You could say I was used to a disciplined life even before I went into residential domestic service with the Morgensteins. But I was so glad to get away from home … I found the piety really stifling. I'm sorry to be prattling on like this … but I can talk to you so easily, Frau Rosensweig. And I'll work very hard for you, I promise."

"Ah so, my dear … and I'm sure you will. But there's no need to overdo the enthusiasm, eh Greschen?"

"No, Frau Rosensweig. And I'm very grateful to be living in this magnificent house. Are all Jewish people very wealthy, like I've heard say?"

"No, no, Greschen … they're definitely not, my dear. We've worked very hard to develop and grow our company over many years, and we've been fairly successful … and fortunate. There are many Jews who also work with commitment and rigour, but who are quite poor. My husband's business interests sometimes take him to cities in Poland. There are hundreds of thousands of impoverished Jews in that country alone. You may know that over recent years, several thousands of Polish Jews have migrated to Germany looking for work and a better life. Economically it's not been good here for them either, what with the Depression, inflation and everything. And the Poles haven't been welcomed by our fellow citizens … far from it. In fact, they've suffered dreadfully for the most part. I'm sure you're aware that there's much anti-Semitism around. The Jews seem to be blamed, quite unjustly, for all sorts of things that have gone wrong in Germany since the war. On the one hand, they're said to be greedy capitalists taking advantage of good German folk. And on the other, it's claimed they're all Bolshevists seeking to impose the socialist system here. History tells us that we've often been used as scapegoats for a troubled nation's ills. But the Polish Jews don't want to return to their homeland, where there may be even more poverty, hatred of the Jews and uncertainty."

"I'd better go tell cook about the number for dinner …"

"Yes, thank you Greschen, you do that now. I'll be here in my study for a while, if cook or you need to ask me anything. Then please deal with the dining room. The florist will be delivering fresh flowers this morning. Perhaps you could try your hand at arranging them in the glass vases."

"Yes I'd like to do that, Frau Rosensweig."

"You know, Greschen, there's so much dreadful news and so many frightening rumours these days that I just want my family and guests to feel happy and hopeful tonight … at least for a few hours."

★ ★ ★

"May I announce Herr Karl and Frau Stella Wartburg?"

"Thank you, Greschen. Sorry we're late, Amelie …"

"That's alright, Stella. We've only just sat down to dinner. Were there any problems, Karl?"

"Merely the usual … our driver had to make a wide detour to avoid some street fighting between Nazi louts and aggressive Commies. Arthur has now gone to visit his mother in the suburb of Wedding. He'll pick us up later this evening."

"Karl … Stella, come and join us at the table. Cook's ready to dish up the soup … You suddenly look fairly cheerful, Stella. Why's that?"

"It's just the thought of piping hot soup, Max. You know it's absolutely bitter outside. Below zero, I imagine. It's lovely to be in the warmth of this beautifully elegant dining room. Thank heavens for my new mink coat earlier … I'll show it to you in detail after we've eaten, Amelie."

"That will be nice, Stella. Greschen … you can serve the soup now."

"Yes, Frau Rosensweig."

"Did you hear Hitler ranting on the wireless last night, Max?"

"Yes I did, Karl. Well, you know there are more elections coming up next month. I think they'll be crucial for the nation."

"I believe you're right, Max. Last month's poll made the National Socialist German Workers Party the second largest party in the Reichstag. If Hitler carries the day, there could be real problems, and not only for us if you know what I mean. What do you think, Herr Mendelsohn? If the madman wins the biggest proportion of votes, do you consider that he'll be made Chancellor?"

"First, I'm not convinced that Hitler is a *mad* man, Karl.

He's certainly a *bad* man, but he's also quite clever in a twisted way. And with Dr Goebbels' warped but shrewd promotional guidance, he's succeeded in capturing the imagination of the people. Secondly, who can blame them for feeling they need strong leadership after the weaklings and failures in the Weimar government."

"But what's your opinion about the Chancellorship, Herr Mendelsohn?"

"I'm coming to your specific question, Karl. Frankly, I'm not at all sure. Von Papen and Hindenburg aren't fools, but they're under tremendous pressure. They're the kingmakers now, but they must have real doubts. My gut feeling is that if Herr Adolf's platform takes the ballot boxes, and his SA louts do excel themselves at electoral intimidation, he could well become Germany's next Chancellor. Maybe the two old farts, pardon the expression, think they'll be able to control him once he's inside the democratic parliamentary process. Tell me, has anyone seen an elephant fly?"

"Enough talking already, Alex … drink your soup before it gets cold."

"Okay, okay, Freda … I'm drinking, can't you see woman?"

"What constantly amazes me is how this one-time mere lance corporal has managed to get so far in the political world that even our great wartime Field Marshall is almost eating out of his hands."

"I think Napoleon Bonaparte was once a *mere* corporal, Uncle Karl … before he conquered most of Europe and became the Emperor of France."

"Yes, you're right Freddie … point well taken. I should've known better than to spout off with a keen historian at the table."

"I think we're all finished with the soup, Greschen. You can clear the bowls from the table now. And tell cook we're ready for the main course dishes."

"Yes, Frau Rosensweig."

"The vegetable soup was delicious, Amelie. Look, I can see everyone nodding in agreement."

"Thank you, Stella. It's cook's own recipe. Please pass on to Frau Midden our compliments, Greschen."

"Yes, I will."

"Just before, you mentioned about Hitler being a mere lance corporal in the war, Karl. But did you know that he was mentioned very many times in despatches, and even won the Iron Cross for an act of bravery at the Front? And I believe his henchman Hermann Goering flew courageously with the Red Baron and his so-called Flying Circus."

"You won an Iron Cross in the war too, Alex. We're very proud of you."

"I know, I know, Freda … but I'm not talking about that, dear."

"I really do seem to be getting it in the neck this evening. Yes, I did know about Hitler's medal for an action in the heat of battle above and beyond the call of duty. Didn't he rescue a wounded comrade? But am I right in suspecting a slight admiration for the fellow, Herr Mendelsohn?"

"I'm afraid that, once again tonight, you're labouring under a misapprehension, Karl …"

"I'm sorry, Herr Mend …"

"… The creature's a murderous swine and a foul anti-Semite. We Jews should never forget that. Or, indeed, be complacent about what he might be capable of doing in the future …"

"Ah, that's wonderful! Greschen has now returned with the steaming trolley and the main course. Please place the platters of hot food on the table, dear. We'll help ourselves as usual."

"Yes, Frau Rosensweig."

"What are we dining on tonight, Amelie?"

"I think cook said we'd be eating one of her Rhineland recipes with roast goose, sauerkraut and potato dumplings. Max dearest, could you pour the wine please?"

"Yes, of course darling. How neglectful of me! I do hope everyone likes Italian red."

"The bird looks really appetising, Amelie. You're very lucky having Frau Midden. Our woman is good, but I don't think she can compete with yours."

"Thank you, Stella. But we've dined many times at your home and we've enjoyed some really tasty meals."

"Okay, if you say so."

"No … I mean it, Stella. That chicken and lamb loaf we had at your place, I think a couple of weeks ago, was absolutely splendid."

"Wine's lovely, Max. It's going down a treat … a real winner!"

"Thanks for that, Karl. As I think you know, I get most of my cellar from a merchant just off the Potsdamer Platz. This case comes from Puglia, in the south of Italy."

"I can almost savour the hot sunshine."

"Dinner's scrumptious, Amelie. The dumplings are heavenly. They melt in the mouth."

"Thanks again, Stella. It's a pleasure when people enjoy what you're giving them to eat. And everyone appears to be tucking in contentedly. Next time you go to the kitchen,

Greschen, please tell cook she has triumphed again. And could you light the candles on the table now."

"Of course I will, Frau Rosensweig."

"Has anyone here been to the cinema lately? What about you, Marleine? You've been very quiet so far … not like you at all, my dear."

"I'm too busy with school work to see any films, Aunt Stella. And, in any case, I'm really scared about going into town. You don't know what could happen these days. A couple of friends of mine, two Jewish boys from my class, were kicked to the ground and pummelled one evening last week. They'd been to see a movie and were on their way home when they were ambushed by a group of uniformed anti-Semites and set upon. My friends were quite seriously hurt, and are still away from school while they're recovering."

"Have you had any problems, Freddie?"

"Thank goodness not personally so far, Grandfather. But like Marleine, some of my Jewish friends have also been cornered and attacked on the street by youths. They told me the young thugs who kept on taunting them and shrieking 'Jew pigs!' had a barbaric hatred in their steely eyes. My pals were battered terribly, and they were very lucky to have escaped without even more significant injuries. I think they'd been to see a new picture at one of the cinemas in town."

"It's ironic that the German film industry has so many creative Jews at its heart. I mean across the entire spectrum, from producers and directors to screenwriters and actors … Don't you have a relative working in one of the major studios, Karl?"

"That's correct, Max. My cousin Paul is a film editor. But he's extremely concerned for the future of Jewish employment, in all fields of cinematic production. If the Nazis attain power at some stage, he tells me he has justified fears. He predicts that Goebbels will head a propaganda ministry which will seize comprehensive control of the film industry, as well as every other cultural medium in the country. I'm sure you must've read in the newspapers, or heard on the wireless, Hitler's contorted side-kick going on about the need to remove Jews from the movie world which, he bemoans and bewails, has been polluted and contaminated by the Hebrews for far too long."

"That's so wicked … there's so much Jewish talent in the arts sphere; and especially in the music field, with composers, conductors and performers."

"I know, Max. And Paul informs me that a number of his creative friends in the film industry have already left for California in the hope of finding work in Hollywood."

"It's all so depressing, though I wonder sometimes whether people might be jumping the gun a bit. We don't know for certain what's going to happen here in Germany. Maybe Paul's departed colleagues were being a bit too pessimistic. Perhaps, Karl, they'll be unable to get jobs in America and be sorry they fled across the Atlantic prematurely."

"You could be right, Amelie. None of us has a crystal ball. But look what's been happening here over the last several years. It has been nothing less than chaos! And the Nazis have thrived because of it. I don't want to be offensive, and I'm not being personal Amelie, but don't they say that there are none as blind as those who will not see. I know it's almost impossible for us to accept the reality of Germany today, especially after we Jews have lived relatively peacefully in this country for a very long time. We've fought for the Fatherland, gained our civil rights as good citizens, been permitted to practice our faith and generally prospered for tens of decades."

"I'm not offended, Karl. Maybe we do sublimate what we can't understand or don't want to believe or accept. You look as if you're bursting to say something, Papa."

"Yes, my dear daughter. *Ich bin ein Deutscher*! I'm very honoured to be a German. I feel extremely satisfied that my family have been allowed to be successful in this great nation. I'm very proud to have fought for the Fatherland in the war. I was fighting for my family and the country that had given us shelter from persecution in the east. And indeed, I won some shiny gongs for my military efforts. There's a wonderful painting in a gallery or museum, I forget where exactly, that shows hundreds of German Jewish soldiers gathered around a rabbi and marking Yom Kippur in the muddy trenches of Flanders. There has always been anti-Semitism in Europe … for two thousand years, active anti-Semitism has come and gone, come and gone! What about the Romans flaying rabbis alive? What about the slaughter of Jews in medieval England? What about the Inquisition in Spain? What about the terrible pogroms in pre-revolutionary Russia … and what about poor Captain Dreyfus in late 19th century France? Ach, the French … the bloody hypocrites!"

"Quite a speech, Papa …"

"Please watch your language, Alex."

"Yes, Freda … but I haven't quite finished yet."

"What? Is there more, darling?"

"Yes my dear wife, there's more. And you, of all people, shouldn't be prodding me like that. You love this country as much as I do. Don't you adore the culture? It's truly unique …

the great writers, artists, composers and musicians. You love its opera houses, concert halls and theatres. You love the Altstadt, the ancient town centres, with their noble merchant houses, beautiful palaces, cathedrals and castles. You love the myths and the legends, the mysterious Rhineland forests, the tranquil southern lakes and the majestic Bavarian Alps. And even though we're Jewish, don't you just love the merry warmth and joyful whimsicality of our wonderful Christmas markets? I do apologise, everyone. I'm sorry for going on like this, but ... *Ich bin ein Deutscher*! I don't think the contemptible little Nazis and their nasty NSDAP can change all that for us Jews ... they're a passing phase, believe me, and they'll fade and vanish into the fog of history like the ancient Romans, the Spanish Inquisitors and the Tsars. A fundamentally civilised, cultured and Christian country like Germany cannot condone any belligerent upheaval of the Nazi genus for too long. And we Jews will get through all this ludicrous nonsense as we've always done. We'll survive and flourish again. I'm finished now ..."

"I can hardly believe it ... Was that silence in the room for the last few seconds! You should've been a politician, Papa. You would've left everyone speechless!"

"Well said, Amelie. More wine, anyone? I'm coming straight away Karl, Stella ... Freddie and, yes, I think you can have another glass Marleine."

"Could you please clear the plates and dishes, Greschen. I hope everyone enjoyed the main course. Oh, so many hands rising ... I'm flattered and I'll gladly take that as an affirmative response, then."

"It was excellent, Amelie ... delectable, in fact. And I've just noticed your beautiful flower arrangements on the sideboards."

# A Dream

"Well thank you so much, Stella. Actually, Greschen arranged the floral displays in the vases this morning. Oh I'm sorry, my child … I've made you blush. But you do appear to possess a natural knack for it."

"Thank you, Frau Rosensweig. You're very kind."

"Not at all, Greschen … credit where credit is due. When you've cleared all the used crockery and cutlery back to the kitchen, please inform cook that we're ready for the dessert now."

"Yes, of course."

"Do you know what Frau Midden has concocted for pudding, Greschen?"

"I think you're having apple strudel, Frau Wartburg. Cook gave me a tiny taster earlier on. And I've got to say it's full of flavour and so mouth-watering."

"Thank you, my dear. I can't wait to get stuck into it. I suspect you'll miss eating at home when you go to university next year, Freddie."

"You're quite right, Aunt Stella. As you know, I'm hoping to attend the Law Faculty at Nuremberg. Maybe I'll be lucky enough to be allocated some accommodation in one of the halls of residence. I sincerely hope so. Then I'll be able to take advantage of the refectory catering. I'm afraid I've no leanings whatsoever towards the culinary arts."

"What about anti-Semitism at the universities?"

"I'm not so naïve as to believe that there isn't any, or won't be any, Uncle Karl. There's no shortage of anti-Semites amongst academics and the so-called intellectual classes. I don't know whether I'm shocked by that, or not. But I'm hoping that, like at High School here in Berlin, I'll be successful in keeping away from any trouble. And also I'm thinking that, on the academic campus, there's unlikely to be the sort of violence that we're witnessing on the streets here and hearing about in other big cities. But, of course, I don't really know. I'm just hoping everything will be calm so that I can get on with my legal studies in peace. But I've got to add that I'm seriously worried about what the National Socialists, if they attain real power, will do about university education for Jews."

"I'm sure everyone here wishes you well and every success in your chosen studies and professional career, Freddie."

"Thank you, Uncle Karl."

"Dessert's here! Lay out the dishes please, Greschen. There's parve cream if anyone wants it. No, I didn't think so … it's quite horrible really, isn't it?"

"Yes it certainly is, Amelie."

"Thank you, Stella. We just try to do what we can."

"I know, and that's very commendable. But as you know, we're not so fussy when it's just us eating at home. Oh thank you, Greschen. Mm, the strudel does look good!"

"And believe it or believe it not, the casing's made without butter."

"Fantastic!"

"What would everyone like by way of a hot beverage afterwards? Greschen will serve it in the drawing room, where we can relax for a while. Is that alright, Greschen?"

"Yes, Frau Rosensweig."

"So that's three black coffees and four lemon teas …"

"Yes, Frau Rosensweig."

"You're suddenly looking very thoughtful, even a trifle sad, Marleine. Aren't you having a hot drink? Don't you like the strudel?"

"Yes I do, Mutti. It's as succulent as always. The apple pieces are heavenly … but I've got a confession to make."

"You've got a confession to make? What confession?"

"Don't worry. It's okay. I'm not pregnant, Grandmother."

"Marleine! Apologise immediately to your Grandmother … and everyone!"

"I'm sorry, Mutti. I apologise, Grandmother … Sorry, everyone."

"What are you talking about, Marleine?"

"I'm just about to say, Mutti. I've read a book …"

"What book?"

"Please don't get angry with me, Papa … at least not until … you see, I've read *Mein Kampf*."

"Wasn't that written by Adolf Hitler, Marleine?"

"Yes it was, Grandmother … he wrote it whilst he was serving a sentence in Landsberg Prison."

"I didn't know he'd been sent to prison."

"He was jailed after his unsuccessful beer-hall putsch in Munich in 1923, Stella. The Nazis wanted to march on Berlin, just like Mussolini and his Fascists had marched on Rome. But everything kind of collapsed. Hitler tried to run away, but he was caught and arrested by the police. A well-disposed judge gave him a pathetically short sentence for what truthfully amounted to treason, and he didn't even have to serve all of it."

"Thank you for the information, Herr Mendelsohn."

"Don't mention it, Stella. Hitler has wriggled out of so many tight corners, even assassination attempts, the fiend thinks that he's divinely protected. Just think about the possible implications of this for a moment …"

"But Marleine … *Mein Kampf*? I don't believe it. Whatever

possessed you to read such nonsense?"

"I wanted to. Has anyone here read it? No, I didn't think so."

"Don't be discourteous, Marleine. And why ever would we wish to read a lunatic's wild ravings?"

"Is Hitler the enemy of the Jews, Mutti?"

"Yes, I suppose it can be said that he is, Marleine."

"Why?"

"It's because he hates us."

"With respect you're exactly right, Mutti. And do you know why he hates *us*, and what he intends to do about *us* if he ever wins power over *us* in Germany? No? I thought as much."

"Don't be impertinent to your mother, Marleine. What are you trying to tell us?"

"I'm sorry, Papa … I'm sorry, Mutti. I didn't mean anything. I'm just trying to say that I'm a Jew and if Hitler's the enemy of my blood, then I want to know all about my enemy. That's why I read his book. It's a sort of manifesto. It sets out everything he believes and what he wants, with a terrifying passion but a malevolent rationality, to accomplish. He writes of the purity and superiority of the Aryan people and the sub-human nature of the Jewish race. He desires to remove us comprehensively from German life and make Germany *Judenfrei*, free of Jews. He also seeks lebensraum, living space for the legendary German folk to expand … and he covets the lands in the east to achieve his nefarious aims. It's black and white to me … Hitler wants a fight, a racial war against the Jews and a devastating conflict for the possession of vast tracts of territory in Poland and Russia. And guess what? Millions of Jews live in those countries …"

"My baby …"

"No Mutti, I'm not your baby. Not any more. You know what? After I'd read Hitler's philosophy and political motives and objectives, perverted as they may seem, I had a dream … no, it was a nightmare. I saw thousands upon thousands of Jews being led to slaughter like lambs. I'm not talking about the massacre of a handful of Jerusalemites by the Romans, or about the burning of a few heretics at the stake by Catholic Inquisitors or even about a Cossack attack on a little shtetl in the Pale of Settlement. I'm talking about the wholesale murder of many millions of Jews …"

"Marleine!"

"Sorry Mutti, but I must go on. Grandfather, bless him, doesn't believe anything too dreadful can happen to the Jews here in this educated and enlightened nation of which we're loyal and upright citizens. I do understand why he says that, and maybe why all of you need desperately to believe it. But do we realise how thin the crust of civilisation is? If we don't accept that soon, you'll see … we'll reap the whirlwind. You know what? I'd really like to go to the cinema to see a nice happy movie right now. But instead, if you'll all please excuse me, I think I'm going to bed … perhaps I'll have a safe and pleasant dream."

# The Beetles

"PROMIŇTE, pane, ale vypadáte úplně jako John Lennon."

"I'm sorry, madam? I'm English ... afraid I don't speak your language. Do you speak English?"

"Yes, I do. I regret disturbing you ..."

"That's okay. I was just admiring this amazing view over the town. The beautiful onion-shaped domes on the church towers are a delight to the eye. It's fabulous the way they gleam in the midday sunshine."

"Yes, it *is* a wonderful panorama from the castle heights here."

"If I may say so, your English is excellent ..."

"Thank you."

"... But can I help you in any way?"

"I'm now feeling really pathetic, and embarrassed, about approaching you like this ... You see, I was a big Beatles fan in the 1960s, when I was a teenager. Though it wasn't always easy being a fan of anything like that during the anti-Western communist regime here. My favourite Beatle songs are *Yesterday* and *Eleanor Rigby*. You could say that I was a raving fan of the Fab Four!"

"Sorry, I don't understand what …"

"Please excuse my stupidity … I was sitting on the wooden bench over there, eating my lunch sandwiches, when I noticed you standing here. I was thinking that you bear a striking resemblance to John Lennon … the Beatle you know. That's what I said in my language just before, when I came over to you."

"Striking resemblance to John Lennon, eh? In a way, I hope not … he's been dead for over twenty years now, I think! Well, that's very funny … no, not my silly and tasteless comment. By a coincidence, only yesterday afternoon I was emerging from a café on the town's historic main square when I overheard one of two youngish guys, maybe students, standing nearby saying almost the same thing about me to the other."

"That's quite a coincidence, but I can readily see …"

"I really don't see it myself. Any likeness to the Beatle, I mean. I think perhaps it's this peculiar hat that I'm wearing, though I can't recall Lennon ever sporting anything quite like it. It's called a Baker Boy. I believe it may've originated in New York early in the last century, though I bought this now rather crumpled example in Poland last year."

"You bought it in Poland?"

"Yes. Since my retirement, I've travelled quite extensively around Eastern Europe."

"Why's that? Wait … what am I thinking? I'm really sorry, sir. I shouldn't be quizzing you … asking you questions, any questions at all. How presumptuous of me! Not only have I rudely interrupted your peaceful admiration of my home town, but …"

"No, no, that's okay. It's no problem. In fact, it's great being able to carry on a sustained conversation in English here with someone who speaks it as well as you do."

"Well, thank you. That's quite flattering. I learned your language part-time at evening classes in the 1990s. And it's very interesting talking to you, too. I don't get the chance to use my English very often. But anyway, I've got to hurry back to work now …"

"Look, I'm a stranger in your town. I arrived only yesterday morning. And, as I said, it's been more than pleasant chatting to you like this. I'd like to answer your question, maybe … maybe over a cup of coffee some time, if you would be free for that. What about after you finish work today?"

"Er … all right. That sounds possible. I have an hour or so before I need to go home to my elderly mother. She hasn't been feeling particularly well of late. I could meet you when I leave the office. That would be just after five …"

"Where …?"

"I suspect you've noticed the large white, double-towered church on the main square?"

"Yes, I have. It's really handsome."

"Directly opposite this magnificent eighteenth century building is one of my favourite café bars. It's got quite a gritty buzz when people gather there after work; but not too much of it, if you know what I mean. I could meet you outside …"

"Fine … Just after five?"

"Yes, that's right. I work around the corner. Sorry, I've absolutely got to dash now."

"Okay … bye. See you later, then."

"Yes, bye …"

"By the way, what's your name?"

"… Sondra …"

"My name's … *Oh, she's gone.*"

★ ★ ★

"Hi there … Sondra, it's me!"

"Hello."

"It's good to see you again."

"Likewise … but please call me Sandra, if you wish. Of course it's the English, and perhaps softer version of my name."

"Right … Sandra it is, then. My name's David."

"Well, this is the café I mentioned. You found it okay?"

"No difficulty at all."

"I hope nobody else has compared you to a Beatle since …"

"Aha. No. Not so far."

"Okay. Shall we go in …?"

"There looks to be a table for two in that corner over there."

"You sit down while I order at the counter."

"No, please let me …"

"That's alright. What would you like to drink, David?"

"Can I have a coffee, please?"

"Of course you can … black or with milk?"

"Black as it comes."

"Fine, I won't be long …"

★ ★ ★

"Hi, again … Please sit down, Sandra. You should've let me pay for the drinks."

"Don't worry, David. I know … the age of chivalry isn't dead yet, but we're quite egalitarian here. Women do sometimes pay for …"

"No, I wasn't suggesting …"

"I know. I'm just teasing. Sorry, David. Anyway, they'll bring the coffees shortly."

"Thanks …"

"Ah, here are our hot drinks."

"That *was* quick!"

"Yes, you might say we've still got that lingering Germanic efficiency … a Teutonic legacy from our long-gone Hapsburg history."

"I know that your country has sustained quite a tortured time-line, including the Nazi occupation during the war."

"Yes, you're quite right of course. The Germans marched into this town in the spring of 1939. But I'm sure you know that."

"Yes, I've done some research on the internet back home. I've got a real interest in that turbulent, if not horrific period of European history. Some of my wife's distant relatives in Poland are believed to have perished in the Holocaust …"

"*Are you Jewish?*"

"Yes, I am. And I'm almost certain that John Lennon wasn't! You look surprised … about *me* being Jewish, I mean. Not about the late Beatle *not* being Jewish."

"A double negative … my English grammar teacher said that it's to be avoided."

"Sorry?"

"Anyhow, you don't look Jewish. But … But you may be even more startled to learn that I'm Jewish, too."

"*What?*"

"Didn't I say …?"

"Well I never … in a town of a few hundred thousand people and a microscopic Jewish community, you have to admit that our casual meeting this morning was a rather extraordinary coincidence."

"Yes, I suppose you're right. My fair hair may've hoodwinked you, too. As I say, I'm Jewish because my mother is Jewish. She's actually a Holocaust survivor, the only one from her family. And you may be interested to know that British troops found her in Bergen-Belsen in Germany, when they liberated the camp in April 1945. My late father wasn't Jewish, though. And I've never practiced the religion to any extent. What about you, David?"

"My wife and I attend our synagogue fairly regularly for Shabbat and festivals. We're not ultra-orthodox, but we do keep up the religion to the best of our ability in all the circumstances. We retain a kosher home, but we'll eat permissible fish or vegetarian dishes in restaurants. You see we travel quite a bit, so eating strictly kosher is often practically impossible. I suppose we fall within the category of what's now vaguely termed Modern Orthodox. It's an expression that can cover quite a spectrum of observance between the polarities of the reform, liberal or progressive movements and the really frum or charedi elements of our faith. Do you know of these words I've just used?"

"Yes, of course. Although I don't practice Judaism, I know quite a bit about it. And I understand exactly what you're telling me. I don't want to offend, but isn't what you've said a tad hypocritical?"

"That's an argument, of course. But, as I said, we try to do the best we can."

"I'm sorry for being controversial."

"Honestly, it's really no problem."

"I'm afraid that I wasn't brought up Jewish at all, if you get my drift. And you might comprehend now, from what I've told you, a little of why that was the case ... though it's probably more complex than you may think."

"What about your own family ... your husband?"

"I'm not married. I think perhaps you knew that ... I'm not wearing a wedding ring. And I've never been married. I'm a fifty-nine year old ... spinster of this parish, as I believe you English might tag me."

"This is very good coffee."

"It's the reason I come here. And I'm sorry if I caused you any embarrassment just now ... with that little outburst about my age and marital status. Do please forgive me."

"There's nothing to forgive. But do you know what? Our conversation seems to be leading quite nicely to the question you posed up on the castle heights earlier today."

"What question was that, David? Sorry, I can't remember."

"You wanted to know why I travel around Eastern Europe."

"Oh, yes. I recall now ... and also why I, a complete stranger, felt presumptuous ... even idiotically forward or familiar about asking you personal questions."

"I didn't take it that way, Sandra."

"You're very kind."

"Not at all, it's only ..."

"As I say, you're very kind."

"Anyway, I trek quite a lot around this part of Europe for two reasons basically. First, my ancestors immigrated to England from Russia and Poland in the late nineteenth century.

Secondly, I'm intrigued to meet up with and observe today's developing Jewish communities in countries like yours. And to discover how, over recent years and with the help of young and dedicated rabbis often imported but occasionally home grown, Jewish people, young and not so young, are evolving a significant interest in learning about their Jewish culture, heritage and religion. In some cities, I've found that the communal infrastructure is becoming quite sophisticated. And quite often, gentiles seem to be sharing the growing interest and helping to celebrate it."

"It's strange you should be mentioning this subject, David."

"Why's that?"

"It's because only fairly recently, and for the first time in my life, my mother has started to tell me about the proper kosher home she was brought up in here in this city, and its thriving Jewish community at that time."

"Why do you think she's doing this now, Sandra?"

"I don't know, and that's the genuine answer to your question. I have asked her, but she would just ignore me. I get the feeling it could be some kind of belated guilt complex. For what, I'm not sure precisely. But as I think I've told you, she has not been too well of late. So it could be something concerning her advanced age and physical decline. I really don't know. Anyhow, Mum's doctor is keeping a close eye on her condition. It's her heart problem mainly …"

"I'm sorry to hear that."

"Thanks, but her intellect is quite sharp for her maturity of years. And although she occasionally has difficulty remembering recent times, Mum can sometimes bring to mind, quite vividly, events from the war and even from her childhood."

"Yes, I know myself of some elderly people with that anomalous kind of memory recollection. Would you like another coffee?"

"No, thank you. I consume far too much caffeine as it is. I'm addicted to the drug. But I've got to be leaving you very shortly. I can just about afford to engage a part-time carer, a neighbour conveniently, for when I'm not around at home. Sonja comes in a few hours a day to give Mum a bit of company for a while, and to make her a meal. Sometimes she takes mother for a short walk to give her a little fresh air. Sonja also keeps a comforting eye on her, just in case … you know. It's not that Mum's physically incapable … she *can* do things for herself, though she does get fatigued fairly quickly now. And when Dad died of cancer three years ago, my mother became quite lonely when I was at work."

"It must be hard on you, too … if I may say so."

"I love my Mum dearly. So in that sense, it's no hardship to me. But, as you clearly appreciate, my life in recent times has been somewhat restricted and preoccupied."

"I'm sorry."

"Please don't pity me, David! It's …"

"No, I'm not offering you any pity at all. I do follow what you're saying. You obviously love your mother very much, and you're doing your level best for her. It's merely that I …"

"I don't believe how I've reacted to you just now. I'm a fool, you know. You're a total stranger … but you've been so kind and indulgent. And I'm being stupidly boorish by continually making you feel self-conscious and uncomfortable. I don't know what to say. Please forgive me, David. Will you?"

"Of course, Sandra … and as I've said, I do understand what

you're telling me … I really do."

"That's very sweet of you, David."

"There's no problem, really."

"Thanks, you're far too tolerant. You know, I've just had a brilliant idea. And I don't get too many of those these days! Would you like to meet my mother?"

"What …? When …?"

"Unless you've got something else scheduled for this evening, what about right now?"

"No, I haven't got any immediate plans. It's …"

"Then why not come for supper? Oh … I could make a salad for you, if that would be acceptable. I'm sure Mum would be delighted to meet with you, a new face for a change. As someone who's interested in the history of Jewish communities in this neck of the woods, you'll surely be keen to talk with her for a little while … before she goes to bed. What do you say?"

"I say, thank you for the thoughtful invitation. Thank you very much indeed. And I accept, gratefully. But how will your mother and I make ourselves understood to each other? Will you be interpreting?"

"Oh, no … Mum speaks perfect English, too. In fact, she's very literary. I taught her and Dad after I'd learned your language myself. You see they loved reading, but a lot of the books written in English that they wanted to read hadn't been translated into our mother tongue."

"Wow! This is quite something, Sandra."

"Thank you. Okay, now. Well if you're ready, let's go then. Hurry now, we need to catch a tram …"

★ ★ ★

"This is where we get off. Come on, David."

"Okay, Sandra …"

"Come along, I'd like to get home before Sonja leaves … that's the part-time carer I was telling you about. I need to have a word with her."

"I'm just trying to look up the tram departure times on the notice board at the stop … for when I leave you later on."

"Don't worry about that, David … I'll chauffeur you back to your hotel."

"That's really very good of you. Thanks a lot."

"Don't mention it. Now we just cross that bridge over the railway track, take the first street on the left and we're home. It's not that far."

"What do you drive?"

"It's a Škoda. What else?"

"Yes, I suppose."

"My car's really old, but I don't need to use the thing that often. And it's very reliable."

"A one-time friend of mine, now sadly deceased, wouldn't drive any other make of car."

"Nearly there … it's the third terraced house on the right, the one painted sickly light green. Quite small admittedly, but it was big enough for the three … and now the two of us. Mind yourself as we squeeze between my Škoda on our little forecourt and the neighbour's rickety wooden fence."

"Will do … By the way, what's your mother's name?"

"Zelna. Come David, let's go in …"

★ ★ ★

"Sonja … *Sonja*! Oh dear, she's gone. Never mind, she probably had to go directly on time. Her husband's a bit of a tyrant. I'm a little late home as well. It wasn't that important … what I had to tell her, that is. I'll catch up with her tomorrow morning, before I get the tram to work. So, come and meet my Mum. This way, David … the living room's through here. She'll be sitting in her armchair waiting anxiously for me."

"I'm sorry."

"For what are you sorry?"

"Well, it's my fault that you're late."

"Don't be silly … Hello, Mum. What? Yes mother, this evening we're going to speak only English. I've brought someone to meet you … he has come all the way from London, in England. His name is David."

"He has come all the way from London … and just to see *me*?"

"No, Mum. Not *just* to see you. He's visiting our town. And he's Jewish, like us. Well, not quite like us. He's a practicing Jew. I'll leave you two to get acquainted while I prepare the supper. I won't be long, and we'll eat soon …"

"You're *Jewish*, David?"

"Yes, I am."

"I'm very pleased to meet with you. May I shake your hand?"

"Of course you can."

"Well I know that religious Jews wouldn't touch a woman other than their wife, not even a hand."

"I'm not *that* religious."

"Take off your coat, David. Lay it across the sofa over there and sit yourself down on this chair beside me. It's where Sonja usually sits. She's a neighbour … and my part-time carer."

"Sondra told me about her. And thank you, M–Mrs …"

"Call me Zelna."

"If I may say so, Zelna, you speak English excellently."

"That's all down to Sondra."

"Yes, I know. She told me."

"Did she tell you that my late husband Pavel, her father, wasn't Jewish?"

"Yes, she did."

"And …?"

"And …? I'm sorry?"

"As a not *too* religious Jew, what do you think about my husband not being Jewish?"

"I don't think anything at all. It was your decision to make. It's really none of my business."

"I fell in love with Pavel. You can't help who you fall in love with, you know. Are you a politician back home in England?"

"Ha, ha … no, I'm definitely not a politician. And you've got a lovely sense of English humour, Zelna."

"I don't think so, young man."

"*Young man* …? Ha, you're very good, Zelna. No, I'm not a *young* man either. I retired from my profession a couple of years ago."

"But you're younger than me … much younger! I was born in 1926."

"You didn't have to let me know your age. In any case you don't look it, if I may say so."

"That's very nice of you, David … but I know you're telling a porky pie."

"Your idiomatic English is … exquisite! But I assure you that …"

"Don't say any more, or you'll be digging yourself into a deeper hole."

"Wonderful! You're great."

"If you say so … But I don't feel so great nowadays. I'm not very well, you know."

"Yes, Sondra mentioned that to me. I'm sorry, and I wish you well."

"Thank you, but I don't think I'm much longer for this world."

"Please don't say that, Zelna."

"But unlike your gentle little fibs, it's true what I'm telling you. My only regret is that Sondra will be left by herself when I go. Are you married?"

"Yes, I am. My wife was unable to join me on this trip."

"Okay … I'm sorry I asked."

"That's alright, Zelna. No problem at all …"

"Supper's ready! How have you two been getting along?"

"Like a house on fire, Sondra. That's what they say isn't it, young man?"

"Ha, ha … yes, Zelna, it's exactly what they say. And you beat me to saying it."

"Could you take your chair to the table please, David? And I'll help Mum up."

"Sure …"

\* \* \*

"The salad's absolutely delicious, Sandra."

"Thanks. It's nothing really, but I'm glad it's something suitable for you."

"The fresh salmon has a great flavour ... quite tangy."

"Our local fishmonger lightly smokes it. We like it, too. Don't we, Mum?"

"Yes, we do. It's very tasty. I appreciate such food, really I do. Because I remember the appalling times during the war years ..."

"Not now, Mum. We're eating and our guest doesn't want ..."

"That's okay, Sandra. I don't mind ... really. In fact, do please allow your mother to continue ..."

"Well, don't say I didn't warn you."

"Tell me about the war, Zelna ... if you want to, that is."

"As Sondra says, it's not very pleasant to hear my horrible story ... though I'm very willing to tell it to you. But are you certain you want to listen to it, David?"

"Yes, Zelna ... please tell me, unless of course it would upset you. I've heard many ghastly accounts of their experiences from Holocaust survivors."

"I will tell you then. But let's wait until after we've finished our dinner ..."

★ ★ ★

"Ah, the coffees ... thank you, Sondra. Well, David, you know we had a good life here before the Nazis came. My father had his own business, a small but successful one in the haberdashery trade. We weren't wealthy, but I reckon you might say that we were a comfortably well-off, middle class family. We lived in a lovely big house with a large landscaped garden in a highly salubrious, leafy district of the town."

"Sandra told me your family were fairly orthodox Jews."

"Yes, that's right. I was brought up with my much prettier older sister Anna and younger brother Viktor to be good Jews. Our home was strictly kosher and we went to the beautiful synagogue for Shabbos, High Holyday and festival services. But all that came to a shocking halt when the Germans invaded and occupied our little country. In common with many other Jewish businessmen, my father lost everything that he'd worked so long and hard to build up. Naturally, the Nazis burned down the community's synagogue. And our property was expropriated for Aryan use. We were virtually homeless beggars when the deportations to Poland began in the autumn of 1941 …"

"As I mentioned to Sandra, some of my wife's distant Polish relatives perished in one of the Nazi death camps, maybe Auschwitz-Birkenau. My own Polish ancestors lived in or near to Lodz."

"There's a coincidence, because that city's ghetto was the destination for many transports from this region. However, it's fairly unlikely I would've bumped into your wife's Polish relatives. People from our part of the world were kept together mostly in our own part of the ghetto …"

"I seem to recall that Lodz was named Litzmannstadt by the Germans."

"You're right. But you can't imagine what it was like to come from a lovely happy home with tons of space, plenty of food, a warm and cosy atmosphere and the freedom to go wherever we wanted … and then to be dumped, the five of us, in a single, one windowed room of a fourth-floor flat dripping with damp in an ancient crumbling tenement."

"It must've been horrific …"

"It was even more than horrific, David. We were stunned, shocked to the core of our very being. It was a … l-living n-nightmare!"

"Mum, please don't go on … you're upsetting yourself."

"No, Sondra. I want to continue. I must keep a stiff upper lip, eh David?"

"Zelna …"

"No, I'm okay … When we were first thrown into that hell-hole, we couldn't believe it. It was impossible to accept … to take in the dramatic change in our circumstances. It was so unreal … almost surreal. The flat had four rooms and as many families occupying them. We all used the one tiny kitchen, so you couldn't conceive the havoc, the shouting and the confusion … the nerve-wracking impossibility of it all. I can't remember the number of apartments in our block, but there were a lot of them. To say the place was overcrowded would be a ludicrous understatement. The lavatories in the inner courtyard were disgusting … always overflowing with urine and excrement, please excuse me. And I don't know what else ran along the filthy open drains, aside from the rats that is. Constantly, there were snaking lines of people waiting to use the stinking facilities. Many of them, particularly the elderly and the very young, just couldn't cope … if you know what I mean. There was no separation for men and women in the hideous toilets, and the putrid stench was awful. You couldn't escape the foul smell … it pervaded everywhere in the building. Sometimes, residents just fainted because of the terrible odour. For women especially, the situation was horrendous … and for young girls like Anna and me, who were not that long into puberty, I cannot begin to describe what we went through. It was like being tortured to the very core of our being on a daily basis. Again, to say that all this was demeaning and humiliating would be a hilarious underestimation. People literally went mad with the shame of it. But this is just how the Nazis wanted us Jews to feel, to exist day in and day out … like we were nothing."

"Drink some more coffee, Mum. Whilst it's still warm."

"Okay … Do you want to hear more, David? I can tell you so much more."

"Please don't tire yourself, Zelna …"

"Don't worry, David. I'll be alright. I spend more than sufficient time in my bed. I've not spoken much about this to Sondra, certainly never to Pavel. Somehow I need now to speak of it. Where was I? Oh, yes … day in, day out. The food was horrible. But having said that, there was never enough of it … Men and women who worked got more in the way of rations, which of course they shared within their families. But there were many people who consumed their meagre portions, which should've lasted a week or more, in only a few days. The outcome was inevitable, David. What with rampant disease, physical abuse and starvation, our numbers diminished considerably. My father, mother and sister had jobs in a ghetto factory producing winter coats for the German army. So at least our provisions were reasonably adequate though hardly nutritious, consisting mainly of potatoes, flour, margarine and some sugar. Also available for collection was some stew, if you can call stew a piss-pot, excuse me, of hot water with some unidentifiable bits of whatever floating in it! Those employed were entitled to a little extra food … not that this was of any real benefit. All in all, our tentative lives, which continuously hung by a thread, were a total and utter misery from morning until evening. And if you couldn't get to sleep, and throughout the long cold night, you would hear coming from the other side of the thin walls your very close neighbours weeping in anguish, crying with pain, shrieking in terror or praying to the Almighty with fervour and hope. At first, I prayed too … but as time passed, I gradually abandoned my faith."

"Please let me hold your hands, Zelna. There … you've been through so much. I often wonder how *anyone* could've survived such atrocious treatment …"

"Believe me, David, few did. My father was the first to pass away. He collapsed at his work bench and died instantly. We thought he'd been keeping fairly fit and healthy. It was more likely the mental hurt for his family's condition, and his total helplessness in the situation, that finally overcame and killed him."

"You must've been devastated."

"I suppose, David. But people were dropping like flies all around us, all the time … It's very difficult for me to say this, but we were becoming like zombies and almost numb, immune if you like to the dreadful suffering around us. It's terrible to think that our feelings may've been icy and callous. But there was an emotional vacuum, an utter black emptiness in our innermost selves. Viktor was the next to leave this world. He had this excruciating pain one evening. He lay doubled-up on the floor. He could hardly breathe with the unbearable agony of it. We took him quickly in a wheelbarrow to the Jewish hospital, but the doctor said he was a hopeless case. My brother died a couple of hours later."

"Oh, Zelna …"

"Yes, David, it was impossibly hard for us to lose Viktor. He was such a good boy, helping everyone as best he could, scavenging ahead of the vermin, running errands and trying to keep his pathetically small corner of our grimly depressing room neat and tidy. He passed on just a few days before his tenth birthday. I'm sorry to burden you with my family album of death, but you did insist on hearing all this …"

"I'm sorry, David. But my mother will need to go up to bed soon. Mum, you're obviously becoming very tired and the … the depressing story you're telling isn't helping."

"You must please let me finish, Sondra. I can't let David go without knowing the full story."

"Okay … but only a little while longer, Mum. Then it's up to bed with you."

"Before the war, my own mother had been a very strong woman, bringing up the children, looking after the home and also assisting Dad in the business. But it wasn't long after our arrival in the ghetto that our environment began to suck the strength out of her body, like a vampire drawing blood. She'd been a fine figure of a woman, but the extensive hours she worked hunched over her bench in the factory, the lack of proper nutrition and the clawing fear for her family, that you could see all the time in her hopelessly dark-rimmed and cadaverous eyes, took their heavy toll. Despite her brave attempts to mentally thwart the insidious onslaught of suffering around her and within her, she became a frail and emaciated wreck. She succumbed in the freezing winter of 1942 …"

"So there were just the two of you remaining … you and your sister?"

"Yes, David. Just the two of us … and I don't know how

we'd managed to survive for so long. I owed so much to Anna. She'd continued to work and get the few additional ration items which made that vitally sustaining edge of difference to us. And I suppose that our youth aided us to an extent. All the while, transports were shifting sections of the ghetto population to what the Nazis and our Jewish Council, which was forced to co-operate with the Germans, declared were better living conditions at work camps in the countryside. But rumours were rife, and we had a compelling inkling that the final destinations were rather more sinister. Ghetto inmates would do almost anything to evade the regular round-ups … even by committing suicide."

"Mum … bed soon, okay?"

"Only a little while longer, please Sondra …"

"Are you sure, Zelna? These sad memories must be so emotionally harrowing for you."

"I'm alright, really."

"I'm truly astonished at how you and your sister found that compelling inner force to carry on, despite the …"

"I believed that Anna was very strong, David … much stronger than yours truly. As I said, she took good care of me. Even though she was just a couple of years older, she was conducting herself like a mother to me. But what I didn't realise was that she was extremely distressed, and suffering what I suppose might be called clinical depression today. Needless to say, we were all thoroughly depressed to varying degrees. But it was different for Anna. I have to tell you something. The gruesome tenement building in which we existed, the drab flats and of course our miserable room were, as you might expect, infested with beetles …"

"Sorry for interrupting, David … Mum calls all insects of whatever kind *beetles*. When she talks about beetles in Lodz, I believe she means bedbugs and lice."

"That's right, Sondra … bedbugs and lice. They were our perpetual companions by day and, particularly, by night. Every morning, Anna and I picked them off each other's naked bodies … there were hundreds of the buggers, excuse me David. It was an unpleasant task, to say the very least. I hated it, but strangely I'd got used to it. It became a kind of routine though pointless hygiene procedure. Perhaps your mind will turn itself off at a certain breaking point. Maybe it's just a question of getting used to anything over time … But what I didn't know was that my sister was concealing from me, possibly for my sake, a fathomless abhorrence of her personal contamination, a mind-twisting, skin-creeping phobia of the sticky brown, blood-swollen creatures. Early one day, I was awakened by what I thought was shouting. Mind you, this wasn't an unusual occurrence. But it was different that morning. It was my sister shrieking. I jumped out of what passed for a bed, a jumble of threadbare old grey woollen blankets on the floor, to see her frantically beating the swarming pests off her inflamed chest with flailing arms. *I can't take this any more! I can't take this any more! I can't take this any more!* Anna kept on screaming the same sentence, over and over again. I hardly recognised her voice. It was so different, so outlandishly deep, hoarse and guttural … not quite of this world. I tried to help Anna, but my sister pushed me away. Her bizarre cries grew louder then deeper, like an animal growling … and then they became high-pitched again. The months and months of stifling yet storing her profound terror of the beetles were now made manifest in shrieks bursting through the black hole of her mouth. It was like a volcanic eruption of piercing sound emanating from the depths of her soul. I clamped my hands to my ears … I couldn't bear to hear my sister's agonised screeches. And I closed my eyes tight to shut out the awful sight of my beloved sister rapidly falling apart at the seams. Then I felt a sudden draught. Anna must've opened the window. I thought she wanted to get some clean air into her lungs and our foetid room. B–But … B–But …"

"Mum!"

"L–Leave me alone, Sondra … N–No, the open window wasn't intended to allow some fresh air to enter the room. I–It was intended for Anna to leave it …"

## A Yahrzeit

"THIS IS Mrs Smolensky's room. She's ninety-five years old, and whilst physically quite fragile she speaks fairly clearly and understands everything that's going on. Sadly, that's more than I can say for some of the other, relatively younger residents here. Though there's only one under the age of eighty."

"It's really very good of you, Matron ... I mean, to show me around the town's Jewish home for the aged like this, introducing me to some of the people and, of course, interpreting for me. Your language doesn't come easy to me. We English aren't the world's greatest linguists. But I have to say that I've been more than impressed by the caring work you and your team do here."

"You're very welcome, and thank you for your kind words. I'm very pleased you're taking the time to visit us as part of meeting the city's Jewish community. By this time of the morning, the staff will have settled Mrs Smolensky into her favourite armchair by the window. She likes looking down into our gorgeous garden at the rear of the building. When she's not sleeping, that is. And understandably, she does sleep quite a considerable amount now. Please knock and go in. I'll revert to our own language now."

"Good morning, Mrs Smolensky my dear. Look, I've brought someone who's visiting us to wish everyone well. He's come all the way from England."

"She looks so small in that large chair, Matron. But she's smiling at me with what looks like recognition in her bright eyes. Does the lady know England?"

"Yes, I believe so. I seem to recall she told me once that her late husband served with a specially formed fighter squadron in the Royal Air Force during the war. It was some years ago that she mentioned this ... usually her memory isn't so good now."

"Will she mind me holding her hands like this? I hope I'm not taking a liberty. The few other residents I've met here today seemed to like it. Mrs Dra ... Draviska grasped my hands in her own and kissed my fingers. I can't tell you how moving that was for me. I freely admit that I needed to stifle a tear or two."

"I'm sure Mrs Smolensky wouldn't mind."

"What did she just say, Matron?"

"Mrs Smolensky said she's very pleased you've come to see her, but that she's thirsty. She would like you to fetch her some water."

"Can I do that?"

"Yes, of course. Please take the glass from the side table next to her chair and half fill it from the tap above the little sink in the corner over there. It *is* drinking water."

"Can I just give it to her? Is she able to hold the glass by herself?"

"Yes, thankfully she can still do that. Please offer it to her. She'll put it back on the table when she's had enough …"

"Could you translate her words for me, please?"

"Mrs Smolensky thanks you very much for the drink. And she wants to know why you've come here."

"Could you please tell her, Matron, that I enjoy visiting Jewish communities in Eastern Europe, seeing how they're getting along and wishing them well for the future … and please add that my great-grandparents emigrated from this area to England more than a hundred years ago."

"Of course …"

"Thank you … and what did she say in response?"

"She said it's interesting that your ancestors lived in this country. And that it's very considerate of you to visit her."

"I think Mrs Smolensky just added something else, Matron."

"Yes, she noted that you're very fortunate."

"Can you please ask her why she thinks so?"

"Okay …"

"And what did she reply?"

"She just said that she's very tired. We'd better leave her now."

\* \* \*

"Behind this door is Mrs Spinek. She was eighty-nine last month. Like Mrs Smolensky, and virtually all the other female residents here, she's a widow. Generally, she's crisp and right on the ball. You can have a really decent conversation with Mrs Spinek. In your case, I mean that quite literally. You'll understand what I'm saying shortly. And in that sense, I'll leave you to meet her by yourself. You said in the elevator just before that this will have to be the last resident you can visit for now. If you wish, please drop into my office on the ground floor before you leave us."

"Many thanks for accompanying me around the home this morning, Matron ... and, of course, for your essential translation services. I'll certainly want to say goodbye to you before I go. Shall I just knock and go in to Mrs Spinek?"

"Please do. I hope to see you a little later on, then."

"Thank you, Matron. I'll go in now ..."

★ ★ ★

"Mrs Spinek ... er, Pani Spinek ... Pani Spinek?"

"It's okay, you can call me *Mrs* Spinek ... You seem to know who *I* am, but who are *you*?"

"You speak English! Ah, I know now what Matron meant."

"I beg your pardon?"

"Sorry ... no, it's nothing Mrs Spinek. It's marvellous that you speak English ... Excuse me for mentioning it, but I can just about see you sitting there at the table. It's rather dark in here. That night-light on the bedside cabinet doesn't give out much illumination. Would you like me to open the curtains at the window? It's a lovely sunny morning outside."

"Alright, you can open the curtains if you must. And by the way, it's not a night-light. It's a Yahrzeit memorial candle."

"I'm so sorry, Mrs Spinek ... I didn't realise. I wish you a long life."

"I've *had* a long life. I'm nearly ninety ... it's enough already.

But you still haven't told me who *you* are and what you're doing here."

"I'm sorry, Mrs …"

"Please don't keep saying you're sorry. We're all sorry, for one reason or another."

"I'm sor … I won't, I promise. I think I *will* open the curtains, Mrs Spinek. Then we'll both be able to see each other clearly … Isn't that better?"

"Not really … but no, no, don't draw them again. It's alright. Sit down here, at the table and tell me who you are."

"Thank you, Mrs Spinek … I'm from London, in England …"

"Yes, I know where London is."

"Sor … I mean, yes of course. I'm visiting the Jewish community in this city. I spent last Shabbat morning at the synagogue service. Afterwards, I was kindly invited to lunch by the rabbi and his wife. And I've now been to the Jewish museum, the cemetery, the school and the cheder. Today, I'm looking around your home, meeting Matron and her staff and talking, with her help, to some of the residents. It's really unexpected, but very convenient to be able to speak with you in my native tongue. Though, as I've mentioned to other people here, my forebears made the journey from this part of the world to England as long ago as the nineteenth century. How do you find it here, in this home I mean?"

"I can't say it's wonderful to be here, though the staff members are very caring and look after all of us very well. Of course, I'd sooner be living independently but it's not possible now. It hasn't been possible for more than five years. I kept falling over in my flat. It's a pity that I didn't fall over for ever."

"I-I'm … er, I regret to hear you say that, Mrs Spinek."

"You're very good … with the synonyms."

"If I may say so, your English is really excellent, Mrs Spinek. Perhaps I can ask you about that?"

"It's simple. I had a brother living in New York. He was a bachelor. He would come to visit me once a year after my husband died. And he would stay for a couple of months."

"Do you know, I thought I detected a slight American twang to your voice?"

"Yes, some people do notice that."

"When did your husband pass away? Is it his Yahrzeit today?"

"It was a very long time ago now. But no, it isn't his Yahrzeit today. I'm Jewish, of course you know that. Otherwise I wouldn't be permitted to live here. My husband wasn't Jewish."

"Oh, right. So whose Yahrzeit are you marking today, if I may enquire?"

"Our son's … I'm Jewish, so he was too."

"I'm so … regretful."

"Good. Yes, that's very good. Would you like a cup of coffee? I could easily ring for some. Room service, so to speak, is okay. They're normally quite efficient in the kitchen."

"No thank you, Mrs Spinek. I had a hot drink with Matron when I arrived here a couple of hours back. But may I ask when you sadly lost your son?"

"You say 'sadly'. And 'lost', eh? Interesting choice of words … you don't know how interesting."

"I don't understand, Mrs Spinek. I hope I haven't said or done anything out of place. I don't want to offend you in any way."

"N-No … y-you haven't s-said or d-done anything out of

p-place. And, believe me … i-it's not that easy to offend s-someone my age."

"You're crying, Mrs Spinek. Please don't cry. Shall I call someone?"

"N-No, d-don't d-do that. D-Do you have a t-tissue, please?"

"Yes, of course … Here you are."

"T-Thank you, kind sir. This time it's for me to say *sorry*."

"Can I help in any way?"

"P-Please allow me a moment to wipe my eyes … and no thanks, you can't help in any way at all. It's just that I had a flood of terrible memories. I don't talk about things … I *never* talk about things."

"Would you want to talk to me about these … these things?"

"You seem to be a very nice man, but I don't know you at all."

"Sometimes, Mrs Spinek, it can be therapeutic to talk to a stranger … though I hope you could say that I'm not a complete stranger."

"What do you mean?"

"Well, you're Jewish and I'm Jewish. I've visited, either alone as now or sometimes with my wife, many Jewish communities around the world. In recent years, I've been focusing on communities in Eastern Europe. You know, whenever I'm with other Jewish people, wherever that is across the globe, I feel just as if I'm at home. It's like we're all brothers and sisters … one big family. We share so much based on our faith and heritage. And what we share comes also from the heart and the soul. I believe that unity of thought and object, and pride in our religion, has helped the Jewish people to survive dreadful oppression and persecution over the ages, not least the Nazi Holocaust of six million Jews in our own era … Oh Mrs Spinek, you're weeping again. Would you prefer that I left you in peace?"

"N–No, p–please don't go yet. J–Just give me a couple of s–seconds … and another t–tissue, p–please."

"Did you lose family, parents, siblings and maybe other relatives in the war … in the camps?"

"Y–Yes, I did … all of them. I–I was lucky to survive the rigours of a labour camp. B–But those weren't the awful memories of which I spoke just before."

"It's something to do with your son, isn't it … the son for whom you have Yahrzeit today?"

"My late husband and I had only one child. But you're right … it's all about our son. And you're also correct about another thing. We Jewish people *should* be proud of our identity, of who we are. My eyesight's not brilliant nowadays, but I read the reports and articles in the newspapers and watch the news programmes on the television. I wonder sometimes whether anti–Semitism, in whichever form it takes and for whatever purpose or motive, will be with us for all eternity. And despite everything that's happened to the Jewish people. We need to be a family, especially for those who don't have any. We need to share our joys and sorrows to make us stronger as Jews together, no matter how weak or strong are our religious beliefs."

"As you've heard, I agree entirely with your sentiments, Mrs Spinek."

"It wasn't always my notion of how things should be. After the unspeakable slaughter of the war, we were in traumatic shock."

"I really can't imagine what it must've been like for you here, as a Jew that is."

"Did you know there were pogroms in this country even after the war's end?"

"Yes, I did know that from my reading. Wasn't it partly due to Holocaust survivors trying to reclaim the homes and other property they'd owned before deportation?"

"Yes, that's so. I was in my mid-twenties. I'd experienced unbelievable horrors during the war; and I was now hearing of more killings after the conflict was supposed to be all over. I was terrified to be a Jew. My family had been traditionally observant, but I made a conscious decision to hide for ever the fact that I'm Jewish. In that respect, it was fortunate I was a girl. You know what I mean?"

"Yes I do, Mrs Spinek."

"I had no family left to care, one way or the other. And when a repressive communist government began to rule this country, it became obvious that the open practice of Judaism wouldn't be permitted. In any event, Jews who were unable to flee the regime went underground, so to speak. And for the most part, they concealed their faith and religious observances. I married a gentile. He was a good man and very kind to me. I suppose that I loved him. But I never told him that I'm Jewish. As I mentioned, we had one child … a son. Why only one, you might ask? That's another easy question to answer. My husband was a carpenter and joiner who worked in the post-war reconstruction of our country, helping to build bleak and sprawling housing estates for the dispossessed. Health and safety weren't top priorities on the ubiquitous building sites. One afternoon, the police came to our flat. My husband had fallen from some high scaffolding, they informed me, and apparently he had been killed instantaneously."

"My goodness … that must've been dreadful for you, Mrs Spinek. How old was your husband when he died?"

"He was just thirty-seven."

"What did you do?"

"What could I do? I carried on as best I could. I had a five-year-old son to look after."

"How did you cope? It must've been so very hard for you."

"I take that as English understatement. Times were extraordinarily difficult, and not only for me of course. Life was an endless struggle. But isn't that what communism's supposed to be all about? The proletariat's continuing struggle … at least that's what those in authority constantly stuffed down our throats. I managed to get shift work in a factory. A benevolent neighbour looked after my boy when he came home from school, and when it was necessary. As he grew to become a teenager, I worried about him all the time. It was such a pity he never had a Dad to talk with, to discuss things with … like football, life and politics. I was always exhausted from work and hardly ever at home when my son was around."

"Didn't his father have any relatives that could've taken him under their wing?"

"Yes, he did have some family and they didn't live too far away from us. But I didn't see them, save occasionally in the street. They never visited us, and never communicated with us in any way. I don't think they liked me. Don't ask me why. Perhaps, I thought, they blamed me for my husband's death. I didn't see how they could do that. It was an accident at work. I really don't know."

"So how did your son manage? Presumably, he would've made some friends at school or at a youth club maybe."

"He never spoke of any such. But as he grew older, he seemed to get very secretive. When he turned seventeen, he told me never to go into his bedroom. I wasn't to go into the room to clean or dust it. Or to do anything else for that matter, like changing the bedclothes or taking down the curtains for washing."

"Why was that, Mrs Spinek?"

"He never said. He didn't want to tell me. He just promised that he would do whatever was required to keep his room neat and tidy. In fact, he fixed a lock on the door and I never had a key. So I couldn't have entered his room, even if I'd wanted."

"What did you think he was doing in there?"

"I really didn't know. I did wonder whether he was ashamed or embarrassed about things he might've kept in his wardrobe, desk drawer or bedside cupboard. You understand what I'm saying?"

"You mean … pornography?"

"Yes. Anyway, I never knew."

"No clues at all?"

"No, there was nothing. One evening I came home from work and I noticed that his bedroom door was slightly ajar. I just peeped inside, no more than a glimpse. But he was in there, sitting quietly at his desk. When he spotted me staring at him, he jumped up suddenly like a jack-in-the-box and slammed the door shut in my face!"

"That must've come as quite a shock to you, Mrs Spinek!"

"Believe me, you're not wrong. Later on, he apologised. But he stressed that he'd asked me politely not to do what I'd done. I said that I'd only glanced in, but he was having none of it. It's not that we didn't get on generally. That may sound a bit ironic or incongruous to you after what I've related. On rare occasions, if I had a little money to spare, we would even go together to see a film at the local cinema."

"Was your son working at this time, Mrs Spinek?"

"Yes, he was. Against the odds, he'd managed to find a position as an apprentice plumber. I was so glad that he would have a steady job in time, and be able to earn some money. I'm sure he would've liked to move out to a place of his own, but obviously he couldn't afford to do that."

"And you never saw any of his friends? Didn't he ever bring anyone home?"

"No, he never did. But once, in the middle of the day, I saw him running down a street in town alongside two or three older men. I had a rare weekday off work and I was doing some food shopping in a nearby market. Each of the men, including my son, was gripping what looked like a bag or a sack. I couldn't be certain. They seemed to be in a crashing hurry. I thought the older men might've been my son's workmates. But they looked quite rough and thuggish, if I can put it that way. Maybe, I thought subsequently, I'd been too judgemental, basing my view solely on their appearance ... though, truthfully, I wasn't very impressed. My son returned home much later that day carrying a Hessian sack. I remember it was after eleven o'clock. Sometimes he would stay out all night. I never knew where he went and, of course, he didn't tell me. Frankly, even though I was his mother I wouldn't have dared to ask him. In a sort of way I was afraid to know, to hear what he might tell me. I mentioned that I'd seen him earlier with the other men. I asked whether his companions were colleagues, and what he had in the sack. He ignored me completely, went into his room and quickly closed and locked the door."

"Must've been mystifying, to say the least."

"Yes, it was. But it was peculiar, really. Although we had these moments of acute friction, and as I mentioned earlier, we had generally what you might call a satisfactory mother and son relationship. We even shared a laugh from time to time. Of course, he didn't make much money as a trainee. But occasionally he would come home bearing a little present for me … perhaps a nice coloured comb for my hair, or a pair of cheap glass earrings he'd bought in the flea market near the main railway station. Of course, it was the thought that counted for me. He wasn't especially affectionate, I mean in a cuddly sort of way. Nor, for that matter, was I particularly demonstrative. But whenever he gave me a small gift, he would plant a quick peck on my cheek. I did love him. He *was* my son, my own flesh and blood, after all. And I really do believe that in his own particular way he loved me."

"We all have our foibles and odd character traits, of one kind or another. Doubtless your son had his own quirks. But it does seem clear to me that you were each bound by an emotional attachment to the other. When I first saw your face in the light earlier on, and you told me you had Yahrzeit for your son today, I thought I read sadness across it. But on reflection, and considering what you've had the strength of purpose to disclose to me, I think what I saw rather was doubt and bewilderment. I was receiving the message that you're not sure, maybe that you've never been sure, about observing your son's Yahrzeit. You must forgive my presumptuous ramblings. It's really none of my business. I was just wondering whether there's any truth in what I've just said, I hope sympathetically, Mrs Spinek?"

"M–More t–than you can ever imagine, m–my d–dear f–friend from London in England … and c–could you hand me another t–tissue, p–please?"

"Here you are. Would you like to talk about it, Mrs Spinek? Or shall I just leave now? As I've said, you really don't have to tell me anything. It's absolutely none of my concern …"

"Nobody here knows what I'm about to tell you. So I beg of you not to mention it to anyone."

"You have my complete assurance on that, of course."

"I want, no maybe I do need, to tell you my fellow Jew about my son, and how and why he died so young. Perhaps I should put into practice what I said before … about sharing sorrow."

"I do respect your feelings, Mrs Spinek. And I'm deeply humbled by your trust in me."

"There was a time when I became seriously ill. The disease I contracted was thought by the doctors to have been caused by my work in the factory over many years. It was something in the dust that lingered around the workshops, and which had affected my lungs. I was rushed to the hospital and they operated on me as a matter of urgency. But the surgeon wasn't clear as to whether his work had been totally successful. He told me it would take a week or so, and some further tests, to obtain the prognosis. I asked him to be honest with me. He said that I was very courageous. I recollect shaking my head at him, and responding that I was scared stiff but an ardent realist. He advised that my medical situation didn't look too sound. Naturally, I didn't tell him that I'd been on the brink of death more than once in the camps. That night, I thought long and hard and came to a decision. I resolved to tell my son that I, his mother, was Jewish and that, therefore, he was Jewish also."

"If I may be so bold, Mrs Spinek, why did you reach that decision?"

"This isn't an easy question to answer. Somehow, I wanted him to know who he really was. I considered it was his basic entitlement and my only legacy to him. There were times during his young life when I'd felt that my son, like many of his contemporaries in the world today, was searching for an identity. I sincerely wished him to know that he possessed one, an ancient and sacred one that I'd been forced by circumstances to abandon, may the Almighty forgive me."

"I see … I think."

"It's more than difficult to explain personal motivation at times, especially if it springs from the heart or the soul rather than the logical intellect."

"You're doing remarkably well, Mrs Spinek … and I assure you that I'm being neither patronising nor condescending. Truly, I'm filled with admiration for you. Please continue but only if you want to, of course."

"Yes, I do. And thank you so much for your kind and comforting thoughts."

"No, I must thank you for your candour."

"In any case, I believed my condition was fatal and that I was at death's door. So the next time my son came to see me in the ward, although he'd warned that work prevented him from coming too often during the restricted visiting hours, I asked a nurse to pull the curtains around my bed for greater privacy. When she'd gone and my boy had sat himself down on the bedside chair, I said that I had something very important to tell him. And that he must forgive me for not having told him much earlier in his life. I implored him to try to comprehend *why* I hadn't said anything previously."

"How did he look when you said this to him?"

"Puzzled but, in a way, curious … perhaps even intrigued."

"Okay."

"So then without further delay I told him point blank that I was Jewish and that, in consequence, he was Jewish too."

"How did he react on hearing that, Mrs Spinek?"

"He just laughed like a hyena, shook his head and continued shaking it. I was dumbfounded, though I'm not sure why I should've been. I do recall being in some pain, despite the drugs they were feeding me."

"So what did you say to him?"

"I said that he had to believe me, that it wasn't a joke."

"But did your son *say* anything to you?"

"Yes, he did. After he'd stopped laughing his head off, he just said that I was very ill and didn't know what I was talking about. Then I advised him where he could find written proof of what I was saying. At that he became a little more serious, frowning oddly all the while. But he persisted in declaring that I had to be mistaken, and that it was the medicine I'd been given which was stirring up my fevered imagination. In spite of my pleas, he carried on with that kind of incredulous theme. In turn, I insisted he went to the place where the proof of my origins and faith could be found. Finally, grudgingly and wholly reluctantly he agreed to go there and look. But I knew he was still self-persuaded that, being on the fatal edge, I was becoming deranged by the fear of dying. Then he left me, his face as white and wild-looking as that of an albino rhino about to charge a hunter."

"I'm constantly smitten by your English usage … I do apologise, Mrs Spinek, please carry on. What happened next?"

"A miracle happened, that's what happened next."

"What miracle?"

"I began to recover and get better, quite quickly too. The doctors were amazed, but really glad for me. The tests showed that the operation had actually been a complete success, and that I was healing well. My surgeon hadn't killed me. But I could've killed him for being so pessimistic! Of course, I wouldn't be allowed to return to work at the factory. But that was nothing compared with the fact that I had my life back. I couldn't wait to let my son know. I still needed to be in the hospital for another couple of weeks. I decided, nevertheless, not to have my son's employer telephoned with the good news. I would wait until my boy's next visit when I could tell him in person. Despite his busy work schedule, I thought it shouldn't be that long before he would come to see me. But he didn't come to the hospital again. I was disappointed, but not entirely surprised. When he'd left the ward after I'd told him he was Jewish, he didn't look very pleased with me."

"So what did you do then, Mrs Spinek?"

"After I was discharged, my neighbour came to take me home in his battered old vehicle. He was a strong man and managed to get me up the stairs to my flat. When we went inside, there was this very unpleasant smell … it was coming from under my son's bedroom door. It was locked as usual. But I was so concerned that I told my neighbour he should smash it down. After a few attempts that weakened the hinges, he succeeded and dragged the broken door into the living room. We couldn't really take in the horrifying sight that met our eyes. I–It l–looked like my s–son had b–built a–a k–kind of g–gallows … and h–he was h–hanging f–from it, s–stone d–dead!"

"What? My goodness! Please, Mrs Spinek, do take a rest. You're overcome … here are some more tissues."

"T–Thank you, but don't worry yourself. I–I'm okay, really. I–It was a very long time ago now."

"But the shock … Can it ever go away?"

"Y–Yes, I was stunned. In fact, I collapsed into a heap on the bedroom floor. My neighbour immediately called the police and an ambulance, and I was rushed back to the hospital."

"What you're telling me is … almost rendering me speechless, Mrs Spinek. But why in heaven's name …?"

"My son had left a brief suicide note, which the police showed me later. It wasn't even addressed to me, his own mother. In it he wrote that he'd discovered he was Jewish, but couldn't accept the fact that Hebrew blood ran through his body. At first, it was like I was dead myself. Nothing seemed real and of this world. And I couldn't grasp the enormity of what my son had felt before destroying his young life. Until a time shortly afterwards, when the police and doctors considered that I'd become more rational. And then they told me what had been found in my son's bedroom at home."

"And what *did* they find, Mrs Spinek?"

"In his wardrobe cupboard, the desk drawers and in cardboard boxes under his bed they'd discovered papers, books, diaries, recordings, badges, emblems and suchlike."

"This sounds fairly innocuous."

"No, they weren't innocent at all. Everything he'd stored

away in his room was related to Hitler, the Nazis and Nazism."

"What?"

"Yes, my son was a dedicated neo-Nazi! He was a faithful member of an active neo-Nazi group. The material the police had found glorified Nazism and incited anti-Semitism, amongst other hatreds. And maybe the ugliest part of it all was my son's diaries. His regular and graphically detailed entries indicated clearly that he was a passionate and vicious anti-Semite. It was quite evident that he'd often put his evil passion into wicked effect. In his diaries, he'd described his pleasurable participation in some brutal assaults on Jews and in the daubing of swastikas, as well as the notorious Nazi demand *Juden Raus,* on gravestones in Jewish cemeteries, on synagogue walls and on other buildings with a Jewish connection. Also from under my son's bed, the police brought out a sack, used brushes and almost empty, five-litre tins of red and black paint …"

"I don't know what to say to you, Mrs Spinek. I really don't."

"You don't have to say anything, my dear Jewish friend … and brother. The bemused expression on your face tells me everything I would wish to know. But thank you for listening so attentively to the troubled story of a very old woman, who may herself learn more about all this in the not too distant future, if you know what I mean …"

# Brothers-in-Arms

"TOM! TOM! Can you hear me?"

"Yes, I can. You're bellowing loud enough to wake the dead! What do you want, Greg? I'm very busy round here at the dugout."

"Come along here, Tom … I think I've found something really interesting at my end of the dig. I'm in the short side-ditch, just off the front trench."

"Tell me something I don't know, Greg … oh okay, I'll be with you in five minutes. Need to bag up a few bullets and cartridge cases I've gathered. And also what looks like the remains of a hair comb and a toothbrush. I can just about read the letters L-O-N-D on what's left of them, so they were obviously manufactured in London."

"Not so surprising, Tom …We *are* excavating a trench in what were the British lines, after all. Come on over as soon as you can, then. I want your opinion on something …"

★ ★ ★

"Right, I'm here Greg."

"Thanks, Tom. As you know, these lateral trenches were multi-purpose, from storage of ammunition to allowing a quiet recreational smoke to relieve the boredom of waiting and watching long hours for an enemy assault that might not materialise for days, or even weeks. They were also employed temporarily to shelter wounded soldiers who'd fallen from the firing steps just over there, and before they were taken to the medical facilities at the rear."

"Nice lecture, Greg. But what's causing you such excitement, my dear archaeological colleague?"

"Look here, Tom … just there, right up against what would've been the plank-clad side of the trench. The wood has rotted away, of course. I've been clearing away the soil, rubble and a century's compacted mud for half a day now. An hour or so back, an arc of human rib bone suddenly poked its way through the surface. I've been brushing very carefully and …"

"So what's so significant, Greg? We've come across the bones of soldiers killed in these Flanders Field trenches several times before."

"This seems different to anything we've discovered previously. See down here, I've exposed what appear to be the bones of two virtually complete skeletons … I reckon they were in their late teens."

"So? We've seen fairly well preserved specimens …"

"Give me a chance, Tom. I know you're itching to get back to your dugout treasures! But …"

"Sorry … please go on, Greg."

"Right, well the thing is these two skeletons appear so

closely attached, even intertwined you could say, that they're virtually fused together."

"That can happen where troops packed together in what amounts to a ditch are caught in an incendiary shell explosion or flame-thrower attack."

"Please don't be teaching your grandmother to suck eggs, Tom. I've seen the results often enough. But the extraordinary thing is this. I consider we've got here the skeletons of a British and a German soldier."

"Why do you think that? Let's take a butcher's …"

"Look down there, Tom … no, a bit further to the left. Notice the scraps clinging to what are clearly two sets of rib cages? Well, I've identified the small pieces of material as coming from infantry uniforms of the German and British military in the Great War."

"I do believe you're right, Greg. I can see that there's not too much of the respective tunics to go on, though I certainly agree with your conclusion."

"Now I know it's just possible that German troops attacking a Tommy trench could be caught up in a rolling but inaccurately located bombardment from their own artillery. But contemporary accounts suggest that a misplaced barrage didn't occur too frequently. In any event, over a decade of excavating First World War trench systems here in Northern France, I've never seen any proof of that kind of thing myself. Have you, Tom?"

"No, I haven't. The oddity is that if this might be a case of incendiary fusion, I don't observe any signs of fire damage on the bones. Is there any clear indication yet of how these two young men met their deaths, Greg?"

"As you can see, I've just brushed down so far as to reveal the two skulls. They appear to be in good condition. I don't want to waste your time, Tom. So why don't you go back to your dugout and let me do a little more work down here … I'll try to seek out a few more clues. Maybe I'll detect some evidence of the specific cause of death …"

"Good idea, Greg. Just give me another shout if you come across anything useful to check over …"

\* \* \*

"Tom! Tom!"

"What is it, Greg? It's only been fifteen minutes since I left you brushing away merrily and with a passion."

"Come quickly, Tom. Just wait until you see what I've found …"

\* \* \*

"Horst, keep up with me … Phew! … Let's take a short breather … Jump into that shell crater over there. Hurry now … our big guns seem nearly to have found the range of the Tommy trenches. Taken them long enough! Come on … Horst!"

"I'm coming, Emil. You're a faster runner than me when it comes to a sprint across No Man's Land … and younger!"

"What? It's only a two-year age gap, my friend. I'm nineteen, not ten! You clearly weren't studying maths at university before enlistment. Maybe it's shell shock! Quickly now, into this hole here … Ach, that's better! Where the hell are you, Horst?"

"Aaach! … I'm here beside you, Emil … left side, idiot! Aaach! But I don't think I'll be going any further, Emil …"

"What do you mean? Are you hit, Horst? Where, where …?"

"No … no, I'm not hit, thank God. I think we've been lucky on this flank of the attack. It seems relatively calmer here than over to our left … machine gun fire appears lighter and more sporadic. Aaach! But I'll not be able to go on …"

"If you're not hit and you're found cowering here, you'll be shot at dawn for cowardice in the face of the enemy."

"No, Emil … Aaach! I want to overrun the British trenches alongside my comrades, but I really can't at the moment … Aaach!"

"What's the matter with you, Horst? If you've not been wounded, why do you keep on groaning like that?"

"I'm sure I've just broken my right ankle hurling myself into this bloody hole of yours, and … Aaach! I'm in terrible pain. That's the fundemental essence of the matter, my dear Emil …"

"Oh I'm sorry, Horst … do you want me to take a look at your leg?"

"No … don't worry, Emil. But thanks, anyway. You've got more important work to do. I'll apply a temporary dressing and bandage from my first aid pack."

"Okay … you rest here, my good friend. You've got some fairly decent cover. You'll be picked up later, of course, and taken back to our lines. But look … Splendid! Our artillery appears to be having its intended effect. It has located the target area with absolute precision now. The Tommies are retreating in droves … Hurrah! Just look at them run. Excellent! It should be easy capturing the front trench now."

"Yes I can see, Emil … Aaach! Look how fast the British are

scampering to their rear positions?"

"That's right, Horst … but keep your head down, my friend. There could be some well-camouflaged snipers around. I think we've been fortunate this time … really quiet and fluid on this part of the line … makes a change. To the left, I can see our massed troops advancing rapidly on the British centre. Hurrah! I've only got to dash another hundred metres and I'll be in their front trench … should be deserted by the time I get there. So you stay here then, Horst. And remember … keep your winkle-picker on, your head low and your trusty rifle close beside you. And be careful the needle sharp point of that bayonet. I'll catch up with you later, please God. Will you be okay now?"

"Yes … Aaach! I'll be fine, thanks. My affliction certainly isn't life threatening … see you later on. Aaach! Good luck, Emil, and don't you take any stupid risks …"

"Don't worry, Horst … I won't."

★ ★ ★

*Over the top again, Emil … Hope Horst will be alright … Of course he will … The stretcher-bearers will be scouring No-Man's-Land for our wounded … When it's safe to do so … Come on, Emil … Focus on the job in hand … Rush like the wind across this treeless, shell-pocked killing zone … Only another hundred metres to the British lines … Zigzag pattern, zigzag pattern, you've learned the drill, Emil … Gun high at port … Huff, puff … Run like the wind, Emil … Champion sprinter at your Hochschule a year back … Won medals for running, yes you did … Hope Horst is okay … Concentrate, Emil … Only fifty metres more and you're there … Lucky devil, it does seem very peaceful on this flank … No firing coming from the Tommies … They've all run off, that's why … No mist … And no drenching rain, for a change … Hell, have I been stuck in quagmires before! … Oh, look at those brilliant star shells bursting high over to the left, Emil … And the orange sun steadily rising … Hurrah! Hurrah! … Our boys have taken the front trench … Nearly there now, Emil … Just a few metres remaining … Trusty rifle and razor sharp bayonet ready, ready … And just in case …* Shema Yisroel, Hashem Elokeinu, Hashem Echad *… And we're here … Over these shattered sandbags … Thrust, thrust into the foul, smelly air … Quick glances, left then right … Military textbook stuff … Abandoned, the trench is deserted! … The Tommies really took off in a mighty hurry, and I saw them … But be careful, stay alert Emil … You never know the score … Seems like I'm on my own … Never mind, looks as if we've routed them anyway … The British have vanished like ghosts, evaporated into thin air, doubtless even now seeking refuge in their second trench line … Have a quick nose in this dugout … Nobody there … Good, so far … Let's move along the trench a bit … Appears to be a side ditch over there … Blind corner! … Take care, Emil … Watch out for booby-traps … Just a peep around here and …*

"Mein Gott! Mein Gott! Hand Hoch! Hands up!"

"Don't shoot … Bitte!"

"Mein Gott! Was ist los?"

"Don't shoot! Don't shoot! … Bitte, bitte! Please. Oh my God … *Shema Yisroel, Hashem Elokeinu, Hashem Echad* …"

"Mein Gott! Was ist das? I'm not going to shoot you, Tommy … you're unarmed, and now my prisoner … B–But, you were just reciting the *Shema* …"

"It's a prayer … You speak English?"

"Ja … I mean yes, I learned it in High School … You spoke a word of German just now …"

"I only know the odd word or two … But how did you know I was saying the *Shema*?"

"And I know *why* you were saying it … because I'm Jewish, too."

"What! … *What?*"

"Yes, I'm Jewish like you … what's so strange about that?"

"But I'm British and … and you're a German, my enemy."

"Ha, ha … you're a bit naïve. How old are you? Have you had your barmitzvah yet?"

"Very funny, Fritz … I'm seventeen, if you must know. How old are you?"

"Nineteen. By the way, where's your weapon?"

"Over by the sandbags there … well out of my reach. But how could you think that …?"

"I know what you're telling me of course … I'm just naturally cautious."

"And you think I'm not?"

"No, it's just … and, incidentally, my name's not Fritz."

"And mine isn't Tommy."

"Touché …!"

"What?"

"Never mind … so what's your name, then?"

"Solomon, but everyone calls me Solly."

"Well, my name's Emil. Good to meet you, Solly … pity though it's not at a simcha!"

"Likewise I'm sure, Emil."

"So you don't think there are any Jews living in Germany?"

"Well, I …"

"There are several hundreds of thousands of us, Solly ... and most of us have been doing quite nicely in the Fatherland for many decades now. But tell me, Solly, why didn't you run away ... sorry, retire in good order with your comrades?"

"I've done something to my ankle ... probably broken it."

"Mein Gott! Sorry ... that's quite a coincidence, Solly. My friend Horst suffered the same problem back in No Man's Land ... during our rapid advance just before. Listen, when I get you back to our lines as a prisoner of war our superb doctors, many of whom are in fact Jewish, will take very good care of you."

"How will you get me back ... I can't walk, or even hobble?"

"You're a slight-looking lad, so I'll probably be able to get you over my shoulders. Don't worry ..."

"I'm not now, Emil."

"Were you still at school before ... before all this?"

"No, I was an apprentice cabinet maker in London's East End ... loads of Jews live there. And that's where I live, in an old terraced house with my Mum and Dad, and my brothers and sisters. I'm following in my father's footsteps, trade-wise I mean. What about you?"

"That's another coincidence in a way, Solly. I'd just finished High School before enlisting to fight for family and Fatherland. My father owns a furniture company in Hamburg. After the war, I'll probably go to university. I hope to become an accountant, then return to work in the family business ..."

"So your family must be very rich?"

"Not so wealthy as you might think, Solly. But we do have a reasonably large house in the suburbs and another place in beautiful Bavaria, where we go for winter and summer holidays."

"Do you have any servants, Emil?"

"Yes, we do."

"It seems to me your family is very well off. How many brothers and sisters do you have?"

"I've got four siblings, two younger brothers and two older sisters, one of whom has volunteered as a nurse at a military hospital ... except for Elsa, they're all at home."

"That's another funny coincidence, Emil! I have two brothers and two sisters, also ... but I'm the youngest. One of my brothers is asthmatic ... he has breathing problems, so he's exempt from military service. But my other brother is serving somewhere else in northern France. I'm not sure where, though. I hope he's safe and well. My parents are worried stiff about us, as yours must be about you."

"I'm sure you're correct, Solly. But we have to fight for what we believe is right. Though I'm sure you and I would agree to disagree about the rightness of our respective causes."

"Ha ha, you're not wrong, Emil. But it feels so strange ... we're both Jews, and yet we're fighting each other."

"I know, Solly. At this minute, I have the same emotions as you. It's no doubt happening all along the front here in this hell on Earth. But sadly it's probably not the first time, and nor may it be the last time this happens."

"I suppose ..."

"And you know what? I think part of our religion's traditional belief is that we Jews owe allegiance to whatever country has given us sanctuary, and our freedom to worship the Almighty according to our faith and Torah. I'm sure that, like me, your forebears immigrated to another land in order to escape persecution in Eastern Europe or Russia. Am I right, Solly?"

"You're absolutely right, Emil. My ancestors came to England from Poland about forty years ago. Is your family religious?"

"Maybe not as pious as once it was. We've assimilated somewhat to the surrounding society and culture ... though my mother keeps up a kosher home. And we go to the synagogue ... it's a really beautiful building. The shul is Reform in nature, and we have an organ and a mixed choir. We certainly attend for the High Holydays and some of the festivals, as well as a few other times during the year. But we don't go on a regular basis. What about you, Solly?"

"We're quite orthodox, and in normal times I would be in our little shteibl every Shabbos. I help also to make up the minyan on weekday mornings ... before I have my breakfast and go to work."

"Can you speak Yiddish, Solly? It has got German language roots. We could converse in Yiddish–German."

"No, I don't have Yiddish ... save for a few odd words. My close family are quite anglicised now. But I've got some friends whose families speak only Yiddish at home. Maybe if I'd gone to yeshivah ... there's one just round the corner from where we live. But my family need me to earn as soon as possible, not learn ..."

"So how have you managed in the army ... with the meals, I mean?"

"It has been very difficult for me ... impossible, really. But I do my best. As you know, to safeguard a life it's permissible under our Halachah to eat treif, non-kosher food. I would starve to death if I didn't eat from our supplies, but sometimes it makes me vomit. I can't help it. What's your grub like, Emil?"

"Grub ...?"

"Food ..."

"Oh, right. Well really it's not too bad. Not culinary perfection, you understand. But it's fairly palatable. What's your favourite dish when you're at home, Solly?"

"That's an easy one. Chicken soup with lokshen and kneidlach followed by cholent, the Polish way my bubbeh makes it ... with a kugel. What about you, Emil?"

"I think we must be related in some way, Solly ... from way back. It looks like we've got ourselves another incredible coincidence."

"You're joking, Emil ..."

"No, I'm actually not ... my Mutti ... sorry, my mother insists that our cook makes the cholent just like your bubbeh does! But look, my dear Solly. You and I are talking together like we're sitting in a peacetime café somewhere in the centre of London or Hamburg, and not in the middle of a bloody battlefield. I've got to consider getting you back to our rear for some expert medical attention."

"Thank you, my dear Emil ... I'm so lucky *you* came upon me."

"You know, Solly ... give me your hand ... we're like brothers. At least you'll be safe now as a POW ... until the end of this terrible conflict. Now I'm going to bend down and get you across my shoulders, alright?"

"Okay, Emil ... I'm ready."

"Ach ... R-right n-now. H-here we g-go, then! Ach! No,

that's fine … you're no weight at all. A bag of bones! No wonder you've broken your ankle. Your legs can't take the strain. How can you find the strength to fight if you don't eat? And you really haven't been eating properly, have you Solly?"

"My Mum would kill me if she knew …"

"Ah so … hold tight, Solly, we're on our way … Ach, slowly but surely."

"Thanks a lot, Emil. I can't tell you how grateful I am."

"Don't worry, I've got you Solly. Ah, look at that … a pack of cigarettes left behind on the sandbags over there … I do smoke occasionally, you know. I'll just grab the …"

"No, Emil! Don't touch that …"

★ ★ ★

"So what have you discovered, Greg? What's that in your hand?"

"Take a look, Tom …"

"Gold necklaces …? You've hit treasure trove, Greg."

"Gold chains, specifically … yes, Tom. But it's more than that. I'll hold one up in each hand. So what do you notice, Tom?"

"Well, let's see what you've got here. There's a kind of gold charm attached to each chain …"

"No, they're not charms … at least, not of the sort you may be thinking about. Take a closer look, Tom."

"You're right, Greg. They appear to be Stars of David. One of them, the rather larger one, is affixed inside a circle of gold. The other's kind of smallish, slightly bent and free-standing. Both are linked to their chains. Isn't the Star of David a symbol of the Jewish faith, Greg?"

"That's correct. Sometimes it's known as the Shield of David, referring to the biblical King."

"A truly amazing find, Greg ... What do you think it means?"

"Well, I've been pondering that question. It seems to me that, extraordinarily, both the German and the British soldier were Jewish. Maybe at the crucial moment they each knew that. I would love to know the precise details of this personal engagement, if I can put it that way."

"Do you think they killed each other?"

"My gut feeling says *No* to that, Tom. But we can't ever know the exact circumstances of their confrontation, if it can be described as such. Maybe they even sat here, where we're standing now, and chatted for a while ... though there *is* the language problem."

"Perhaps they spoke Yiddish to each other, Greg."

"Yes ... of course. You could've hit the proverbial nail on the head, Tom."

"It seems possible that, as the German infantry were attacking this British trench, the Jewish Hun could've taken the Jewish Tommy prisoner. I've diagnosed that the Brit had succumbed to a broken ankle bone. That might be why he couldn't retreat with his mates and would've been captured fairly easily. This is all speculation, of course."

"Yes, I understand. But it sounds highly plausible. So how do you think they died?"

"I'm really not sure, Tom. It's just a fanciful thought ... but I've also noted that both their skulls, which I found just centimetres apart, reveal a serious shrapnel hit. So there may've been some kind of proximate explosion. If the British frontline had just been overrun by German troops, it's unlikely that German shells would be exploding around them. Their long-range artillery would've been silent at that stage of the battle. And with the Tommies having only just pulled back, it's equally unlikely that their rear-based big guns would be firing shells into their very recently evacuated positions."

"So what killed them, if your gut reaction tells you that they didn't kill each other?"

"Well, I haven't discovered any evidence of bullet or bayonet wounds ... there's usually reasonable evidence of that on the legacy of bone material."

"You're trying my patience, Greg ... I'm on the metaphorical edge of my seat."

"You know ... whenever troops, whether British or German, hightailed out of a trench in the face of an overwhelming infantry assault, they often left behind some vicious little booby-traps to entice and kill unwary, usually rookie enemy soldiers. I've just got this notion that they were killed by some sort of anti-personnel device."

"What, the Hun and the Tommy together?"

"Yes, Tom. The Sherlock Holmes in me envisages a scenario where the Tommy didn't retreat alongside his buddies because of his broken ankle. He was captured and made a prisoner of war by the German infantryman. I infer that he decided to carry the POW back to his own lines. Remember, they are seemingly both Jewish and may well have discovered this fact. The inter-relationship of the skeletons suggests to me that, because of the Brit's evident foot injury, the German was carrying him slung across his upper back and shoulders. The proximity of the skulls is somewhat indicative of that positioning. It's all conceivable."

"Great deduction, Greg ... it seems to me you've worked it all out. And you opined earlier that they were both killed by a powerful booby-trap explosive of some kind. Is that so?"

"As I say, it's only a tentative opinion but I believe one worthy of consideration. I have the idea that, while starting off to carry his prisoner to safety, the German may've spotted something he fancied taking with him, reached out to grab it and ... whoooosssh-bang! Wallop! Game over! And a quick but awful end to two young lives, two of millions mind you that were terminated prematurely on the Western Front between 1914 and 1918."

"You may well have the complete story, Greg."

"Perhaps, Tom ... but as I say, we'll never know for sure. What I was thinking, though, is that these two teenagers were, in more than a manner of speaking, brothers-in-arms. And maybe more accurately, Jewish brothers-in-arms ..."

## *"Where am I?"*

"WHERE AM I? Why's it so startlingly bright in here?"

"You're on our mother-ship."

"What?"

"On our mother-ship ..."

"What do you mean? I was just walking across Hampstead Heath ..."

"You've been asleep here for a while."

"Asleep? I know I was walking across the heath just before dawn ... but that's because I couldn't get to sleep at home! Where am I? ... Who are you? ... And why am I strapped down to this bed thing?"

"So many questions but I do understand the need, Alan ..."

"H-How do you know my name?"

"First, let me just say that you've been secured for your own safety ... and let me assure you, Alan, that your wellbeing is our primary concern ..."

"What are you talking about?"

"Allow me a chance to explain, Alan ... and please don't worry."

"Should I have any cause to worry? Am I in any danger? Why are you wearing a white coat? Is this a hospital? Am I in an operating theatre? Did I have an accident?"

"No, you're not in a hospital. And I'm very glad to say that you haven't had an accident. But as I've just remarked, your health, welfare and comfort are of prime importance to us."

"Who are you? What am I doing here ... wherever *here* is? What do you want with me?"

"Again so many questions, Alan ... though of course, it's natural and totally valid and understandable. We expect a lot of queries from our guests. Please permit me a few moments to satisfy your ... your, shall we say, *curiosity*?"

"Look, whoever you are ... I'm losing my patience fast! Not that I'm able to do much about it, trussed up like a chicken and tethered like a goat. But what I'm experiencing right now isn't exactly *curiosity*. It's actually absolute terror! Has my wife been informed of where I am? I'm not deceased, am I?"

"No ... you're not deceased, Alan. And I would urge you not to struggle with the straps, please. You might hurt yourself and we don't want that, do we? Look now, you've made your palms quite lined and red. As I noted earlier, the bindings are for your personal safety ... like seatbelts on one of your airplanes, if you wish."

"Seatbelts ... What in heaven's name are you going on about?"

"Don't be alarmed, and please accept my apologies. But you'll be unable to speak for a short period whilst I explain, without interruption, your presence here on our mother-ship, a term you may well comprehend. Of course you'll be able to hear everything I say, Alan ... Our onboard computer, for want of a better technical term, targeted your image as you sauntered across the deserted heath. You conformed precisely to our fact-finding research parameters. It may come as a real shock to you, and I regret that, but we've journeyed from a star system millions of light years from Earth, as your astrophysicists would say. We've visited your neck of the Milky Way, as you call your galaxy, several times in carrying out our investigations into life forms across the cosmos. It has been … how can I put it? Yes, rather mischievous of us. But we've borrowed human beings from your planet at various stages of their development, and over quite a lengthy period. We hope the outcome will ultimately be beneficial, universally speaking. That's the redeeming feature of our quest for information, as we see it … a bit like readers seeking knowledge by borrowing books from one of your public lending libraries … though, of course, we've observed that a lot of you Earthlings now do something still rather primitive, known we believe as surfing the Internet, to obtain data etcetera. There's little point in my informing you of the complex procedures involved in your delivery to this spacecraft … or, indeed, the intricate science and technology of its propulsion drive and means of inter-galactic travel. Incidentally, our ship is now orbiting temporarily one of the outer planets in your solar system. But what I *will* tell you is that you'll be returned home to your wife before she awakens, just as you'd intended originally. And if you don't believe me, then believe your great theoretical scientist Albert Einstein. There … I've now enabled you to speak again, and I regret your enforced vocal hiatus … I said you can now speak again … Why aren't you saying anything, Alan? You're just staring wide-eyed at me. I realise that what I've just told you may've further rendered you, but still temporarily, speechless … All I can say is, please don't be afraid of me … of us. We're just collecting statistics, if you like. And, for sure, we mean you no harm. I promise …"

"Oh, my Go … I-I've been abducted by aliens! … I've read about such things, outlandish firsthand accounts … huge craniums, bulging almond eyes, spindly legs. But I-I never believed them, of course …"

"Personally, I wouldn't use the word *abducted*. And do you know what, Alan? You're just as much an alien to me as I may be to you."

"Hmm … I-I suppose. But what's strange to me is that you don't look like an alien. In fact, and I'm assuming you are of the male gender, you appear, at least at first blush, no different from our masculine species on Earth …"

"In order not to frighten you with my authentic appearance, I've morphed into a humanoid … with all the attributes that allow me to communicate with you."

"Oh, my … Please don't hurt me."

"Listen Alan, there's really no reason to distress yourself. I've said it before, and I'll say it again. You'll not be harmed in any way. That would not be in our own long-term interests. And shortly, you'll be back in Hampstead as if by taxi, and like you'd never been away. And you'll be in good time, as usual, to make up the minyan for Shacharis at your shul. Okay?"

"O-Okay … B-But how …? I'm profoundly astonished, shocked even. Your civilisation must be *so* advanced … intellectually, technologically and scientifically. What can you learn from us relatively primeval creatures, who can just about rocket a man onto the surface of our nearby moon? What could your researches and scientists possibly gain from studying us

Earthlings, and especially from this Earthling ... this *Jewish* Earthling, noch? Yes, as I'm satisfied you've gathered, I'm a middle-aged Jewish man from North West London with a wonderful wife, two marvellous children and four delightful grandchildren. Doubtless as you know, there aren't many more than seventeen million Jews in our entire world ... out of a global population of around seven billion. I'm hardly representative of Mankind, now am I?"

"My dear Alan ... and I do hope you won't mind me addressing you affectionately thus. As you might imagine, we now know a great deal about your little blue planet, the third in line from the fairly ordinary star you've named the Sun. And if I may say so without any intent to embarrass, we've now learned quite a lot about *you*. If I can just add something else, and honestly without meaning to sound superior, arrogant or assertive, maybe the point is that you might learn something from and about us ..."

"I–I'm sorry. I suspect you may've detected a note of hubris in my comment."

"Not at all, Alan ... You've got every right to be inquisitive, if not suspicious of our motivation."

"You keep addressing me by my name, but I don't know yours."

"You can call me Lenga, if you wish."

"Okay ... Lenga."

"You appear to be a tad calmer now, Alan. I'm very pleased to note that. You have nothing to be upset or fearful about."

"Thank you, Lenga. But I'm sure you've understood my apprehension. This ... this encounter is hardly what was forecast when an insomniac left home, as he sometimes needs to do early in the morning, for a walk across the heath."

"But isn't that a dangerous exercise? Can you be certain you wouldn't be attacked by muggers or drunken louts?"

"Or spacemen! No, I guess you can never be absolutely assured. I don't know about yours, but there are no guarantees in our lives. However, in the comparative scheme of things on Earth these days, and by the law of averages in our rather more genteel segment of London, what you've mentioned is highly unlikely to occur."

"I believe that I know what you mean by the *scheme of things on Earth*. With great sorrow, we've witnessed your world wars, revolutions, civil wars and other conflicts for centuries. They've become more gruesome, brutal, bloody and mercilessly inhuman as your so-called developing *Humanity* has increasingly regarded itself, somewhat paradoxically and even ludicrously, as becoming more civilised. We know all about the Nazi Holocaust and the murder of six million Jews in the Second World War; and, indeed, subsequent attempts at genocide."

"I can see where you're coming from, Lenga. I really don't disagree with you, as doubtless the vast majority of my planet's population wouldn't either. But I have hope and faith in the Almighty, the Creator of the universe. I'm certain you're already aware of that. But do you … does your people believe in a God … in the one God?"

"Yes, Alan, we do believe in the existence of the omnipotent Supreme Being. Though, unlike in your faith and other religions or beliefs on Earth, our faith, or should I say devotion, dedication or commitment doesn't stem from any Divine revelation or messianic individual or event. We don't possess a book of holy scripture from the ancient past, nor any body of sacred ritual, governing laws or codes of good and bad, right and wrong …"

"So how do you know …?

"It's intuitive to us … Throughout our evolutionary generations the knowledge of Him has been inherent in our intellects and philosophical makeup. We have no doubts …"

"Are you saying such belief is innate and instinctive for everyone in your world? Surely your people have different views and opinions about this, whether positive or negative."

"Yes I *am* telling you that my people are, as you might say, of one mind and unanimous about this. I accept that it's hard for you to grasp such a notion coming, as unhappily you do, from a world where there's so much tension, strife, aggression, divisiveness, segregation, conflict, racial hatred, internecine jealousy, covetousness, resentment and an overriding destructive fear of *the other*."

"You know what, Lenga … as I walk the heath in the middle of a clear night I gaze up at the sprinkling of stars glittering in the blackness of the firmament. I think about the vast and eternal majesty of the Almighty's Creation. And then I meditate on our tiny blue ball of rock hurtling around, as you say, our rather run of the mill sun at the insignificant edge of a quite average spiral galaxy. I don't have to tell *you,* but I appreciate that one day in the far distant future our life-giving Sun will explode catastrophically to become a supernova and destroy the solar system and all Mankind. Unless by then we've acquired the kind of technological ability you possess to journey enormous distances from your own solar system. So I ruminate on all those dreadful elements you've just listed, and I wonder why … And now I wonder, though without any real conviction, why Earthlings can't seek to be more like your people. I'm sure your way of life has benefited immeasurably from the philosophical unity of your belief system, as you've described it briefly to me."

"You're right of course, Alan. Though let me say at once that we're not all clones of each other. Just like humankind, we're all different … every last one of us has his or her own character and personality. But we know the place from which we all come, and it's recognised that we're all working towards the same goals for the commonweal. Inexorably, there are problems from time to time … but we seek to overcome any obstacles with original wisdom and without resorting to counter-productive violence against each other. Who would we advantage if we destroy ourselves and our home environment? It would certainly not be us. What is the point of mindless war and conflict? I don't want to give you the impression, Alan, that we're all infallible goody-goodies … that would be entirely boring, and untrue. But if we do something which, objectively, might be regarded by others as let's say a bit *naughty* … like borrowing you for a very short time, we hope that our motives are altruistic and hopefully replete with loving kindness. In the end, only the Supreme Being can judge us on that."

"It's truly wonderful, miraculous even, to hear you speak of all this. So many questions are flooding into my head, Lenga. I want, no I need to ask you about so many things … What's your planet like? What resources does it possess? Do you have cities? What kind of structures do you live and work in? What sort of education systems do you have? What food and liquid do you eat and drink? What kinds of work are your people engaged in? How do they transport themselves? What sorts of leisure and cultural activities do they enjoy? In what way do you worship the Supreme Being? And maybe most intriguingly, what other kinds of life, if any, have you located in the universe?"

"Ha ha, Alan … I can see that I've whetted your appetite for knowledge about us … so perhaps you can now acknowledge, a little more, our own inquisitiveness about the existence and nature of other forms of life in the universe. No, it's not merely inquisitiveness. This may be very difficult for you to get your mind around, Alan … please forgive me for saying so. But it's also a real concern we have for all the inhabitants of this awesome cosmos."

"Yes. And if I wasn't lying stretched out on my back like this, I think I would be hanging my head in shame for harbouring …"

"No, Alan. You really shouldn't think like that … I understand, implicitly. But I would like to believe that we, you and me, can be like brothers in eternity …"

"There is a question I have to ask you, Lenga. Have you discovered the secret of eternal life? On Earth, we're mere mortals with a gradually increasing but limited longevity and life span. You've probably gleaned that, as a religious Jew, I believe that after our physical bodies pass away our eternal souls return to the Almighty."

"Let me put it this way, Alan … we live on, too."

"What about my other questions, Lenga? Are you able to answer them?"

"I *am* able to answer them, naturally. But I'm afraid that we just don't have the time right now. Our mission is complete. All I would say, finally, is that I come from a happy place, a place full of love … and I'm anxious to be returning home soon … just like you are, I would presume. So I'll say goodbye … at least for the present, Alan. It was a great pleasure meeting you, and I wish you and yours all the love in the …"

★ ★ ★

"Darling … darling, wake up! Rise and shine, Alan. It's past seven … and you've overslept."

"W-What …?"

"Get up, Alan … And hurry up about it, or you'll be late for shul this morning!"

"W-What, what's that? W-Where am I?"

"What do you mean, *Where am I?* You're wallowing in bed, Alan … For heaven's sake, get up already!"

"Shul? Shul!"

"Yes *shul*, darling …"

"But I was just …"

"Just, shmust … get up now!"

"Okay, okay Esther … I'm getting up right away. I must've been dreaming."

"Careful Alan, you don't seem too steady on your feet. Give me your hands …"

"I'm okay Esther, leave me alone for a …"

"Alan … what are these red marks on your palms?"

## *"Honey, I've shrunk the cab!"*

"B-BABS! B-BABS! W-Where a-are y-you …?"

"I'm in the kitchen feeding the washing machine."

"O-Oh, t-there you are …"

"What's the matter, Danny? Looks like you've seen a ghost … what's wrong?"

"B-Babs, y-you'll n-never b-believe w-what j-just h-happened … I, I …"

"Calm down, Danny … you're getting me really worried. What just happened? You were in the garage washing the cab. What could happen? Speak to me, Danny … Are you having a heart attack, God forbid … you're only thirty-eight!"

"B-Babs … I-I've … I-I've …"

"You've what? Pull yourself together, Danny. This isn't like you, not like you at all. I'm going to call Dr Spellman if you don't stop whimpering and spluttering, and tell me what's going on."

"Babs, honey … I've shrunk the cab!"

"You've what? What are you talking about? Look, Daniel …

grown men don't play practical jokes when their wives are up to their necks in soiled underwear, yours mostly, and the kids are due home from school …"

"I know … I know what you must be thinking. *You* don't believe me. *I* don't believe me … but I'm telling you, on my life, it's true. Please come with me, O Sceptical One!"

"Careful, Danny … you're pulling my arm out of its socket! What's the rush? Where are we going? I've got …"

"We're off to the garage, Babs … where else?"

★ ★ ★

"Why have you pulled the up-and-over door down, Daniel? You don't usually do that when you're cleaning the cab in here."

"Careful that bucket … a-and t-that c-can of s-spray p-polish!"

"What's with the jangling nerves again, Danny. What's up? And how am I going to trip over anything in here … it's bright enough with these neon ceiling strips to illuminate an Olympic stadium! And by the way, where *is* the cab? You were cleaning it five minutes ago!"

"That's what I'm trying to tell you, Babs …"

"Tell me what? I'm losing the plot fast, Danny. I've got piles of dirty washing waiting for me on the kitchen floor … and our lovely but nonetheless ever-hungry children Ben and Joni, if you remember them, will be home from school and demanding a tea-time snack at any moment now!"

"You ask me where the cab is, honey. Well take a gander down there, yes there … in the centre of the floor. And don't forget your microscope …"

"Don't forget my what?"

"Just look, Babs!"

"What's that shiny black object? Wait a minute ... it's that little model black cab you got for Ben last month. I'll murder you, Danny. Wasting my ..."

"No, don't pick it up ... Babs, p-please! For crying out loud, put it down ... right now, and very carefully. I know it's incredible, but that four-inch object represents many thousands of pounds' worth of hackney carriage. Put it down, Babs ... I'm begging of you!"

"Okay, okay ... keep what's left of your hair on, Danny. I'm putting the toy taxi right back down on the floor, just like you say. Now look here, *you* may be two sandwiches short of a picnic, but *I'm* quite sane and normal thank you. Now explain this lunacy, or else I'm ..."

"Please bend down ..."

"What?"

"... and take a peek under that small black thing's bonnet. Well, just humour me, then."

"If you ..."

"Please do it. That's right ... so why the shattering silence, Babs? And you look as if *you've* just seen a ghost. I wonder why ..."

"D-Danny ... D-Danny! Oh my God, you've shrunk the cab!"

★ ★ ★

"Look at us Babs, pathetic pair that we doubtless present ... sitting here staring pitifully boggle-eyed and drop-jawed at my livelihood, all four inches of it, perched forlornly in the middle of the kitchen table."

"H-How did it happen, Danny? I-I just can't get my head around this …"

"It's simple …"

"Simple!"

"Please, Babs. I'm just as bewildered and befuddled, maybe even as bewitched, as you. It's simple in that I was using a sample can of spray-on wax polish that a fare gave me yesterday. I applied it to the cab and was just about to buff when, suddenly, the vehicle began to get smaller and smaller … like Alice in Wonderland, after she'd swigged from that bottle labelled 'Drink Me'! You know the rest of …"

"Forget about Wonderland! What are you going to do about this, Danny?"

"Suppose I could become a minicab driver."

"I-I really don't understand you. How can you joke about this? It's serious and it's amazing, I know … amazingly serious, inexplicable, unbelievable, shocking, whatever! But as you've just groaned, it's your … it's *our* livelihood, for God's sake. And don't forget, it'll be Ben's barmitzvah next year."

"No I haven't forgotten, Babs."

"I-I'm sorry, Danny. I'm not helping, am I?"

"Not really. And I'm at my wit's end, too. How could this …?"

"What's that noise …? What am I saying? It's the kids! Listen to me, Danny. I'll phone Mum and see if she can take them for the evening. I'm sure it'll be okay. In the meantime, while I'm driving them there, you put on your thinking cap and try to come up with a solution … if I can use that word. I'll be back soon. And remember, Danny. We're in this together, and I love you …"

"Well here we are again, sitting around the kitchen table gawping at our … our little problem."

"I was thinking in the car just now, driving back from Mum's. How do we know this miniaturisation was caused by the spray-on wax, Danny?

"What else could it have been? It happened right after I'd used the can."

"I guess you're right. But I think we should try the spray on something else … just to confirm, you know. What do you suggest?"

"When's your mother coming round?"

"Very amusing, I'm sure. If this wasn't so damn tragic and you didn't look so stressed out, I'd box your bloody ears!"

"Okay, okay … enough already, Babs. We've got to sort this out somehow. Let's try the wax on the bucket in the garage. Come on then …"

"Aim the can well away from me, Danny. I don't want to be a Borrower or some diminutive character out of Gulliver's travels, if you don't mind."

"Oh, my …"

"How long did that take?"

"Just seconds, Babs …"

"And now it's as tiny as a thimble! Fantastic, but I don't understand any of this. It's all way beyond my primitive comprehension … and absolutely terrifying."

"Don't worry … I'm locking it away in the wall cupboard over there right now. Do you have any other bright ideas?"

"Perhaps we should phone 999, Danny. No, don't shake your head. I really think we should do that."

"Ah yes: *Which emergency service do you require, sir … fire, police or ambulance?* Well, maybe I should request an ambulance, Babs … to take me to the nearest psychiatric hospital, and a comfy padded room."

"Well, what then?"

"I think I've got to find the passenger who gave me the spray can. He gave it to me instead of a tip. Like you, I can't grasp any of this but there has to be an antidote."

"Who was this guy? Where did you pick him up and drop him?"

"I collected him from Heathrow. He was Chinese, slim, short and looked to be about sixty or so, with slicked back grey hair and spectacles. We had a little chat as I drove him into London. He said his name was Woo. He'd just flown in on Cathay Pacific from Hong Kong. We were chatting, and he told me that his company manufactured a variety of wax products. I was taking him to a restaurant off Gerrard Street, in the heart of Chinatown. When I dropped him, he paid with a credit card, said he didn't have any small change for a tip, took what he said was a sample can of car polish out of his suitcase and gave it to me …"

"Do you remember which restaurant, darling? There are so many Chinese eateries in that area."

"Sure I do. And that's precisely where I'm going tonight."

"I'll drive you to the West End, Danny."

"No, that's okay. Let me take your car. Phone your Mum and ask whether she would let Ben and Joni stay with her overnight. She'll relish the chance to spoil them rotten. Then please keep the mobile clamped to your ear, just in case I need to talk …"

"And don't forget to take that stupid spray can with you!"

"What do *you* think, honey? And never tell another living soul about this."

"And what do *you* think, darling?"

★ ★ ★

*Right, so I'll be leaving Babs' Metro here in St James's Square. Now I'll head across Piccadilly and along Shaftsbury Avenue towards Chinatown …Well, here we are … This is it … I'm certain it's the restaurant where I dropped Mr Woo. Windows are quite steamed up, but I can just about make out the rows of glossy red Peking duck rotating on their skewers. That chef is shaking a seriously massive and sizzling wok of stir-fry something or other! Okay, in you go, Danny my boy …*

"Can I help you, sir … a table for one?"

"No thanks, but is there a Mr Woo here?"

"Are you the taxi driver who brought Dr Woo here yesterday morning?"

"Yes, I am. Sorry … Dr Woo? I didn't know he was a doctor."

"Yes, he's a doctor. Please to come with me, sir. Down these stairs … please follow me along this corridor. I regret the illumination isn't so good down here. Please take care."

"Where are you taking me?"

"Just over here. Please knock on this door and go inside the room. I have to leave you now and attend to my hungry diners …"

## "Honey, I've shrunk the cab!"

*My goodness, where am I? This is quite some room, more like a large chamber ... even a cavern. Thankfully, it's quite brightly lit. I've always wondered what lies beneath London's Chinatown. I've driven fares to this lively area often enough. Just look at these red walls covered with graffiti. No, wait a minute, it's not graffiti ... it's that stunning black calligraphy of Chinese writing. And what about those beautifully illuminated lanterns suspended from the exquisitely carved wooden ceiling ... What's that aroma? Yes, it must be some kind of incense ... burning incense. Fascinating ... But where the hell am I? For the love of ... who's the man sitting on that platform? Looks like a Chinese ancient garbed in a red robe with a dragon motif ... Could be a character out of a martial arts movie! What a magnificently flowing white beard he boasts ... And who are those two similarly dressed, elderly gentlemen sitting on either side of him? Hold on, the ancient's beckoning. Appears to be saying something to me ...*

"Please sit down on that chair facing us, Danny."

"How do you know my name?"

"We're very glad you came to us, though we'd almost discovered your home address."

"My home address ...?"

"Please don't be concerned. I'm afraid that Dr Woo gave you something by mistake. I believe you're aware of what I'm referring to."

"Y-yes, I-I certainly am."

"Please don't be alarmed, Danny. I'm sure that, very sensibly, you've brought the spray can of wax polish with you in that bag you're clutching. I would be very grateful if you could kindly hand it to Number One, seated to my right ..."

"Yes, of course."

"Thank you, Danny."

"No problem."

"You say *no problem*. But from your obviously concerned expression, you have clearly used the wax spray on some object. Am I correct? And I can see you removing something else from your bag."

"Yes, you're right. And this *is* the object."

"It's your black cab?"

"Yes, it is."

"I have to tell you that Dr Woo completed his business in London this morning. At this very moment he's flying back to Hong Kong. But you must go there and see him in person, do you understand?"

"I think I do. My wife and I were in Hong Kong on holiday a few years ago. I'll need to tell her ..."

"Then you'll probably remember your way around the city."

"Yes ... possibly."

"A flight leaves from Heathrow in five hours. You must be on it with your little taxi cab. You must now go direct to the airport. Your tickets will be awaiting you at the airline's sales desk. We've booked you into a luxury Kowloon hotel for one night, and you'll return to London tomorrow evening. The restaurant manager upstairs, whom I believe you've already met, will hand you an overnight case with a change of clothes. We've estimated sizes etcetera from Dr Woo's description of you."

"You've thought of everything ... that's incredible!"

"Don't mention it. There's just one more thing, Danny. I ask you not to be frightened or upset please but Number Two, seated to my left, will painlessly prick your right index finger with a sterilised needle right now and draw a tiny amount of blood. This we will retain in a vial. The procedure is a necessary sign between you and us. It signifies your promise to forget everything that has happened since you picked up Dr Woo at the airport. I'm sure you know what I mean. We've assumed, of course, that your wife knows about all this. But if you break your implicit vow, you will definitely be hearing from us again. However, we know that you're a sensible and intelligent young man … so you have no reason to worry unduly."

★ ★ ★

"Is that you, Babs?"

"Isn't the phone line clear enough? Don't you recognise your own wife's voice any more? Who did you think it was, darling … *Minnie* Mouse?"

"Funny, but not ha, ha … Listen, I've got to fly to Hong Kong tonight."

"What!"

"I'll explain everything when I return, day after tomorrow. No, I can't tell you anything right now. Just trust me, darling. Believe me … I need to go to the Far East to sort things out. You'll have to come to the West End to collect your car if you don't want a costly parking ticket. I've left it in St James's Square. And better tell your parents, the kids and anyone else if necessary that I've had to visit a sick old school friend living in, I don't know … in Belfast. And I'll say it one more time: do not tell anybody about any of this, otherwise the family is Chop Suey! Unbelievably I've been supplied with a suitcase of clothes, and I'm about to ride the Tube to Heathrow then catch a flight to the Far East in a few hours. See you soon, honey, please God. What? Yes, I'll take care and I love you too …"

* * *

*Wow! It's quite a view from this deluxe sixth floor suite. Nathan Road, here in Kowloon, is just as I remember it from our holiday … hectic, smothered with neon-illuminated advertising, congested with traffic and milling with pedestrians. That American buffet breakfast in the hotel's restaurant was really excellent, wasn't it? And didn't Dr Woo's secretary sound very pleasant when I rang a short while back to fix an appointment for later this morning …?*

*Well, that was an interesting trip … Star Ferry boat from Kowloon to Hong Kong Island with its exciting Manhattan skyline surrounding the famous hilly Peak, where a lot of very rich people live, including Dr Woo … Then a taxi from the stand outside the Mandarin Hotel to the doctor's villa high on the commanding hillside … and now here I am at last. This is quite something, eh Danny? What a magnificent panorama of the city and its tremendous harbour you get from this high point! Well, the cab has dropped and left me in front of this rather impressive residence … there's a high perimeter wall, and an iron-grilled gate topped with swivelling CCTV cameras. I'll just press this … Oh my, the gate's opening by itself! And who's this coming from the villa to greet me? She must be Dr Woo's secretary. Yes, very …*

"I'll just close the front door … Now if you would please care to follow me, sir. Dr Woo will greet you in the library."

"The oil paintings in this hall are beautiful, if I may say so. English landscapes?"

"Yes, eighteenth century. And they are, as you say sir, quite lovely. Dr Woo is an avid collector of that period's European art. Well, here we are ... I'll leave you now, sir. Just open the door and enter, please. Dr Woo will be with you shortly."

"Thank you."

*This is quite some place, Danny. Dr Woo must be an exceedingly wealthy man, indeed. Just look at this astonishingly elegant room. There must be thousands of books on those shelves! And this is a desk and a half ... looks like an extremely expensive antique to me. Perhaps it's French. But what do I know about such things, apart from the Antiques Road Show? A DIY flat-pack from IKEA is more my line in furniture! So what? It's nicely designed ... and good value for money, too. My goodness, the landscaped tropical garden looks remarkable through those French windows ... just look at all those towering palm trees ...*

"Ah Danny, my London taxi driver ... I'm sorry to have startled you."

"T-That's okay, Dr Woo."

"You have a good strong handshake. I'm glad ... I hope you're feeling better and that you're fully reassured that we can help you out of your little problem. I observed you looking through the window at my garden. You like it?"

"It's stunning. You're a very fortunate man."

"Ah well, maybe. So we meet again, though in rather stranger circumstances."

"Yes, you could say that. You must help me, Dr Woo. T-Take a g-good l-look at w-what h-has h-happened to m-my c-cab!"

"Please stay calm, Danny, and put the taxi back in your bag.

Let's sit down here on this settee and talk for a moment or two. Now don't be anxious. I appreciate what you must've been going through. And I do sincerely regret my silly error. I can only express my profoundest apologies for the stress and trouble I've caused you and, I believe, your wife Barbara. However, let's now look on the bright side. I can readily restore your taxi to its normal size …"

"Oh Dr Woo, that would be really marvellous. Thank you so much. I just knew there had to be an antidote."

"My company is engaged in very secret, revolutionary research work into miniaturisation and nanotechnology. I believe you've been advised about, how shall I put it politely, the consequences of disclosure?"

"Yes, Dr Woo."

"Good. Please wait here, Danny. I must retrieve something from my laboratory in the basement …"

\* \* \*

"Come along, Danny. I've got what I needed from the lab. Follow me, and please bring your bag with you. We're going to the garage at the side of the house. I've had my chauffeur remove the Rolls Royce and the Bentley for the time being. Now we just go through this door, and here we are …"

"This is an impressively spacious garage, Dr Woo."

"Yes, well … Please place your tiny cab in the centre of the floor over there … on the spot marked in white chalk with a cross. That's right. Thank you. Now please step back here alongside me. Okay, Danny?"

"Okay, Dr Woo."

"Close your eyes, Danny."

"Close my eyes?"

"Yes, please. It's necessary. That's right Danny, eyes closed now …"

★ ★ ★

"Open your eyes, Danny."

"W-What …?"

"You can open your eyes now."

"W-What …?"

"Wake up, wake up! Open your eyes … it's all over."

"I-Is that y-you, D-Dr W-Woo?"

"Dr Woo … Dr Who … Dr Shmoo! You're still a bit under … woozy, eh Danny?"

"W-What …? W-Who are you?"

"You don't remember me, Danny? Ha, ha. Well it's Gary, your long-suffering brother-in-law."

"W-What …?"

"Come on, Danny. I've got another patient waiting outside. I don't know, I've just done two extractions by gas … and that was *your* choice, Danny."

"What! Gary?"

"Oh goody, goody … you're now in the land of the conscious living! Yes, I'm Gary. It's nice to meet you again. Now out of the chair, if you would …"

"Do me a favour, please Gary."

"What? I'm really busy today, Danny."

"Could you look out of the window, and say if you can see my cab parked in your driveway …"

"Oh, okay."

"Can you see it?"

"Yes, I can see your cab. What about it? It's quite safe left there, you know."

"How big is it?"

"What?"

"Please tell me, Gary. How big is my taxi?"

"Well, I know that gas extractions can sometimes have odd effects when patients come round. But you're acting more than a tad weird, Danny."

"Please, Gary."

"Okay, I'm looking out of the window. How big is your cab? Its size I would say is … normal. Unlike you, it would seem. Anyway, clear off and go drive Babs crazy, eh Danny?"

"Okay, Gary. I'm going now. But you've made me a very happy man."

"I'm really glad about that. We do aim to please. So go now."

"But you know what, Gary?"

"What now, Danny?"

"Small isn't necessarily beautiful …"

# Life Changing

"I STILL can't believe it. Pinch me, Jan … I'm not dreaming, am I? It's like I'm in a constant state of shock."

"Me too, Neil … it's hardly sunk in yet, but let's *try* to get some sleep. Look at the bedside clock. It's past midnight and we've got another big day tomorrow."

"But I can't get to sleep. How can I? I'm far too jangled and excited!"

"Don't you think I'm thrilled, too?"

"So can *you* sleep, then?"

"I'm mentally exhausted but no, you're right … I can't sleep, either. Why? Well, there are a million reasons!"

"Very good, Jan …"

"Yeah, okay."

"We've won a million pounds on the National Lottery! Jan, we've actually won a million pounds on the Na …"

"I know, I know! It'll be life changing for us, Neil … life changing! Luckily, we've hit the jackpot in our mid-fifties rather than our dotage. So it really is life changing, eh?"

"Of course it is. You know, next month I would've been driving a cab around London for twenty-five years … I can't believe that, either."

"So can you believe two married sons and four grandchildren bless them?"

"Yeah … David and Ian have done us proud. My parents, God rest their dear souls, would never have believed it of me. It's just so sad that …"

"When I phoned Mum, right after we'd discovered our numbers had come up, she said the same thing …"

"What, that she never would've believed I could raise a family?"

"Don't be funny … or daft, rather! She loves you, even more so since Dad passed away last year, what with all you've done for her. And as you well know, she was going on about how sad it is that her Morris is no longer with us to hear the incredible news."

"If we're going to stay awake all night, can't we talk about happier things? We've just become richer, a relative term you understand, by one million smackers! And we collect the cheque tomorrow. My long-suffering bank manager, bless him, will be very impressed. It'll be the first time he'll have had any positive thoughts about my account since I opened it a very long time ago. Maybe I'll take him a bottle of bubbly for tolerating all my overdrafts these past many years …"

"Do you think we can afford to give away champagne, Neil?"

"Nice one, Jan sweetheart. I'll ask my financial adviser."

"I *am* your financial adviser."

"Just remember who came up with the numbers, darling …

I told you we should keep to the birth dates … yours, mine, David's and Laura's, Ian's and Emma's."

"I was wondering when you were going to bring that up. What are you saying, that *you* own all the money and that *you* will make all the decisions about it?"

"Oh, Jan … I'm being as serious as you were when you just mentioned your money bags role. Stay cool and hang loose, woman …"

"What are you staring at? If you're referring to my pyjama's top, I'll kill …"

"Come give us a kiss, you … you loose woman, you!"

"Get off me, Neil. You know I've had my hair worked over this afternoon. Marion fitted me in … of course she did, even though it was a busy Saturday. I wanted it coloured and styled to look its best for the photos …"

"Marion has done an excellent job, Jan. Your hair looks marvellous!"

"Thanks. But as you well know, Neil, after my hair is done I sit in bed virtually upright all night so as not to spoil it."

"Sorry about the grabbing, sweetheart. You look so scrumptious, and I feel quite …"

"You'll *feel* something in a minute. Now get back to your side of the bed, and let's just think about the things we can do now with all that lovely, life changing money!"

"Well, first off we've got to give some cash to the kids."

"Naturally, and they've had it quite tough these past few years. David's manager of his estate agency … and Ian's manager of the menswear shop now. But they don't earn huge salaries, and our lovely daughters-in-law have both been taking time out of work to look after the children …"

"The guys are literally bursting out of their flats, Jan. They're very nice apartments, but you can't fit two adults and two fast-growing children into two-bedroom, one reception room accommodation for too long."

"They've both been saving like squirrels for deposits on houses …"

"I know that, Jan. And as David and Ian have often told me, the financial goalposts keep on moving. Do you know how much money you need to put down now, just to buy a very ordinary three-bed suburban semi with a small garden?  I suppose the mortgage companies are much more wary of potential borrowers since the credit crunch? They need to see a big initial capital commitment nowadays. But house prices are constantly rising because of the heavy demand and lack of supply. It's a Catch 22 situation! I wish we could've helped the boys."

"Well now we can, Neil. How much should we give them?"

"I think they've got some equity in their flats, though I'm not sure what it amounts to now."

"How much could they have?"

"Not much, I agree. Perhaps we should give each of the boys £200,000. It won't buy a mansion in Hampstead Garden Suburb, but with what they've managed to put aside in their building society savings accounts it should assist them towards buying something reasonably suitable outright."

"Why not make it a round quarter of a million each, Neil? They're good boys struggling to do the best for their families. I know it's not a fortune when it comes to buying property these days. When we got married, we were lucky that our parents could help us to get on the housing ladder. Now at last we can help David and Ian to each put a foot on it, too."

"You're absolutely right, Jan. Let's do it, if only to see their faces light up when we hand them the cheques to bank. Remember when they were babies, and how their eyes would sparkle when we gave them new toys?"

"S-Stop it, Neil. Y-You're making me cry. H-Hand me a tissue from that box."

"Here you are, sweetheart. Now give us that kiss, Jan."

"Careful my hair ... just a peck on the cheek for now, okay darling?"

"Okay, my love."

"A million quid, a million quid ... it'll be life changing for us! There's still a kind of mental block about it. What time do we have to be at the local newspaper offices tomorrow afternoon?"

"The reporter said three o'clock. She's coming in especially with a photographer. And she urged us to definitely drive there in your taxi. I take it they want to take pictures of us holding the cheque and standing in front of the cab. Makes a better news story, I suppose. Can you imagine the headline: *LOCAL CABBIE WINS A £MILLION!*"

"We'll be famous."

"Yeah, our fifteen minutes of fame ... at least in North East London."

"On the other hand, Neil ..."

"What, Jan?"

"I've got some reservations about the publicity. Why did we agree to it? You never know who might be reading about us these days ... and all those begging letters we'll get! I don't know about this, Neil."

"I'm sure it'll be alright. And it could be fun. We're not the first, by a long shot. And I've never heard any alarming stories as a result of this kind of exposure. Anyway, I'll make sure the paper doesn't print or give out our address, and our home number's ex-directory. Besides, if we happened to get any requests for donations we'll judge their genuineness on a case by case basis and maybe even give a little something here and there, particularly to worthy charities."

"Yeah, I reckon. But in any case, won't we be giving something to the Jewish charities we send a few pounds to every Pesach and Rosh Hashanah?"

"Of course … I've always said that I wish we could send them larger amounts. But before we get to these very good causes, perhaps we should think about our grandchildren …"

"You're not wrong, Neil. After all, that's what they say … charity begins at home."

"Only it wouldn't be charity, would it Jan?"

"No, it certainly wouldn't. So what should we be giving our little darlings Amy, Ellis, Susie and Glenn?"

"First … do you think you could move your head occasionally, Jan? If you keep it as rigid as that against the headboard all night in aid of your truly fabulous hairstyle, you'll lock it into that position for all time, God forbid! Secondly, and in answer to your question, I think we should let the kids have some little gifts straightaway … nothing too extravagant, you understand. We don't want them to learn the wrong lessons about gelt, do we now? They'll just be small tokens of our love … possibly some nice new designer wristwatches."

"So what else do you have in mind for them, Neil?"

"Look Jan, perhaps one day they'll want to go to university.

They might decide otherwise, of course. But do you know how much it costs nowadays, what with fees and loans?"

"Yes, I read and see the news. I think most colleges now charge about £10,000 a year in tuition fees. Isn't that right?"

"Not far off. Who knows how much it will be in the future? In any event, it must be extremely doubtful whether our dear grandchildren's parents could ever afford to support them all at university. Apart from the fees, students graduating today and tomorrow could be burdened with many thousands of pounds' worth of debt, repaying the loans they've needed to take out to survive for three years away from home."

"I know they only pay back the loans when they're earning above a certain amount. But it can't be good to have such a huge debt hanging around your neck, especially when you're striving to make a life for yourself in our very uncertain and troubling world …"

"You know what, Jan … you're a philosopher, and you don't know it."

"If you say so, darling … now *you* engage in a bit of philosophising, and tell me what we're about to do for our grandchildren's future."

"We should put some capital aside for each of them until they're eighteen years old, and in savings accounts paying as decent an annual interest as we can find."

"How much do you think?"

"Well, taking into account inflation etcetera, what about … £40,000 each?"

"Make it £50,000, Neil. It's your *etcetera* that I'm worried about."

"Fifty thousand each it is, then."

"You're the best Grandpa ever!"

"Yeah … well it's *your* money, too. So let's have my accountant scout around for the best interest rates, and do the business as soon as possible."

"Perfect! Do you fancy a cuppa, Neil?"

"What? Look at the clock. It's coming up to the wee small hours …"

"Well, I'd like one."

"Right, I'll go down and brew you some tea. Maybe I'll make myself a coffee."

"Coffee … that'll certainly keep you up all night."

"I'll refrain from making the obvious response. But it does look as if we're going to be awake for the duration. I won't be too long. Please don't smirk at me like that, Jan …"

★ ★ ★

"I really enjoyed that, Neil."

"I take it you're referring to the tea, Jan."

"Shut up, clever dick!"

"I like it … but not as much as the million pounds we've just won. Oh, my goodness! One million pounds! I can't believe it. It'll be so life changing for us."

"Can we be serious for a minute?"

"Okay, Jan. What do you have in mind?"

"I'd like to offer some of the money to Mum, if that's okay."

"Sure it is. And I think I know why you say *offer* and not *give*."

"Yeah, Mum could be rather sensitive about it. I realise you've helped her a lot since she lost Dad. I'm very grateful for that … and I know for sure that Mum is, too. But she's of the old school when it comes to actually handing her money."

"I appreciate that. Listen Jan, your Mum's what … seventy nine now? Perhaps we could set up some kind of fund for her. So if anything happens, you know what I mean, she'll have something in the coffers to help her along. I know that, thank God, she can look after herself in the flat at the moment … what with the home help and all. But I think we should foresee a time when that might not be a practical possibility."

"She'll never go into a home … she often says that, as you know."

"I appreciate she says that now, but things change for the elderly, sadly. I've noticed her memory isn't that marvellous these days."

"You're right. It's strange, really. She often reminisces about the good old days, fairly accurately I think. Though it's true Mum sometimes can't remember what happened yesterday. I *am* a little anxious about that, but she won't go to her GP about it. I'll need to work on her stubbornness. Thankfully she seems reasonably fit physically, apart from the occasional aches and pains. The doctor says they're nothing other than creeping old age. But I can readily see where you're coming from, Neil. We'll have to watch her carefully. Unfortunately, as you say, there may come a time when …"

"Don't let's depress ourselves about that right now, though good care of the elderly does come rather expensive these days. We know that from your uncle's situation. I think we should put aside £50,000 from our win for your Mum, and of course continue to provide her with whatever she wants or needs. And incidentally, let's arrange for your uncle to receive, say, £10,000?"

"Thank you, darling. That's very sweet, generous and considerate. You may've won a million pounds, and I know it's going to be life changing for us … but you've certainly won your place in heaven, God bless you."

"Now you're making *me* cry. W–Where are those tissues? And what did I tell you about keeping your head too rigid?"

"Okay, okay. Give us another kiss, then."

"You've got it … But listen Jan, I haven't got much in the way of family myself, have I? Basically, it's only the odd cousin or two now … people we haven't set eyes on for years, anyway. Well, shall we just put up … let's say £5,000 for some appropriate presents for friends, and the few other relatives that might expect something from us. What do you say?"

"Frankly, it sounds a bit too big-hearted to me, Neil. But … okay then, let's do it. It's only point nought five percent of a million, not a lot really."

"Your maths is brilliant as usual, Jan. You *can* be my financial adviser!"

"Well as you know, I do indulge in a bit of bookkeeping at the dress shop. Those night classes at the institute came in very useful."

"Yeah, you're right."

"So what charities do you think we should give donations to, and how much for each? It doesn't need to be the same for all of them, of course."

"That's true, Jan. But somehow I feel like we should give them equal amounts. They're all very worthy, and they do some tremendous work."

"Which ones do you want us to donate to, then?"

"I think they have to be the charities we normally send a

small cheque to twice a year. As I've always said, I wish we could've given more to them. Now we can."

"So that means the care charity, blind and deaf and the home in Israel that looks after orphans ..."

"Yeah, those are three very good causes ... and if you agree, I'm mindful we should write a cheque to one other."

"Which one do you have in mind, Neil?"

"It's concerned with dementia. The organisation provides support for those who suffer with this dreadful problem, and for their carers. It also promotes and encourages research into mental health."

"You really didn't need to ask whether I would agree. Of course I do. We've seen the terrible results of this increasingly widespread disability. What about ...?"

"Ironically it seems to be due, in large part, to people generally living much longer now than, say, even twenty years ago. The benefits of modern health care and the longevity it brings appear to be having a growing downside."

"You're not wrong, Neil. I read a magazine article about this recently. Apparently, there's some pioneering research being undertaken somewhere or other. I can't remember ... oh dear, early signs ..."

"Please don't joke about it, Jan."

"Sorry, I didn't mean ..."

"I know. I apologise, sweetheart ... but yes, I recall the piece. You gave it to me to look at. So far as I can recollect, a scientist they interviewed said the research was using stem cells to try to engineer new cells in the brain. Maybe I've got that all wrong. Though I think the boffin went on to say that the laboratory work is in its very early stages. And that we shouldn't expect a cure, even if that's possible, in the near future."

"I believe we should give dementia provision and research a substantial amount, no less than you propose giving to the other very commendable causes."

"You're right. I think this mental disability problem is one of the most horrific of our time. It seems to be a kind of plague. And witnessing the mind of a close relative, or anyone for that matter, disintegrating in front of your eyes, losing their capacity to understand what's happening around them and being drained of the sense of who they are must be horrendous. If, God forbid, anything like that happens to me ... well, you know what to do."

"More depressing talk ... and *you're* the guilty one this time! We're supposed to be having only happy thoughts today, aren't we? We've just won a life changing one million pounds on the lottery, for crying out loud! Let's enjoy only pleasant musings, eh darling?"

"I'm sorry, Jan sweetheart. So shall we say £50,000 to each of these four really valuable causes?"

"Yes ... absolutely."

"Is that the lot, then?"

"Should we give something to the shul?"

"Apart from the occasional simcha, we only ever go to our synagogue a couple of times a year ... Rosh Hashanah and Yom Kippur."

"But we've been members since we got married there. Our boys were barmitzvah there, Neil. And the rabbi was very good to us when we were sitting shiva ..."

"You're quite in order, Jan. I'm an idiot ..."

"No, Neil ... it's just not the first thing on your mind."

"How much should we give them?"

"I think five thousand would be about right."

"I agree, and thanks for reminding me about this. Is that everything now? I'm bound to have forgotten something or someone else."

"I can't think of anything or anyone for the time being, Neil … no, wait a second. There are two people I'd like to give a little something to … one's Mum's home help. Anna is really helpful, and she has got a great personality. I think she comes from some small town in the Czech Republic. In fact, she's been more than just the normal everyday home assistance to Mum. I don't think I've told you, and I won't go into the details now. Suffice to say, she's been wonderful. Can we give Anna £500, just to show our appreciation for her being such a good-natured and thoughtful person?"

"No problem, Jan."

"Lovely."

"And who's the other person?"

"Sorry?"

"The other person you want us to give some money to …"

"Oh yes, to Bill I think … he has been our punctual and trustworthy gardener for so long now."

"We pay him for his work every fortnight during the gardening year, don't we? What has his punctuality got to do with anything?"

"No, it's not his punctuality specifically. Though he always turns up when he says he will, which is useful. It's difficult to say how old Bill is. He could be fifty or so, though I can't be sure. He lives with his widowed mother. I don't think he has ever been married. But he often talks about his Mum. He obviously loves her dearly, and it may be that she's the only other person in his life. He told me that they haven't had a holiday since his Dad died. And I believe that was a very long time ago now. I know he couldn't possibly afford to take his mother away for even a week's break in this country, let alone abroad. Sometimes he mentions his dream of going with her to the Costa del Sol one day. I'd like us to give him a couple of thousand pounds so he can take his Mum to Spain next summer. What do you say, Neil?"

"What do I say? I say hand me another tissue, Jan."

"I'll hand you something, if you're not careful …"

"Nice one, Jan my sweetie pie. Of course we can give old Bill a couple of grand."

"Not so much of the *old*. Don't forget, he may be younger than us."

"Oh dear …"

"Oh Neil … you can't seem to help putting your foot in it, can you?"

"What about a truce, my own true … and very *young* love?"

"Well give us a kiss, then …"

"Nice one, Jan."

"Okay, that's everyone now."

"What?"

"I can't think of anyone else we should be giving part of our million pounds to."

"No, I think that's it. Brings music to my ears those words … a *million pounds,* a *million pounds*! I can't believe it. However much I say the words, I still can't credit we've won so much cash. It's life changing for us, Jan. I wonder how much we've given away so far. I'm afraid that I haven't been keeping a tally.

You're the numbers person, Jan. Add it all up and let's have the total."

"Well, we've given quarter of a million each to David and Ian, so that's £500,000. Then we've set aside £50,000 for each of our four grandchildren. That makes £200,000 which, together with the half a million for our boys, gives us £700,000. Next, we decided to find a way to get £50,000 to mother and another £10,000 to Mum's brother. So far, that amounts to £760,000. After that, we agreed to donate £50,000 to each of our four favoured charities, and to give £5,000 to the shul. Finally, we thought £500 should go to Mum's lovely home help and £2,000 to our faithful gardener. Therefore … er, the grand aggregate of money we've given away from our fantastic winnings is, let me see, Neil … yes, £967,500."

"What was that figure again?"

"£967,500, Neil …"

"Ha, ha … that's what I thought you'd said, Jan. So, by my calculation, that leaves us with precisely £32,500. At four percent interest, say, that should make us the unimaginable sum of £1,300 per annum, less tax of course."

"Sounds correct to me … and that's what we've got left from our one million pounds, Neil."

"Brilliant! Maybe we'll be seeing Bill and his Mum in Benidorm for our holidays next summer. Didn't we say our win would be life changing for us?"

"We did, darling. But do you know what we've got that makes us even happier than one million pounds?"

"What's that, sweetheart?"

"We've got each other. That's what we've got. Now give me a really big kiss, but be careful with the hair …"

"Yes … I'll give you a really big kiss, Jan. And I'll be careful with the hair. But first, could you please hand me another one of those tissues?"

# On a Wing and a Prayer

"HEAR THAT, Smiley? Skipper says the Lanc has just cleared the Lincolnshire coast ... Can you hear me back there, Smiley?"

"Tail air gunner to mid upper gunner, I'm receiving you loud and clear on my headphones."

"Bit formal, aren't you Smiley? I know that I'm squashed into this Perspex blister on top of the plane with my two .303 inch Browning machine guns. And I also know that you're squeezed into the rear turret with your four Brownings. But you *can* just call me Stan, you know. And it'll take less time, too."

"Sorry, Stan. I know that. I seem to get the collywobbles when we leave Blighty behind ... you must have a terrific view up there. What about testing our guns now, Stan? Get it over and done with."

"You don't half crowd in your thoughts, Smiley! Yes, I've got a grandstand three hundred and sixty degree panoramic view up here on the roof. Jolly useful when a Bf 110 is diving at me from above or the sides, though the German night fighters have

learned to sneak up on us from below or behind. Next, I don't
know about procedures aboard your last ship, but let's just await
the skipper's command to test fire our Brownings, eh? We
should get the nod from the skipper fairly soon now."

"Right, Stan ... it was kind of a routine standing order on
my previous crate. As soon as we were over the North Sea, we
could trigger the guns."

"We'll wait. It'll just be a minute or so till we gain a bit
more height."

"Sorry about the eagerness to get blasting, Stan. As I
mentioned to you at briefing, this is just my fourth sortie over
Germany. And now they've called me in as a replacement for
your tail gunner ..."

"Yeah, poor old Johnny has got appendicitis. They rushed
him to hospital this morning. Sorry, Smiley ... but I sort of miss
him being on board the ship. We've been gunnery partners for
over fifteen trips to the Fatherland. In fact, the entire crew has
been together for the best part of ..."

"I understand, Stan. And Jimmy, the flight engineer, told me
just before we climbed aboard that, with this sortie, you'll have
completed thirty operations. That's ruddy marvellous, Stan. Bet
you can't wait to get back on terra firma again, at least for the
six months off flying duties before your next tour."

"You can say that again. It's been quite hairy the last few
months, and that's the understatement of 1944. We've had some
terrifyingly close shaves. Maybe the war will be over before I
need to go up into the wide blue yonder again."

"You've been really lucky, pal. The word going around is
that the average survival rate for Bomber Command aircrew is
six or seven missions now. And it's said that a bomber is pretty

fortunate if it outlasts some twenty sorties. All this does my head in … but I try hard to focus on the job in hand and forget about these awful statistics."

"You've got to, Smiley … else you'll go off your rocker! I've heard of blokes who couldn't take any more of the stress, and asked to come off flying duties. They've had their service records marked LMF … lacks moral fibre. I think that's quite tough on these lads. After all, they're only in their late teens or early twenties generally, like you and me … Maybe they've got even more vivid imaginations than we have? But the blot on their copy books won't help them when they get back to Civvy Street after the war, eh?"

"I suppose not, Stan. Listen, I know a lot of the boys are superstitious about newcomers like me on board … or Jonahs, as I think they call us! I'm no different really when it comes to superstition. Every time I go up, I wear this old scarf that my Mum gave me when I began flying. But I'm not here because …"

"You don't have to say it, Smiley. I know. Incidentally, I don't need to ask the reason for your nickname, do I? You were grinning even when you climbed aboard."

"I don't know. I think it's a flipping misnomer. A grimace of mine seems to come out like a grin. I heard what you just mumbled … thanks, but I do possess a mirror back at base, you know."

"Look Smiley, we're all scared to death every time we climb into this old bus. Anyone who doesn't admit to that is either a fool or lacks imagination. But I think we're all realists. You might say that many of the boys are even fatalists. There's no reason to go that far … and, frankly, they depress me no end. Practically all the time in the Mess, whilst knocking back their pints of ale, they make black jokes about dying. These chaps are always saying they know they're going to get the chop sooner or later. Naturally, the casualty figures aren't unknown. The guys realise there's a high probability they won't make it anywhere near to completing a tour ... and that they'll never have a chance to fall in love with a beautiful girl, get married and have children."

"Oh Stan, now *you're* depressing *me*. But I've got to say, you seem to have kept your balance. Although I did overhear you talking to yourself before we got ready for take-off tonight. What was all that about, if you don't mind me asking?"

"I don't mind, Smiley. You said just before that I'd been really fortunate to have survived for so long ... against all the odds. Look, I appreciate that many of the boys in Bomber Command feel that whether or not you're in the wrong place in the sky at the wrong time is a question of fate, random chance or Lady Luck, whatever you care to call it. Well personally, I don't quite see it that way. I'm Jewish, you know ..."

"No, I didn't. You don't look Jewish. I'm Church of England ..."

"Okay ... Well anyway, I come from a traditional Jewish family. You said you heard me muttering to myself before we got ready to taxi down the runway for take-off. I was actually repeating the *Shema*, over and over again ..."

"What's the ... er, what you just said?"

"The *Shema*? It's a Jewish prayer, in Hebrew, acknowledging the sovereignty and Oneness of the Almighty. It starts like this, *Shema Yisroel, Hashem Elokeinu, Hashem Echad*. That means 'Hear O Israel, the Lord our God, the Lord is One' ... You could say that the words represent the essence of our Jewish belief."

"It certainly seems to have worked in safeguarding *your* life."

"I do have faith in the Almighty."

"But I take it that a lot of Jewish boys in the Royal Air Force, or in any of the other armed services for that matter, have been killed in this war. Might that be because they didn't say the prayer you just mentioned ... er, the *Sh* ... *Sh-e-ma*? Or is it that they didn't possess the strength of faith in God that you have, Stan?"

"You're right. I mean about many Jewish lads being killed in the service of their King and Country. But the truth is that I don't know why some people have been killed, but not others. That applies to all serving men, and women, of course. And also to the many thousands of civilians who've lost their lives in German bombing raids and suchlike. I believe in the Almighty, and I'm sure that many of those Jewish servicemen and servicewomen who've bought it in the air, on the ground or on and under the sea had faith, too. The point is that we're in the hands of the Almighty. We're all mere mortals. We can't comprehend the reasons why things happen, or don't happen, in this world. And by the way, the *Shema* is often recited by a Jew who may be about to pass away. Perhaps there's an element of that involved in my saying the prayer just before we get airborne which in itself, and as you know full well, is a potentially hazardous manoeuvre."

"Okay, but ... hold on a mo, Stan ... that's the skipper calling. Hurrah! We can now test fire our guns ..."

*Rat-a-tat-tat!*
*Rat-a-tat-tat!*
*Rat-a-tat-tat!*

*Rat-a-tat-tat!*
*Rat-a-tat-tat!*
*Rat-a-tat-tat!*

"Guns seem fine."

"Yes Smiley."

"Hundreds of Lancasters heading east tonight, Stan … I don't think I've ever seen so many crates in the air at the same time, though admittedly I haven't been up here that much yet. It's a really clear night … so far, but I can't even see the stars for airplanes."

"And apparently we're going to be joined by two streams of American bombers somewhere after we've crossed the Dutch coast. Ross, our navigator, will tell you when … if you want to know that badly. Personally, I would leave him alone to get on with his job. I understand we've also got some USAF Mustang P51 fighter cover for this raid on the Ruhr."

"The heart of German industry …"

"Yeah, we should be giving the area another real pasting … you know, most of Germany's cities are almost complete ruins now. We've certainly been paying them back for the Blitz … and in spades! That's been down to Bomber Harris and the so-called area bombing! But this isn't going to be the end of their sorrow, believe you me. Now that D-Day and the Allied invasion have been successful, and with Paris liberated a week or so ago, surely the war can't last that much longer. Eisenhower and Montgomery seem to be hoping the Germans will be routed and surrendering unconditionally by the end of the year. Who knows though …?"

"No, no! F–For Christ's sake … W–What the bloody h–hell!

That plane came a bit too close for comfort just now!"

"That was a bit of a sudden jink ... What was it, Smiley?"

"A Lanc nearly gave us a right old prang from below, Stan ... luckily, our skipper must've spotted it drifting up and astern and pulled the nose up sharp-like ... j-just in t-time, if you a-ask me!"

"Take it easy, Smiley. Nothing has happened ... thank God. We're still in one piece. And that's the main thing."

"Perhaps your prayer ... the *S-Sh-ema* is protecting us, Stan ... I realise this is only my fourth raid, but I'm petrified about all these *friendly* aircraft flying together in such a large and tight formation. I don't know how ..."

"None of us is that happy about it, either. But if we don't keep to some kind of disciplined and harmonious pecking order, planes could just swan off ... and these strays and stragglers can be picked off easily by Kraut night fighters. Nonetheless, I've witnessed a couple of nasty accidents I can tell you."

"What do you mean, Stan?"

"Well, as you may be aware, we often rendezvous with other flight groups. It's quite a complex procedure to choreograph, as you might imagine. And if the weather's not too brilliant, with thick low cloud for example, pilots can be confronted by frightening difficulties. Anyhow and sadly, I lost one of my best chums, a wireless operator, in a mid-air collision between two Lancs. They were flying close together in a mass formation over the English Channel and making headway for France. I actually had the horrible misfortune to observe the horrendous impact. The fireball was huge, what with the full bomb loads ... and both planes disintegrated before my eyes. I prayed to see at least a couple of billowing parachutes from the total of fourteen crewmen. But it was hopeless … all of them must've perished instantly. That's the only good thing you can say about such a catastrophe. The explosive flash of death stays on your retinas for quite a while, just like if you happen to glance at the sun for a moment or two. But I'm sure it'll be imprinted on my mind for ever. My friend Alex was Jewish, too. He was such a handsome young man. His parents were absolutely heartbroken, and I don't need to tell you that. They'll just never recover from their irreplaceable loss. Alex was their only child … they had him fairly late. He'd just turned twenty-three when he was killed, and he was about to be married to a really cute girl. Alex showed me a photograph of her … he was so much in love with Evelyn. And what's more, his Mum and Dad didn't even have his body to bury and grieve over …"

"Bloody hell …! That's very sad, Stan! But it certainly doesn't help me stay calm in this great wave of aircraft … what with their thousands of tons of bombs onboard!"

"I'm sorry, Smiley. I shouldn't have …"

"Don't concern yourself, Stan. If your number's up, I suppose it's up! There's not much you can do about it."

"That's life."

"Or death."

"Okay, Smiley … enough already."

"By the way, I'm an old married man you know. Gwen and I got hitched two years ago. She's a really great lassie. And we're hoping to start a family when the war's over."

"It's none of my business, but why do you want to wait?"

"Somehow I don't think it would be right, Stan. I know the wives of a lot of the married crew have given birth in recent times. Maybe the chaps think that if anything happens to them, you know … they'll have left behind some human legacy of themselves. Perhaps their spouses want a baby for that reason, too. I don't know really. In a way, I can grasp these thoughts to some extent … But as I say, I feel emotionally unable to bring about a situation where my widow would be lumbered with a child to bring up all by herself … And you never know, but it might spoil her chances of marrying again."

"I do see your point of view, Smiley. But God forbid the circumstances should ever arise, if you do happen to become a Dad … while the war's still raging, I mean."

"Thanks, Stan … but what about you?"

"Excuse me?"

"Are you married?"

"Oh, I see. No. Not yet, anyway."

"Do you have a sweetheart, Stan?"

"Yes, I do have a young lady. In fact, she's my fiancée. I've known Sally since we were children. She lives only a couple of houses away from us. I've always loved her … and I know she feels the same way about me. I think it was always taken as read that we would wed one day. I had an ambition to train as a newspaper reporter, but then the war came and I was called up eventually. I wanted to join the RAF because my best chum, that was Alex, had already enlisted in the junior service. In fact, he'd joined the Air Training Corps when he was fourteen years old. Airplanes were his passion. But Sally and yours truly, with our parents' blessings, are waiting for the war to end before we go under the chupah …"

"Under the … what was that word, Stan?"

"The chupah … it's the canopy under which a Jewish wedding takes place in a synagogue. It's held up by four posts, one at each corner. It's erected in front of what we call the Aron Kodesh, the Ark … in effect it's the large cupboard in which the Sifrei Torah are kept."

"I'm sorry Stan, but I don't know the lingo … the *what*?"

"Sifrei Torah … they're the scrolls containing the Five Books of Moses. A portion is read from them every week on Shabbos, that's on a Saturday which is the Jewish Sabbath. And the whole lot is completed by the end of each Jewish year, which starts with Rosh Hashanah or, literally, the head of the year."

"Many thanks for the explanation, Stan. I've never been to a Jewish wedding."

"Okay, Smiley … well, please God you and Gwen will come to mine."

"Thanks Stan, we would really like that … er, please God."

"Gwen and I were married in a church near to where we live in south London. But we're not that religious, Gwen even less so than me. Of course, our vows to each other mean everything to us, though we would've been just as happy getting spliced in a Register Office. I suppose it was our parents who'd really hoped for a white wedding with all the trimmings … such as they were, what with wartime austerity and belt-tightening you know. Anyway, even with the necessary adjustments, it turned out to be a really wonderful day and not only weather-wise. Gwen looked terrific in her bridal gown … it was made from parachute cotton! And we've got no regrets about the religious wedding."

"I'm glad you had a nice time, Smiley. And I'm sure you and Gwen have some marvellous memories. I'm sure they'll carry you through the darkest of days, and nights …"

★ ★ ★

"Half a mo, Stan … it's the skipper again … seems like we're approaching the Dutch coastline."

"Yeah … Skipper says we'll be crossing just to the north of Amsterdam. I'd really like to visit that city sometime. They say it's very picturesque with its canals … Don't they call it the Venice of the north?"

"I don't know, Stan. Anyway, we're not going to see much of it up this high. From what I can see back here, it looks like the formation has been ordered to spread out a bit …"

"Yeah, Smiley … and I think we're going to be joined by the American wings soon. Some of us are bombing Dortmund, others Essen and more cities on the other side of the Rhine. They said many of the German gun batteries in western Holland have been neutralised. Those 88s were murderous! We're probably quite safe from anti-aircraft fire until we near the German border. But you can never know for certain. Obviously, the safest course would've been plotted for us. But Jerry's right on the ball when it comes to swift reconstruction, if given half the chance … you've got to keep pounding the bastards. And there are still quite a number of Luftwaffe airfields en route to the targets."

"I've only known you for a few hours, Stan. But I don't think I've heard you swear before now. No, please don't apologise …"

"I wasn't going to, Smiley. I was just going to say that, when it comes to the Nazis and the atrocities they've perpetrated on the Jewish people and others, swearing at them is the least I would want to do. Haven't you heard the rumours about the mass shootings of Jews in Eastern Europe and Russia … and the horrifying stories of concentration camps and worse? Jews from across occupied Europe have been transported to them by railway trains, and slaughtered in their hundreds of thousands?"

"Yes Stan, I've heard some terrible rumours about that. I can't understand how a supposedly civilised nation could …"

"The writing was on the wall for the Jews as soon as that monster anti-Semite Hitler and his evil cronies began to impose their will on Germany."

"The buggers will get their comeuppance. We're all fighting for a just cause."

"Yes, we are indeed Smiley. And the sooner we succeed in destroying the Nazis the better … for everyone. But what I don't follow is why our politicians and top Brass haven't decided to bomb the railway tracks to the camps. At least that might have slowed down or even blocked the deportation transports from the ghettoes. Our leaders must be aware they're taking place …"

"But surely the Jews in peril are praying for salvation. Why isn't God saving them, rescuing them from mortal danger … just like he brought the Israelites out of Egypt a few thousand years back? You see, Stan … I did learn something in RE classes at school!"

"Ha, ha … you certainly did, Smiley. But seriously, you've raised an important question that I'm sure millions of persecuted Jews have been agonising over. I'm afraid I haven't got an answer to it, and for the reasons I've mentioned earlier. No one on Earth knows why it's happening … other than that, as a matter of undeniable fact, depraved men are having their wicked sway. But I think we agree, Smiley … they'll pay heavily for their dreadful crimes soon enough. And maybe someday we'll understand more about why all this is happening ..."

★ ★ ★

"Stan ... did you hear that?"

"Yeah, Smiley ... the skipper's just given us a couple more minutes before we need to keep a keen lookout for any enemy night fighters breaking through our air cover. Some of our planes will shortly be dropping tons of that clever stuff. I think it's called 'Window' ... it jams or disrupts radar and radio communications between Luftwaffe controllers and their pilots. Still, there's always a few of the blighters that can get themselves up and make a bee-line for us. And with all these planes carrying heavy bomb-loads and lumbering onwards like some massive moving herd of metal cows, we can be easy meat on the hoof for the German night fighters!"

"At least we've got a good chance of seeing them off with our Brownings, Stan. I've already been credited with one probable ... at the debriefing after my last trip. But I was told you've sent packing to fiery hell more than a few of the Krauts during your twenty-nine sorties. You're a hero, Stan. Do you know that? They're likely to stick a gong on you sometime."

"No, I'm not a hero, Smiley. I'm just doing my job as an air gunner. I'm not brave at all ... far from it. But you're right about our ability to fight off the Bf110s, JU88s and whatever else they throw at us. It's those damn searchlights scanning the sky that you can't really deal with. Once one of the radar-controlled beams cones your plane, all the others jump on the bandwagon.

It's not very easy to escape from them, however much your skipper tries to wriggle out of danger. As soon as a bomber's illuminated in that intense circle of light, a whole barrage of flak comes up. One of my chums in another Group told me about a really scary incident he was involved in …"

"What was that, Stan?"

"I think we've just about got time for me to tell you quickly, Smiley. Well briefly then, his aircraft was on a bombing run over Bremen. The plane was suddenly trapped in one of those powerful sets of linked searchlights, like a fly caught in a spider's web. The bombardier had dropped its load and the Lanc was making a wide turn for home. Up came a terrifying bundle of flak, shells bursting close all round the crate. Two of its four engines, one port and one starboard, were hit and shredded by a packet of shrapnel and started brewing up. My pal Benny thought he was a goner for sure. But his captain was brilliant. He knew almost instinctively what to do, though it wasn't without serious risk …"

"What did he do?"

"Well, the very experienced pilot put the bomber, with its engines roaring and flaming, into a steep and rapid dive. Could've meant chips for the entire crew, but Benny's skipper clearly considered there was no other alternative to their sizzling down to a black crisp …"

"Pretty picture you're painting for me, Stan! I can see why you wanted to be a journalist."

"Anyway, the ear-splitting almost vertical descent paid off. The fires in the engines were extinguished. And with the flight engineer's steady support, the skipper managed to pull the bus out of its screaming dive before it hit the deck. He had less than a few hundred feet to spare …"

"Wow! That was quite a tale. I take it all the crew got safely back home to Blighty to tell it …?"

"Yes, the plane trundled home on two engines without ditching in the drink. But the pilot did have to make a crash landing somewhere in the flat wild fenlands of East Anglia. Miraculously, there were only some cuts and bruises. Thankfully, and it was all down to the boss's incredible flying expertise, there were no fatalities."

"Marvellous!"

"And thank God we've got a really excellent skipper, too. He's pulled us out of many a pickle …"

"Speaking of the devil, Stan … orders from the pulpit. Skipper says no more chitchat, and to keep our eyes peeled for the night fighters! A few of the bastards have been spotted weaving around the northernmost edge of the formation …"

"We're on the extreme southern flank, Smiley. So if any of the Nazi sods heads in this direction, we'll be the first to engage them."

"Right … Can't see anything yet … Wait a minute … What's that, Stan?"

"Skipper's calling 'bandits at ten o'clock'. Let's keep a keen look out for those Jerry blighters … Quick, Smiley … there's a 110 heading down your way …"

*Rat-a-tat-tat!*
*Rat-a-tat-tat!*
*Rat-a-tat-tat!*

"Missed him blast it! Stan … I think the 110's going to

climb back over the top again … Do you see him, Stan? No, half a mo … the bugger's making a rolling turn astern … I see him! I see him!"

"Watch out, Smiley. There's another 110 descending fast … No, hold your horses … he's going after Pete's aircraft on our port side … the Nazi swine's zapping it, raking the starboard wing! Guns are returning fire at the bastard from the Lanc … but wait. Oh no! Oh my God, the bomber's been hit bad … Oh, no … oh, no! The starboard wing's been sliced through … it's falling away …"

"I can see it … the plane's going into a flaming corkscrew spiral, Stan. It's out of control! Can you see any parachutes coming out?"

"Not from here … Can you see anything?

"Wait … yeah … I can see one."

"Who is it, Smiley?"

"I can't make him out from this distance."

"Is it just the one chute, then?"

"Afraid so, Stan … But, oh Christ … the chute has caught fire …! Oh my God, please no!"

"Oh, Smiley …"

"Stan … it's just too horrible to watch!"

"Concentrate, Smiley. Take care … another bloody 110's coming down … your end again!"

"Spotted the Kraut … I've got a bead on him, Stan."

*Rat-a-tat-tat!*
*Rat-a-tat-tat!*
*Rat-a-tat-tat!*

"I think you've hit him, Smiley …"

"I don't know, Stan. He's under the … Hold on … the bastard's coming round again … your neck of the woods. Nail him, Stan …! And what's that? There's another fighter following him … Is it one of ours, Stan? Hell, no! Christ … it's a Jerry! You Nazi bastards! What the hell are our bloody P51s doing up there …?"

*Rat-a-tat-tat!*
*Rat-a-tat-tat!*
*Rat-a-tat-tat!*

"Did you get him, Stan?"

"I'm not sure … I'm not sure, but … here comes his mate now …!"

*Rat-a-tat-tat!*
*Rat-a-tat-tat!*
*Rat-a-tat-tat!*

"Got the sod …! I've nailed him! The tail fin's flying off … Can you see, Smiley? The Nazi swine's baling out!"

"Good shooting, Stan!"

"Watch yourself, Smiley … his mate might just pop up in front of you!"

"Y-You're right, Stan … I see him. I see him …!"

*Rat-a-tat-tat!*
*Rat-a-tat-tat!*
*Rat-a-tat-tat!*

"Any luck, Smiley?"

"No, the bastard corkscrewed down and away … He should come back under and around your side of the crate … Get the Kraut, Stan!"

"Yeah, there he goes …!"

*Rat-a-tat-tat!*
*Rat-a-tat-tat!*
*Rat-a-tat …*

"Aaargh …! I'm hit, Smiley … I–I'm hit …!"

"… Skipper, skipper … Stan's been hit! … Okay, I'll take over his guns … I'm coming to you, Stan … Ah! … Blast these piles of ruddy cartridge cases …! Hold on, Stan! I'm coming …"

★ ★ ★

"Aaargh …!"

"I'm here Stan … I'm with you now. Where are you hit, Stan? O–Oh, my God …!"

"Aaargh …! Smiley, S–Smiley … I–I f-feel s-so c-cold …"

"I'm here Stan … I'm going to give you a shot of morphine right away. Here we go … There, you'll be alright now. Don't worry, Stan … you're going to be j-just f-fine … O–Oh, Christ …!"

"H–Hold my … h-hold m-my h-hand, S–Smiley …"

"What did you say, Stan? I can barely hear you …"

"H–Hold m-my h-hand, please …"

"Sure, Stan … What's that you're saying? …"

"*Shema Yisroel, Hashem Elokeinu, Hashem Echad …*"

# Contradictions

"*MI SCUSI*! I mean, excuse me. Is this chair free, please? It's really busy here at the café this morning, but I don't want to disturb you."

"Yes, of course … do sit down, signora. But how did you know that I'm English?"

"I recognised you from the sinagoga … you were visiting us for Shabbat yesterday. I saw and overheard you talking to our rabbi. I'm sure you know how starkly strangers in a community stand out around a Kiddush table."

"I'm sorry, but I didn't see you … in the synagogue either. I suppose I was too preoccupied admiring its stunningly beautiful interior. I know I should've been concentrating on my Siddur. By the way your English is excellent, if I may say so …"

"I teach Linguistics at the university here. I've been teaching the subject since I gained my doctorate about ten years ago now …"

"Yes, do please sit down. It's such a charming spot out here by the waterside, and the Art Nouveau buildings are a delight to the eye. I can understand why all the café bars along here are quite lively. What would you like to drink?"

"Thank you, but that's okay I'll …"

"No please, allow me … in fact, I insist. It'll make up for my not noticing you on Shabbat."

"A Lungo, please. That's very kind of you."

"Not at all, I'll call the waitress. Ah yes, there she is … *Uno Lungo, per favore.*"

"Why should you have noticed me?"

"Beg pardon?"

"Why should you have noticed me in the sinagoga?"

"Well, it struck me that the congregation was generally over the age of fifty, including me … just over, if I might add."

"You certainly don't look it …"

"Very good of you to say so, I do think it's important to keep fit. But you're a very attractive young woman. I should've noticed you … ah, here's your Lungo. *Grazie.*"

"And thanks for *your* compliment."

"I have to say that I personally prefer a black Americano. A Lungo, which I know is quite popular here even if the name strikes me as not particularly enticing, is rather too condensed for me as a mid-morning drink. Though maybe oddly, I do enjoy an espresso after an evening meal. Perhaps I should be more open to trying new experiences."

"Life's full of contradictions, do you agree?"

"Y-Yes … I suppose."

"Take our community, for example. It's ostensibly orthodox, but most of its members are secular or cultural Jews

... only a small percentage come to the sinagoga on a regular basis; and those that do aren't necessarily strictly observant. There's been a lot of inter-marriage. There are a whole host of differing views and philosophies about the Jewish religion and life styles, and indeed about Israel and the Palestinians. And sometimes I wear trousers on Shabbat. Our minister is fairly non-judgemental, he doesn't preach fire and brimstone from his pulpit ... he's *aware*, that's the word I would choose to describe his persona. Yes, our rabbi is intellectually *aware* ... and he has therefore achieved much in holding the community together. On the High Holydays and some of the festivals, like fast-approaching Pesach, many more members of the community will attend services."

"For the last few years, I've journeyed around Europe quite regularly in my work, and I've come across this pattern so often nowadays ... You know, I've visited cities in Eastern Europe at Purim time when the synagogues are often filled with young families, the children in fancy dress boisterously waving their noisy rattles whenever Haman's name is read aloud from Megillah Esther. They then attend sometimes lavish communal entertainments with buffets piled high with Hamantaschen. Early on in these travels, I thought I'd arrived in religiously committed communities. Only to discover that on Shabbat there was often barely a minyan. I've become more knowledgeable now ... but it shows that not all is as it sometimes seems. Perhaps that's a kind of contradiction ... even ambivalence. There are many young rabbis in these cities who believe that the soft approach is to be preferred to down-your-throat antagonism. Many of these Jews have had enough of being dictated to for half a century by now defunct communist regimes. They've relished a newfound freedom to make their own decisions in life, openly and for good or ill. Especially when it relates to ideas, concepts or philosophies … and, I suppose, religion comes down to these sorts of things. The tactics, if such consciously they are, of these conscientious rabbis that I've mentioned appear to be working. More and more Jews, especially women I've found, seem to want to learn about their faith, its history, heritage and culture."

"Are you here for work reasons?"

"Kind of … I'm attending a week-long legal conference. And what a great place to hold one. I'm a commercial lawyer. I'll be returning home on Tuesday."

"I see that you're married. Does your spouse … I love the sound of that word, we don't have an exactly similar non-gender, matrimonial noun … does your *spouse* ever accompany you on these jaunts?"

"No, never has done. Leslie's also a lawyer … an extremely busy one too, specialising in family law. You don't wear a wedding ring, so I take it you're not married."

"That's correct, I'm not. I was living with someone for a few years, but it didn't work out. We're still good friends, though. Do you have any children? Sorry, I'm prying …"

"No you're not … it's a normal kind of question to ask someone who's married and that you've just met. In point of fact, we haven't acquired any children. We lead such hectic professional lives that we've never got round to it. My brother's the one in our Jewish family who's proved to be fruitful and has multiplied. He has four children, a well thought out two boys and two girls. So I've a lot of nieces and nephews to buy gifts for on birthdays and Chanucah."

"Has not having children ever worried you and your *spouse?*"

"No, I can't say that it has … largely because we don't have the time to dwell on the absence of offspring. I know our religion frowns on a lack of procreation activity … though the ultra-Orthodox, the Charedi, seem to be making up for the rest of us slackers. But I don't know that in today's world there's any serious stigma attached to not having children, even to not getting married."

"I agree, though in this country there does linger a cultural stigma if not, at least for some reactionary elements, religious dishonour in failing or refusing to propagate the species. I've even heard some insensitive brethren asserting that it's necessary for all Jews to make up for the six million murdered by the Nazis in the Holocaust. I think that's a hit well below the belt!"

"I've heard the same kind of mind-set expressed, too. So basically, I'm inclined to go along with your sentiments on such crassness. Look, I believe in the Almighty as I think you do also. I feel that we can only follow our personal consciences in the circumstances we find ourselves, whether the situation is of our own making, whether it's something that our lives have inexorably brought us to or even whether it's part and parcel of our very being. You know, as a child I was very shy. My parents were very outgoing and were totally unable to comprehend, or rather accept, how they could've launched such a miserably reticent child into the world. Instead of providing me with help and reassurance, they sidelined me. I grew to understand them; but they refused to understand me. Eventually, I pulled myself out of my introversion in order to achieve what I wanted or needed to accomplish in life, not that such a trait is of itself bad or harmful to anyone. There are some people who will remain timid all of their lives. It's an integral part of their nature, their very essence, and impossible for them to subdue or overcome. Despite having accepted their natural make up, they'll frequently suffer from the unsympathetic attitudes of those who can't grasp such a negative attribute or whose own elemental, intellectual, spiritual or emotional being prevents or inhibits comprehension. Maybe we have to understand that also."

"That was quite a speech ... but I do agree with everything you've just said. I love this meeting of our minds ... oh I'm sorry, I shouldn't have used such a word."

"What word?"

"Love ..."

"Why? Sorry, I don't follow you?"

"You're married."

"So? The context and application is different."

"Maybe it's a cultural thing."

"Maybe ... Would you like another coffee?"

"No, thank you. It's such a typically lovely warm spring morning here ... we're very fortunate climate-wise ... I think I'll take a stroll along the promenade. In fact, I do that on a Sunday morning in any event. Listen ... if you're not doing anything special right now perhaps you might like to accompany me. I would certainly wish you to do that, if possible."

"I've got some papers to read for the conference's final session tomorrow afternoon, but I suppose that can wait until later. This beguiling town's situated so picturesquely, its handsome buildings ringed by the greenest of wooded hills and the most tranquil of azure waters. Yes, I would love to take a walk."

"There you are ... you're doing it, too."

"Doing what?"

"Using that word ..."

"What word?"

"Love ..."

"Ah, yes ... very amusing. But do you know what? Whenever I visit a Jewish community, attend its synagogue on a Shabbat or whenever, I do feel as if I'm surrounded by brotherly and sisterly love. Perhaps that's a bit of an exaggeration. But I certainly do feel something akin to that somewhat amorphous emotion."

"That's really good to hear. I have to confess that I was watching you in the sinagoga on Shabbat, I mean during the service ... before I saw you with our rabbi at the Kiddush. Forgive me, but I can confirm that you were indeed peering up at the magnificent domed interior when you should've been following, in your Chumash, the reader's leyning. But I also noticed that from time to time you were gazing, albeit discreetly, at your fellow worshippers. It was just the way you were looking, kind of respectfully but at the same time with a sort of familial sincerity."

"You appear to have been wandering off the pages of your own prayer book, too ... even as much as I was. I'm flattered by your attention. Though it's true to say that I tend also to be somewhat fascinated by the occasional overseas visitor to our shul back home ... I can't see the waitress hovering around, so I'll just pop inside to pay the bill. Back in a moment ..."

★ ★ ★

"... Okay?"

"Yes, it's amusing you know ... the proprietor and his

waitresses know me already. I've been to this bar a number of times during the past week. You could say that I'm almost a regular here!"

"I thought we might amble around the bay to the marina and the faro, the lighthouse I mean. Will that be alright?"

"Sure. That would be wonderful! It's such a fantastic day … it has definitely brought your fellow townsfolk out into the brilliant sunshine."

"We'll see many more of our citizens soon, when they flood out of the numerous churches. And the cacophony of bells will almost deafen you."

"There are some magnificent churches here. I've been inside to view a few of the gorgeous interiors."

"That might be frowned upon by some orthodox rabbis."

"Yes you're right, but I can't see the harm in admiring the noble and artistic work inside … it's highly unlikely that I'll be converted to Catholicism or Greek Orthodoxy by gazing at the amazing paintings, glorious stained glass windows and other decorative stone and intricately carved wood features. I'm always struck by the almost mind-numbing contradiction of a devout Jew nailed to the cross and the fact that the rest is history, as they say … Christian history!"

"We're so much alike in our thoughts and notions, it's unbelievable."

★ ★ ★

"Did you see that?"

"I'm sorry … See what?"

"Those two teenage girls walking along hand-in-hand …

Since I've been here, I've seen quite a few pairs of young women strolling like that about the piazzas and along the public piers, particularly in the evenings and just before sunset."

"I know what you're thinking, but it's not normally the case here. Basically, it's a cultural thing ... a customary display of close friendship and affection. You may also have noticed macho young men, even three or four together sometimes, promenading arm-in-arm. It's a token of warm camaraderie rather than anything remotely suggestive."

"I understand, of course. But if you see that sort of thing in England, it can mean ... well, you know what."

"Yes, I know what ..."

★ ★ ★

"Can we stop for a while, perhaps sit on that vacant wooden bench and admire the wonderful view? I just want to drink in the landscape ... or seascape, whatever. It's absolutely remarkable. The water's shimmering with light like a sparkling starry night sky. And it's surprisingly hot for this time of year, at least for me. I'll be back in my draughty old office next week with April's rain-showers slashing against the windows. And all this will be as if in a dream."

"Of course we can dally here ..."

"Thanks."

★ ★ ★

"I love your wavy hair."

"Er, thank you."

"Oh, I'm sorry if I've just embarrassed you by saying something explicitly personal … I suppose it's that cultural difference thingy rearing its head yet again. You know what I mean?"

"Yes, I think I do …"

★ ★ ★

"You've been very quiet for the last few minutes. I hope it's nothing I've said."

"No, not at all …I was just thinking about Passover … we'll be going to my brother for the first Seder night, as usual. There's generally quite a crowd there. Lots of kids, of course … Mum and Dad don't feel able to organise the service and the dinner any more. If my brother didn't make it, I suppose our parents would spend Pesach in one of the increasing number of hotels around the Mediterranean that now cater for the festival. What about you?"

"I go to the communal Seders arranged by our rabbi. They're really very good, from a social as well as a religious point of view. I've learned quite a lot from them, and from my general reading about Judaism."

"Like what?"

"Ha, ha … you seem to be learning too."

"Sorry?"

"Never mind … Well, I've learned that women played just as important a role as men in the story of Egypt, the Israelites and the Exodus. Perhaps they actually played an even more significant part, but it hasn't generally been recognised fully in our male orientated Old Testament."

"How do you mean?"

"Well, first, if it wasn't for Miriam successfully persuading her father to have more children, despite his fear of Pharaoh's order to kill the Israelites' baby boys, Moses would never have been born. Secondly, Moses' mother Jochebed constructed the cute little ark or vessel in which baby Moses floated to a safe discovery amongst the reeds on the Nile. Thirdly, Pharaoh's daughter Batya found the bobbing crib and brought Moses into the royal palace, where he was soon to be coincidentally if not miraculously tended by his mother, who'd been engaged as a wet nurse to care for him."

"As you say, you've learned quite a lot. I was certainly aware of the inspirational Miriam, and you've just reminded me of the name of Moses' mother. But you've trounced me with the name of the Egyptian princess who came upon Moses' watertight cradle in the bulrushes."

"Which only goes to prove what I mentioned earlier … in a man's world, the exploits of often heroic women tend to be given less kudos or exposure than is their due."

"You're a feminist?"

"If you like, though I'm not one for labels. Maybe male adherents to the Jewish faith, or to any of the monotheistic religions, have much to think about so far as concerns the role, standpoint and identity of women in communal society. That's not to say that some progress hasn't been made in these areas. Though, personally, I believe there's some way to go yet … depending on the surrounding culture. I'm not saying that women should seek to make inroads to the religion that our Scripture can't possibly bear without negating its eternal quintessence. But I do consider that some aspects are genuinely open to interpretation."

"I believe you're not alone in that way of thinking. Obviously there are some passages that, in my opinion, are abundantly clear. But throughout history our greatest rabbis have argued with each other, well I suppose they would, about the true construction of the Torah … and that's particularly the case in our modern era, when its interpretation and application in the context of a rapidly changing world is being debated endlessly by a sadly fractured community."

"I'm trying to think of a good illustration to put to you … as someone, like me, who's inclined to Orthodox Judaism."

"About what …?"

"Those young girls you've seen here, walking hand-in-hand at sunset in demonstrative friendship. Do you approve of that?"

"I can't really see anything wrong with it."

"What if they were Jewish girls, as indeed some might possibly be?"

"Again, it wouldn't faze me. Why should it?"

"What if they were actually Jewish lesbians? … Ha, ha. I can see your brain whirring!"

"Okay, my response wasn't instant … though it's not that I haven't thought about this previously. I've read articles on the subject in the Jewish Press from time to time, just like on same sex civil partnerships and even marriage. I'm sure you've seen similar pieces in the Jewish media here. And I do have a reaction."

"Which is?"

"Yes, there may well be arguments based on a particular analysis of certain biblical verses. They could possibly be open to a more lenient meaning."

"Quite so … and do you know what?"

"What?"

"I find you extremely attractive. I think that I see something of me in you. And I've got the tentative feeling that such a perspective is reciprocated. Earlier this morning, you said I was attractive. That must mean that I'm attractive to you. And you did say something about trying new experiences."

"My earlier remarks concerned coffee. And as I've mentioned, I'm married."

"And your point is?"

"My point is that I'm a faithful ... *spouse*."

"But surely there are different kinds of fidelity. As I intimated before, love is a cultural thing not to be confused with attraction in certain immaterial circumstances."

"And what are these *certain immaterial circumstances*?"

"I think that's self-evident, don't you? ... Ha, ha. I sense yet another pregnant pause, if I can put it that way."

"I regret that my answer wasn't instant. But, again, I do have a response."

"Which is? My goodness ..."

"What?"

"You know we've been chatting merrily together for quite a little while now, yet we haven't exchanged names. Mine's Paola. What's yours?"

"It's Alice."

# His-story

"YOU'RE ADMIRING the swamp cypress on the little island …"

"Ha ha, not necessarily *admiring* … it's rather skeletal at the moment, being that we've only just passed the first day of spring. No, my father just told me in an email that he has planted one beside the pond in the garden at home."

"Where's home, if an inquisitive old man may ask?"

"That's okay … it's in Hertfordshire."

"It'll take a goodly while for the tree to get up to the height of that one over there."

"I know … it kind of dominates this venerable college's lovely lake, doesn't it?"

"It certainly does. You seem to be fairly clued up on arboreal matters."

"Not really."

"But you did identify the cypress …"

"Dad attached a series of seasonal photographs of the mature tree, just to give me some idea of what it would look like in years to come. Mum and Dad are fanatical gardeners."

"Ah, there we have it then … the wonders of modern technology!"

"Yes, it's as simple as that. I'm afraid I haven't inherited any green fingers … though my parents did try, eminently unsuccessfully as it turned out, to indoctrinate me in the horticultural arts when I was a little girl. But I would rather play with our dogs and cats. Oh yes, didn't I say … Mum and Dad are also much taken with domestic pets."

"Am I right in presuming that you're a student here?"

"Yes, you're assumption is correct. I'm a first year undergraduate. This is my second term."

"Why don't you sit beside me here on this bench for a little while … it's Sunday after all, the day of rest from work … and studies. And having turned ninety a few months ago, I promise not to make a pass at you … though I've got to remark, you're a very pretty young lady."

"Well thank you, kind sir … Okay then, I've got some time before I meet my friends for lunch in town. And I'm sure you're a true gentleman."

"Well, I don't know about that. But I can assure you my vow will hold good."

"Ha, ha … you're quite the charmer."

"It's a strange coincidence, you know. Just before you came along, two elderly men were sitting on the bench next to this one. And they were talking about trees, too. I had the impression they may've been students here a long time ago. One mentioned that he'd wandered into the Fellow's Garden, and he said that in such a matter of fact manner, to look at the oriental planes. It wasn't difficult to assume he was referring to trees rather than the Mongolian Steppes. And his companion immediately recalled a number of walnut trees that had once stood in these grounds, but had been removed. I've been visiting this, my favourite college of all those in this sublime town for some time now. But I don't recollect any walnut trees growing here, though that's not too astonishing at my age."

"Are you well up on the world of flora?"

"Not particularly. But I did tend a vegetable garden for a time ... that was quite a while back, in another world almost. I've forgotten most of what I knew about plants and flowers. Well, I am in my tenth decade now. I've always found watching plants grow very calming, I know that much. I can't generally recall the names of flowers any more ... save perhaps for the very common ones, like daffodils and crocuses. Have you seen the magnificent array on the banks down by the river?"

"Yes, I have. But I'm amazed that you're a nonagenarian ... you look at least fifteen years younger! I hope that I look like you when I get to ninety, if I should live so long!"

"I don't think you mean that exactly."

"Sorry?"

"Well, you are of the opposite sex ... so you couldn't look like me anyway. At least, I hope not."

"Sharp as a pin, aren't you?"

"What are you studying?"

"I'm reading History ... actually, modern history."

"Ah, history ... Excuse me for saying so, but didn't the motor car company founder Henry Ford once say that history is bunk?"

"Yes, so I understand. I suppose it's because different interpretations can be placed on the available facts, the evidence from the past ... whether it's the words in a document or the nature of particular artefacts. And that history is what an individual might subjectively make of it. Sometimes it boils down to which of the recorders of history you consider to be the most trustworthy or credible, for whatever reason."

"I can relate to what you just said ... when it comes to battles and wars, for example, isn't it the victor's version that tends to become established as the truth?"

"Are you a Philosophy Fellow here?"

"No, no ... no! But I've got plenty of leisure time on my hands to reflect on history, and I often do cogitate. I read books too, even though my eyesight isn't what it used to be. I also ponder other things ... like this lake. Get the pun?"

"Pardon me?"

"*Ponde*r ... lake!"

"You're incorrigible ... and totally unbelievable."

"No, but it's true. I come here fairly regularly to feed the ducks ... they're mostly mallards, as I'm sure you know, with a sprinkling of moorhens and the odd white call duck. Well, you know ... occasionally, I have these lucid intervals and can run off names just like that! I must be having one right away."

"That's great. Keep it up!"

"The dripping feathered creatures were besieging my gangling old legs just before you arrived on the scene. I think they all know me now. And I'm getting to recognise a few of the little creatures ... you know some of them have certain noticeable characteristics and behaviour, like you and me. Well not quite the same, of course. Unlike the people, mostly mothers with young children who bring bread for the ducks, I give them only swan and duck pellets. I get them from the pet shop near to where I live. It's so much healthier for these waterfowl."

"I agree with you. Come to think of it, I've spotted you on a few previous occasions … standing here beside the lake and scattering feed into the water, just like farmers used to hand-sow seeds in their fields. And I've seen you smiling and nodding in an oddly noticeable kind of way, I've thought … do forgive me for saying so … as the mallards flap each other with their wings and squabble over the showering pellets, pecking and poking the poor little moorhens and our solitary call duck out of the way, so they can scoop up your largesse with their snapping bills. I know it's impolite to ask, but why do you smile and nod so oddly at these antics? It's as if you enjoy seeing them fighting with each other over the food."

"I used to sow seeds in the fields a long time ago. My parents had a small piece of farmland … not in this country, though."

"I thought I'd detected the hint of an East European accent …"

"Well done … you're right. I've never quite lost it. I was born and brought up in Czechoslovakia … more particularly in its eastern part, now known as the independent state of Slovakia. It separated from the Czech Republic in the 1990s. Please correct me if I'm wrong, but you're Jewish aren't you?"

"W–Why, yes … though I'm not very observant. How did you guess? Are *you* Jewish?"

"No, no … no! But I didn't guess. That's a Star of David hanging from your gold necklace, isn't it … the national emblem or icon of Judaism?"

"Yes, I suppose it is in a way. It's sometimes called a *Magen*

*David*, a Shield of David. It was one of the gifts my parents gave to me when I came of age at twelve, according to the rites of the Jewish faith that is."

"So you received it on your batmitzvah …"

"Yes, indeed. You're very knowledgeable about my religion. How does that come about?"

"As I mentioned, I read a lot … well as much as I can nowadays. But at one time, in the distant past, I worked alongside Jewish people. It's very eye-catching …"

"Sorry, what is?"

"Your Star of David … it glints so brightly in the sunshine. Do you like gold?"

"Yeah, it's okay. Actually I prefer silver jewellery. Why do you ask?"

"The talisman looks to have a certain age about it. Am I right?"

"Yes, you are … and it has a precious sentimental and family value. This beautiful pendant belonged to my late maternal grandmother. She and her mother, my great-grandmother, fled to England from Vienna in 1938. Her father needed to stay behind to clear up some business or financial affairs, something like that, before he could get a permit to leave Austria. By then, as you probably know, the country had become part of Hitler's Reich. Sadly and along with many other relatives who remained there, for one motivation or another, he perished at the hands of the Nazis during the Holocaust."

"Ah yes, the Holocaust."

"You know about that terrible time."

"Oh yes, I know about that time. It's history now, of course … as we were discussing before. Just like the walnut trees."

"Sadly, genocides have continued to happen in the world and anti-Semitism still persists. Will people never learn any lessons from history, even with all those monuments and museums in Germany and elsewhere, and remembrances like Holocaust Memorial Day here? Many schoolchildren I've spoken to, even my cousins, have shockingly never heard of Auschwitz. So I suppose ignorance shouldn't be so surprising. But tell me, when did you work with Jewish people?"

"I didn't actually say that I *worked* with them. What I said was that I worked *alongside* them. There's a difference, you know."

"You never fail to amaze me. I don't know when you came to this country but your manipulation of the English language, if I can put it that way, is extraordinary. And for someone of your mature age, if I may be so bold, you possess a wonderfully acute mind. I appreciate we've been conversing for a very short while, but sometimes you sound to me like a lawyer…"

"No, no … no. I've been several things over my years, but never a lawyer. However, your compliment is very kind. Many of my fellow residents in the care home, if I can call it that, are ravaged by the new plagues of dementia, Alzheimer's and other dreadful mental deficiencies that seem to accompany increasing longevity. I can't have a decent conversation with them. They've got no lives, they're just vegetating. I think it's so cruel that they should exist in such misery … and not only for themselves. You should see the heartbreaking numbness and disbelief in the eyes of their unrecognised children or other relatives who visit them. I've been extremely lucky, I suppose …"

"Thank the Almighty."

"Well who knows, eh? I do keep as mentally and physically

healthy as I can for my advanced years. I've always been a keen walker, and probably that's helped my bones and muscles and allowed me some useful continuing independence and mobility. The members of staff are quite supportive ... and they do endeavour to encourage mental and physical activities and pursuits. But regrettably their efforts frequently fall on stony ground, so far as concerns the majority of my fellow residents. As I've said, I borrow books from our library ... crime novels mostly. I relish trying to solve the clues and work out whodunnit, before the author reveals the perpetrator. I also enjoy doing crosswords, especially the cryptic one in The Telegraph ... and I do complete it sometimes."

"That's really cool, and I've got no doubt about it. But tell me something about those Jewish people you worked alongside."

"I don't think you would be very interested."

"Try me."

"Well, if you insist. I don't think it's a problem for me ... not now, anyway. But don't say that I didn't warn you ..."

"Please go ahead."

"Before I start, I want to assure you that I'm not anti-Semitic and never have been. I'm sure that I wouldn't be chatting here like this to you, my newfound Jewish friend, if I were such."

"O-Okay ..."

"My upbringing was in the countryside of eastern Czechoslovakia, as I'm sure you know an artificial state created out of the defunct Austro-Hungarian Empire after its defeat in the First World War. My parents owned a small farm, mostly arable with a few animals and a vegetable garden. I had three older sisters, no brothers. I was given some education in the village school, but mostly my sisters and I worked on the land. My father was a strict disciplinarian and I often got a beating for shirking. Sometimes he caught me reading a book in our barn when I should've been doing some boring chore or other. So I accepted that I deserved the thrashing, according to the parental way of thinking at that time. My parents believed that the only beneficial knowledge I needed in life was provided by them and our priest in church. Nonetheless, I gradually became more adept at avoiding being caught when my head was buried in some literary tome ..."

"I'm sorry for interrupting you, but I have to say that I admire your tenacity in seeking to educate yourself in a difficult situation ..."

"Thank you. During my early teenage years, as a very enquiring lad, I was keen to find out about the big wide world beyond our austerely closeted little one. So I supplemented my sparse secular learning with the clandestine reading of books supplied by a sympathetic teacher. He also paid my father to allow me to do a bit of work in his garden. That provided an opportunity not only to borrow books, but also to discuss current affairs. I learned about Hitler and the rapidly developing might of Nazi Germany. Even when I'd finished formal schooling, such as it was, and I was working on the farm, we continued to debate what was happening politically in Europe ... always under cover of my few hours' work once a fortnight, digging out the teacher's weeds and nurturing his plants ..."

"I can see where your gardening knowledge would come from ..."

"Yes ... well anyway, my father was ignorant about my

growing knowledge of things other than smallholding agriculture and the content of our priest's sermons. As a student of modern history, and as a Jewish person, you don't need me to tell you about the Nazis' philosophy and empire-building aspirations in the 1930s. I'd read Hitler's *Mein Kampf*, so I was well acquainted with his policies."

"Yeah, our weak and appeasing politicians virtually surrendered your poor little country to Hitler at Munich in 1938. He quickly ordered the annexation of the Sudetenland in western Czechoslovakia, which was largely occupied by ethnic Germans. Edvard Beneš, the Czech president, fled for his life. And in March 1939, Hitler invaded the remaining Czech lands and declared them the Protectorate of Bohemia and Moravia …"

"You know your history well, young lady … and, as I'm sure you could go on to inform me, Hitler permitted the collaborative Slovakia to become an autonomous region headed by the Catholic priest Jozef Tiso. He'd been head of the L'udáks, the Slovak People's Party, before the war. Now he was the leader of Slovakia or, loosely akin to his friend in Berlin, Führer of the Slovak state. My father seemed quite pleased with these developments, as news of them filtered through to our remote neck of the woods. He would have his mates round to drink themselves under the kitchen table, toasting the transformation in their new nation's prospects for the prosperity that they hoped would flow from Hitler's Reich."

"How old were you when Tiso was helped to seize the reigns of power, or as much of it as the Nazis would permit him?"

"Seventeen … not too much younger than you are now, I expect. But my father was laughing on the other side of his face when I was conscripted and sent to the barracks in Bratislava. You see, my three sisters had got themselves married and, apart from mother, I'd been the only one available to assist him on the farm as cheap labour. That's until I was ordered to leave home. I can't tell you how happy, even excited, I was to go ... I could see new possibilities opening up to study more, and to maybe one day have the opportunity of getting a job that would allow me to use my brain rather than my hands."

"Bratislava? I think that was where the great Jewish rabbinical authority, the Chatam Sofer, lived and taught in the eighteenth century ... odd facts one picks up sometimes!"

"You're correct, on both counts ... though I believe that, before the Velvet Revolution, the communists transferred his grave to a subterranean mausoleum to make way for a new highway in the city."

"I didn't know that ... no reason why I should've, I guess. So what did you and your fellow conscripts get up to in the big city?"

"Not a lot, really ... we were mostly waiting and drilling, drilling and waiting ... I thought until Tiso, or rather the Germans, told us through him what they wanted us to do for them now they'd conquered and annexed or occupied much of neighbouring Poland. But being in the town certainly opened my eyes to what was going on politically. From time to time, I found myself amongst huge crowds of people who attended open-air public meetings in the old town square at which Father Tiso made pronouncements. It seemed incongruous really ... the fact that he wore a clerical collar and gave the Nazi raised-arm salute! Of course, it wasn't long before anti-Semitic legislation, modelled on the Nuremberg laws, was enacted by the Slovak parliament. The *Jewish Code* prevented your brethren of that time from owning property and any luxury goods. And they were generally excluded from education, economic activity and cultural events. In public they were forced to wear the Star of David on their outer clothing. I suppose that's what I noticed most on the occasions we were accorded some time off in the town centre."

"And what did you think about the things you saw?"

"In the barracks there was a lot of talk about what was transpiring. But there was a good atmosphere of camaraderie there. I have to say that the boys were like a family to me. We had some good fun, despite the depressing make-up of our surroundings. It was ironic, really. Back home, my environment had comprised fields, forests, flora and fauna, the cheerful sounds of birdsong and the alluring scent of plants. Yet I preferred our cramped grey concrete living quarters. I was so much more content than I'd ever been at home, except for those short interludes of gardening for my teacher. Practically all my comrades didn't see anything wrong with what was going on out on the streets. In fact, they thought it was no more than a natural consequence … though being largely from rural areas and without much formal or worldly education, you know what I mean, they didn't quite express their opinions in that restrained way. I often overheard them laughing and making jokes about what they'd observed. But any free time that I enjoyed in the barracks would be spent devouring any books that I could buy cheaply in the town's flea markets."

"So when did Tiso or his German friends get you actually to do something for them?"

"After Hitler's invasion of the Soviet Union in the summer of 1941 …"

"That was *Operation Barbarossa*, wasn't it?"

"Yes, that's right. Anyway, a platoon of us was sent to a partially constructed prisoner of war camp in Poland. Most of the military personnel stationed there consisted of German special troops and their auxiliaries. Our task was to assist in guarding the thousands of Russian POWs being shipped in from the east. They were forced brutally to finish building the wooden huts into which they were to be crammed to the ceilings. They were a pathetically vanquished and bedraggled heap of men ... and things didn't get much better for them, especially when a bitterly cold winter marched icily over the eastern horizon."

"So what were your particular duties?"

"Well, for a time I was part of the squad patrolling the perimeter of the camp ... but I also sometimes helped, with a few of my comrades, to guard the barely subsistence rations that were available to feed the shivering prisoners. We transported the provisions from the kitchens to the various encampments within the extensive laager. There was a murky looking liquid in large tubs that the cooks told us was soup, but I wouldn't have fed it to the dogs on our farm. On one supply trip, I saw a guard urinating into the tub then stirring the foul concoction with a long wooden stick. Nearly everyone fell over themselves laughing their guts out. The Russkies are so hungry and thirsty, the man said, that they'll eat and drink absolutely anything. What could I do ...?"

"You could've protested, upset the contents of the tub onto the ground and returned for some fresh, untainted soup!"

"I may've been caught up in a kind of madness ... but I was quite sane myself! If I'd protested in the manner you suggest, I would've been shot at once. Nothing could be done, I'm telling you. I accepted, rightly or wrongly, that the pee would be just another dubious but harmless ingredient of whatever rubbish was already in the food container. Didn't I say you wouldn't necessarily enjoy hearing what I might describe?"

"Go on."

"If you want me to …"

"Yes … go on, please."

"Mindful of the random beatings and executions of weak and defenceless POWs that I'd witnessed, the urine in the so-called soup was the least of their problems. And there were other things too … We carried bread baked in the kitchen ovens, a few dozen loaves for hundreds of men. Some of the guards would delight in breaking up some of the loaves into small morsels and hurling them over the lofty wire fences to the gathering mob of famished … no, ravenous prisoners. And I would observe my comrades smiling and nodding as the Russians fought each other to get at the meagre scraps, several of them usually being trampled to death or seriously injured in the frantic tearing scrum …"

"Horrible, horrible …"

"Yes, it was indeed horrible. I can't tell you how glad I was to receive the sporadic furlough home … though, in fact, I didn't use it to visit my family. I wrote them from Poland and lied that leave was impossible to obtain in the war situation. What I actually did was to remain in Bratislava for my few days of so-called rest and recuperation. Early in 1942, I noticed that the authorities were beginning to organise the construction of further camps to adjoin the POW enclave. In the distance, I could just make out some large buildings being put up, one or two of them featuring tall redbrick chimneys. They looked like factories to me. I'd heard about the many labour camps being established in German-occupied territories."

"I think we know what those chimneys were all about, don't we?"

"I get what you're saying ... and you're right about the chimneys. But you're not correct in assuming, if that's what you're doing, that I understood what they amounted to at the time. They could quite easily have been part of an industrial complex ... such schemes were numerous in other parts of the Nazi camp system in Poland ... By the way, what about your friends?"

"Sorry?"

"You were supposed to be having lunch with your friends in town."

"O-Oh my goodness, I quite forgot. My wristwatch tells me I'm late ... I'll send them a text to say that I'm not coming ... please give me a moment ..."

"Of course ... but I don't see why ..."

"That's okay, don't ... there that's done. Please continue. What was happening to the Jews in Slovakia at this period?"

"On one of my time-off trips to Bratislava in the spring of 1942, I heard that the deportation of Slovakian Jews for resettlement in Poland had started. I thought they would be transported to the labour camps. Apparently, this was after the real Führer had summoned Tiso to a meeting in Austria. Subsequently I discovered that, up to the early summer of forty-two, over 50,000 Jews had been removed from the country, ultimately and mainly to Auschwitz-Birkenau. We learned much later, of course, what happened to them there. Then, for some reason, transports to the concentration camps began to diminish. And finally, they dried up altogether. From talking to various people during my leaves, it seemed to me that a head of steam was growing in Slovakia against the deportations of its Jews. Some said that even Tiso had been bullied by Hitler into following Nazi policy on European Jewry. I really don't know. There were also rumours that the Vatican had intervened with the priest about the persecutions."

"But there's a great deal of controversy about the attitude of the Holy See towards the Nazis' excesses …"

"Maybe, though there must've been some reason why the authorities were no longer deporting Slovakian Jews to the camps in Poland."

"Perhaps officials were being bribed handsomely with money smuggled into the country from Jewish relief agencies."

"It's possible. But I believe it can be said that Slovakia was the first state to halt the deportation of Jews from within the Nazis' sphere of occupation or influence."

"That's not saying very much … must be that a huge proportion of Slovak Jewry had already been despatched to their deaths!"

"I can't disagree with you … it could've been as high as seventy-five percent of the Jewish population. But be that as it may, from that time until, if I remember accurately, nearing the end of 1944 Tiso's Slovakia and Hitler's ally became, paradoxically, something of a safe haven for Jews. Especially for those who'd managed to escape from neighbouring German-occupied countries like Poland and the Protectorate."

"I take it from what you've just said that the deportations began again towards the close of 1944?"

"Very good, you've presumed correctly."

"You mentioned earlier in our conversation that you had worked *alongside* Jews, but not *with* them. You were very clear about that. Now that I know the context to which I infer you were alluding, what exactly was the connection?"

"It's nothing sinister, I can assure you. I mentioned that additional camps were constructed adjoining the POW camp to which I was dispatched to be a guard. In the summer of forty-two, whilst performing my patrol duties, I could see that the inmates of a lot of these laagers were mostly Jews ... others separately held gypsies and possibly other groups. Don't ask me how I knew about the religious or ethnic origins of these prisoners ... I don't want things to sound stereotypical, but it was reasonably obvious. So as I patrolled around the edge of the Russian POW encampment, I was also, but only in a sense, working alongside Jews."

"In a very tentative sense ..."

"Of course ... I meant nothing by my semantics. Actually, as we moved into 1943, the turnover of Soviet army prisoners diminished substantially. Rumours were spreading that the war in Russia wasn't going too well for Hitler ... and that's English understatement. But the German rout at Stalingrad was a crucial turning-point on the Eastern Front, if not for the war generally. We kept quiet about this, and we didn't speak openly about Soviet military advances ... expressions of defeatism could have harsh and spiteful consequences."

"What about the renewed transportation of Slovakian Jews to the Nazi death camps in the autumn of forty-four?"

"By that time, I'd been reassigned to duties in my home country."

"What were these duties?"

"The Nazis had occupied Hungary earlier in 1944, because Hitler couldn't trust the Magyars' leader Horthy not to make peace with the Soviets. Could be he felt similarly about our priest, particularly when the Russian army had fought their way to Slovakia's eastern border. German troops marched into the country and took over the government … but they retained Tiso as the titular head of state. I was deployed with others to guard the train station from which Jews were again being transported for resettlement in Poland. I think that more than 10,000 were despatched in cargo wagons over a relatively short period. The platforms were heaving with humanity … it was almost like watching a huge organic entity writhing around the building. Hindsight is a marvellous commodity, young lady. But I believed they were being sent to industrial camps of the sort that I thought I'd observed being constructed not far from the Russian POW stockades."

"Mothers with children and babies …?"

"It would've been inhuman to split families, or so I may have considered … if I did actually and honestly consider it. There were so many things happening. What could I have done? What could any individual have done? There were SS and Gestapo all over the place. I can see you shaking your head. But let me tell you, young lady, that my last questions were more than rhetorical ones. I actually did do something, something really dramatic … at least for me, a veritable bookworm!"

"So what did you do then?"

"You say that in such a sceptical, even derisive manner … you know, for the first time I saw a Jew, in fact it was a Jewess possibly close to your own age, killed in front of my own eyes.

She'd been shuffling with hundreds of other Jews into the interior of the railway station. The young woman clutched in her arms a baby that was screaming its tiny head off. A guard made to seize the shrieking kid and remove it from the mother's grasp. She tried to resist by lowering herself to the ground, covering the child with her body and crying out pitifully for mercy for her flesh and blood. A bullet through the back of the head stopped her bawling for all eternity. The baby was dragged from its mother's enfolding grip and quickly taken away. I don't know what happened to it, but I can imagine. You don't know how difficult it is for me to tell this to *you*. I could barely catch my breath … I stood numb with emotion. In the barracks that night, I thought about everything I'd witnessed … in the POW camp, on the streets of Bratislava and around the train terminal. The regular and familiar comfort of my books couldn't help me any more. But the knowledge I'd derived from them could … and it did. I knew that I had to do something, and quickly. So I made the decision to desert …"

"You deserted from the army?"

"Yes, over that long and sleepless night I'd worked up the courage to run away … but not aimlessly. I managed to slip off whilst on another assigned guard duty, this time at an ammunition dump on the outskirts of the city but close to the Danube. Actually, it was the river that aided my escape. After a while, I located the group of people I was seeking and became a tiny cog in the Slovak National Uprising. The rest, as they say, is history. At the end of the war, the Soviets occupied the reunited Czechoslovakia. And a communist regime under Moscow's heavily guiding thumb began fifty years of grindingly repressive rule. After a post-war trial of sorts, Tiso was sentenced to death, hanged in Bratislava and buried in some secret place so that the grave wouldn't become a shrine for any of his dedicated followers."

"So what did you do after the war … and when did you come to this country?"

"I went back to my home, but it was a wreck. For some reason, the villagers weren't very pleased to see me. They told me that my parents had died in a blaze at the farmhouse. I went to the churchyard to visit their graves … then I tried to locate my three sisters, but strangely without success. I gave up seeking out any other relatives and, to cut a very long story short, ended up here in England. Not that I didn't wish to be here. With the shortage of manpower, I easily obtained work on a farm and set about seriously learning the English language. I was still a young man. I took various correspondence courses that were gradually becoming available. I studied mathematics and then accountancy. Eventually, I was able to move to London and luckily secured Articles with a prestigious firm of Chartered Accountants in the City. After a number of years, I qualified professionally. A decade later, I became a salaried partner in the concern. I married an English woman, but we didn't have any children. Looking around at the world today, I can't say that I've got any regrets about that …"

"What about your wife?"

"I'm a widower … my wife died a long time ago. When I retired in the 1980s, we came to live in this lovely old university town which we'd often visited on day trips. You know what … I think that's about it. Thank you for listening to my rambling memories. I don't often get the opportunity to talk at length with an intelligent person. I should let you go to whatever you do on a Sunday afternoon, maybe catch up with your friends and have a spot of lunch with them after all. You've now heard my story, my personal history if you like …"

"In a way, I'm not surprised that mathematics became your forte."

"What do you mean?"

"Well, I think you're quite calculating … and that's not just an echo of your beloved word play."

"I'm sorry, but I don't follow what you're trying to say."

"What I'm trying to say is that I believe you largely tell only half-truths, if you respond at all to certain questions. You've already admitted to me that you're a liar."

"When …?"

"In relation to your letters home from the Russian POW camp …"

"Well, that was just …"

"Just what …? I have to say that you're very plausible, with a vastly superior memory and ability to juggle words than I'd thought or expected initially."

"As I've said, I do have intervals when I can rattle off a whole string of facts and figures … But why are you saying all this to me? Why are you doubtful of what I've told you? What reason do you have for doing this to a very old man with recollections and reminiscences, and some bad memories that he will never be able to forget?"

"I trust my judgement. It's got me this far … to this great and ancient college of learning. But it's something in particular I'd observed, and something you've spoken about from the past, that I think gives your little game away."

"What are you talking about?"

"Remember I mentioned seeing you, on other days, feeding the ducks here by the lake? I asked you earlier about your strange smile and the nodding that I'd noticed when the waterfowl were squabbling and fighting, biting, pushing and pecking each other over the pellets of feed you'd thrown into the water … You completely ignored my query, just like you judiciously ignored one or two other questions I'd raised."

"So what …?"

"So what …? So what about when you witnessed your fellow camp guards smiling and nodding approvingly while the Russian POWs trampled each other to death, struggling to get at the scraps of undoubtedly stale if not rotten bread they'd been thrown over the wire? I suspect you weren't merely a moral bystander, but one of those smiling and nodding guards. And if I'm right about that, which I think I am, I suggest that you were the guard who urinated into the soup. And, if that's correct and however much I don't want to believe it, it was probably you who murdered the Jewess in cold blood and then killed her baby at the station. Despite the innocent assertions that, so to speak, some of your best friends are Jewish, I believe you are an anti-Semite and always have been … from your formative childhood, I feel, and certainly since you overheard the drunken, anti-Semitic ranting of your father and his mates from the village. And I suspect it was your Nazi village teacher that deliberately supplied you with *Mein Kampf*. Strangely enough, I've got the impression that you were telling the truth about joining the Slovak National Uprising against the German occupiers of your country. But it's your motivation for doing so that I would question. Obviously, you knew that Hitler was losing the war. Your side-changing was more than likely a kind of Monopoly Get-Out-Of-Jail Card for you, and your little game seems to have succeeded. Though, apparently, the villagers weren't terribly impressed, eh? It occurs to me that your maybe age-related lack of inhibition now, about talking of your wartime experiences, has backfired on you somewhat."

"I'm off. And you can't prove anything, you … young lady."

*There he goes … his-story is, indeed, bunk!*

# A Restaurant in Paris

"PARIS? ... I love her and hate her."

"*Do you love her and hate her in equal measure, like you might a woman?*"

"I haven't got a clue, and I don't have a woman ... well anyway, I've not had one since my twenties. And that was nearly forty years ago. Wait a moment. What I just said is untrue. No, not about women ... that *is* true. I love Paris, without any reservation, without any intrusive psychology. Paris ... Je t'aime. I've always adored this most inspirational, charming even sublime yet emotional of cities, the City of Light ... climbing breathlessly to the glowing ivory of Sacré-Coeur, scanning tearfully a sunlit rooftop vista with its glinting skyward pointer of steel, grinning nostalgically at bright-faced kids proudly sailing their model boats in the shimmering Luxembourg water-basin, sipping pensively a café espresso beside the solar-splashed bell-tower of Saint-Germain-des-Prés, jiggling adeptly the curvy handle, shiny silvered from constant use, on a Métro train door. Yes, the City of Light … an impressionist's palette of urban luminosity."

"*But it's the City of Darkness for you, too … at the very least, an ambivalent greyness … neither black nor white.*"

"My Jewish soul has struggled long to redeem this city, despite everything … Dreyfus, the Occupation … everything."

"*Bit before your time, eh?*"

"It's the *every* thing … that includes the restaurant massacre, of course. Remember?"

"*Yes, I understand of course … and how could I forget? But that was more than thirty years ago.*"

"It will be with me for ever, like my skin … or, maybe more relevantly, my soul … Take a photo of me right here, on the terrace of the Trocadéro … with the city's toweringly symbolic icon in the background … use your smart-phone camera … I'll stand on this spot. You know, it's where Hitler stood admiring his metropolitan conquest after the Blitzkrieg invasion by his armies. It wasn't long before this country's Jews felt the heavy black jackboots and an eager collaborative regime crushing their heads to pulp, just like their compatriots were suffering in the Nazi-overrun lands further to the east."

"*Stand still! I don't need a lecture on the Defeat of France 1940. And do stop gazing around at the sky as if you can't believe that it's there, that it's yours now and that's it's more than a conquerable but transient object of desire. It's all those things, and you need to accept that. Believe me. And stop fidgeting. Look, I'm trying to focus the camera. It's not easy keeping it steady with all these jostling tourists after the same shot, striving eagerly to encapsulate a* miniature *tower between thumb and forefinger. Here we go again, then. How about giving me a nice big smile?*"

"You're joking, of course! And by the way, I'm sorry for walking you off your feet this morning … and possibly out of your mind, in a manner of speaking. You know it has been a very long time. But I've needed to return … to reconnect, if you like … it's all part of this inordinately lengthy redemption process, I suppose. Maybe it's like waiting for Moshiach, eh? You of all people should understand this."

*"I do, and there's no need to apologise. Despite your darkly thoughtful, even occasionally sullen comments as we've strolled around the city since dawn, I've enjoyed, yes enjoyed, this tour d'horizon of Paris' main sights … l'Opéra Garnier, La Madeleine, Palais de l'Élysée, Place de la Concorde, Jardin des Tuileries, the incongruous glass pyramid at the Palais du Louvre … backtracking up the Champs-Élysée to L'Arc de Triomphe and then here, along a radiating beam of L'Étoile, to the Palais de Chaillot by the Seine. Have you enjoyed the trek?"*

"How can I have? What are you saying? I acknowledge it was thirty years ago, but it wasn't a million miles from here … You know I couldn't stop trembling for six months! The sudden catastrophic, reverberating noise of the grenades exploding combined with the automatic gunfire was like a shocking cacophony in a surreal dream … no, more a terrifying nightmare! I was so close to my destination, the restaurant, now and out of the blue an unbelievable, blood-drenched wreckage of concrete, brick and glass … largely Jewish blood, of course. You know I haven't *enjoyed* the trek, as you put it. Though I've got to admit the alfresco coffee was excellent at the Café de la Paix, its tiny and close-packed tables spilling onto the Place de l'Opéra as appealingly as ever."

*"I'm sorry."*

"Don't be. Do you see those dark roiling clouds building up, scudding behind Eiffel's amazingly conceived and enduring showpiece, smothering the fragile spring sun and gathering a menacing if not sinister strength, like another miscreant army of the night advancing from the east?"

*"Very literary even poetic, I'm sure. So there's going to be just a prosaic rain shower, probably thunder and lightening. It's April in Paris, after all! No problem. I'm carrying an umbrella."*

"No, I didn't mean that. And you know it. No … it's all in my mind, too. And I'm not saying that in any way fancifully, as you might expect. Okay, so it's also a metaphor. There've been many days when the thickly assembling clouds have churned around my head, a maelstrom of fearful turbulence nailing me to the wooden bed, stifling liberty of thought and barricading exit routes."

*"Please don't confuse pretentiousness with freedom. It doesn't become you."*

"All I'm saying is that, although I wasn't hurt physically, it was a close run thing … like Wellington said of Napoleon's defeat at Waterloo. Yes, it was a narrow escape for me, but only in one sense. I felt like an innocent but hunted animal that had managed, agonizingly, to break away from a trap by the skin of its teeth … almost literally. Others weren't even so lucky. Six were killed … murdered, I mean. And more than twenty were injured, some maimed or scarred for life."

*"A miss is as good as a mile, don't they say? But possibly you're feeling the same kind of guilt that Holocaust survivors experienced after losing their close family and friends in the Nazi death camps."*

"No cause for levity …"

*"I didn't mean …"*

"Perhaps you're right about there being an element of culpability. I really don't know. Who can say for sure? In this world, there's no such thing as an absolute certainty. You can plan only for so much. It's all a question of the degree of probability. However, I do recall hearing about some of my relatives who'd survived deportation from Drancy to Auschwitz, while other members of their kith and kin had perished in the gas chambers. And I did come very close to death myself that day. Was it good fortune, fate or something else beyond human comprehension? Consider a potential passenger who for one reason or another misses a flight that, a few hours later, crashes into the ocean killing all on board. Maybe his or her taxi to the airport was caught up in an unexpected, unpredictable but horrendous traffic jam. Why? Don't bother to ask let alone answer the question, eh? Or maybe ponder the case of a single solitary Jew who crawls, smothered in filth and soaked with the blood of other Jews yet bodily unscathed, from a stinking pit containing thousands of his buried brethren, shot to shrieking death by SS machine-gunners. How do you explain such random and inexplicable things? It's impossible, at least for us mere mortals. So what really affected me, I believe, was a profound but confused and confusing sense of deliverance. Ironically, the experience nearly killed me later … as you well know. But I was like the legendary golem of Prague …"

"*The golem …? Sorry, but I don't follow you.*"

"Yes, I'd been made from neutered, unfeeling but tremulous clay on the Potter's wheel then given the breath of life … again, in my case."

"*Come, let's walk a little more … maybe have a spot of lunch somewhere.*"

"Okay, whatever you want."

"*Do you have anything particular in mind … in this Aladdin's Cave of sparkling gourmet treasures?*"

"Ha, ha … that's a very good question. I've been trying to work that one out for quite some time now … that is, whether I have anything particular in mind."

"*Don't be so clever at playing with words. I know you relish doing that, no food pun intended … but I think you appreciate what I mean. So, what do you say about finding a little something to eat, eh?*"

"We could jump on the Métro to the Rive Gauche … maybe eat lightly amid the Left Bank ambience at Les Deux Magots by Saint-Germain …"

"*Why don't we go to the old Jewish Quarter around Rue des Rosiers … Didn't I read something in the hotel last night that the local authority in the Fourth Arrondisement has been seeking to gentrify the street? They're apparently struggling to fashion, or rather to clone the pedestrian-way to imitate other parts of the trendy Marais, with its upmarket designer boutiques and atmospheric cafés.*"

"No, I'd prefer not to go there … I'm sure you understand."

"*Oh, yes … I get your drift … but why ever not? As you mentioned earlier, it all happened a very long time back …*"

"I thought that I'd explained … obviously, I didn't make myself crystal clear."

"*To me or to …?*"

"Sorry for interrupting, but listen. If you want to eat Jewish, alright kosher, why not one of the eateries along Rue du Fauberg Montmartre or its offshoot Rue de Richer, close by the Folies Bergère? Funny how I can recollect … but you know what, I don't want to … I really don't understand why I've come back here … to this city."

"*You know why … but I'm not sure that I fancy North African kosher at the moment. Though I accept there's much to be said for scrumptious turkey shwarma in a tastily pliable pita wrap or with French fries … even salad and rice or couscous. Come on … what do you say to Rue des Rosiers? Perhaps you should revisit your ghosts of the past, and also exorcise those lingering shades or shadows of the present … it could help with the redemption exercise. What do you think?*"

"I don't know. I can't concentrate my focus on the notion. It's difficult to be philosophical. I have to confess there's a certain or should I say probable temptation in your food descriptions. But I don't know whether I'm hungry enough for poultry and chips."

"*That's very good … so come on, then. How about des Rosiers? You'll see. After all the years of that murky inhibiting haze, you can pull yourself free of the billowing black clouds at last. You can do it! Believe me. Isn't that really why you're here … in Paris? Be honest with yourself. You know it, don't you?*"

"Do I know it? The picture is somewhat vague at the moment. Well, you may be right … or you might be wrong. I *am* here in Paris … that's an actual fact I can't dispute. Though as I've endeavoured frankly to say, I'm not entirely sure of the motivation …"

"*I think you are. Anyway, if you're not famished I recall that one of the kosher bakeries in Rue des Rosiers produces some delicious onion baguettes bursting with a smoked salmon filling. Let's buy a couple of the rolls, and consume them sitting on one of those wooden benches in the lovely Place des Vosges. You remember, don't you? It's that gorgeously proportioned and arcaded, royal square with the enchanting 17th century buildings … just around the corner from semi-gentrified des Rosiers. I seem to remember that the evocative open space boasts some wonderful*" *trees ... shades of the Revolution? Did you ever get that tumbrel and guillotine feeling when hanging around Place de la Bastille?"*

"You know that's where *the* restaurant was situated ... in Rue des Rosiers?"

*"Yes, of course I know. That's why ..."*

"Okay, okay. You've said quite enough."

*"Does that mean you're coming?"*

"Perhaps I have to, need to ... maybe in the final analysis it's the authentic reason why I'm here, in the city of light ... and of darkness."

*"That was quite a sigh. Anyhow it's a bit too far to walk from here, now it's coming up to lunchtime. Let's amble along to the Métro and take a train."*

"Yes, I agree. But let's get off a stop before, say near to Les Halles and the deliberately inside-out pipe-work of the Centre George Pompidou arts complex ... the Beaubourg, as I believe the locals call it."

*"Why get off a stop before?"*

"I really think I need to approach des Rosiers gradually and on foot, just like I did that fateful summer's day thirty years ago or so. But I'd really wish it to be like Zeno's paradox. You know what I'm talking about. You journey half the distance to your ultimate destination so you have half way to go. You walk half of that, so you have the remaining half to go before reaching the objective ... and so on. In that way you never attain your goal, at least theoretically. But I can only theorise for now. Anyway, perhaps a measured approach will help put me in the right practical frame of mind to, how did you put it, exorcise those past and present ghosts of mine. Or perhaps not ... let's just see what happens, eh?"

"*Okay, so let's go. You've got nothing to lose.*"

"Famous last words …"

★ ★ ★

"*Right, here we are then … outside the entrance to the Rue Rambuteau Métro on the edge of the stylish Marais. How do you feel?*"

"A bit wet … is it starting to rain?"

"*I don't think so. There's a lot of moisture in the air, though. And it feels quite heavy and humid, like being wrapped in a blanket on a steamy night. The sky looks a bit threatening, too. I don't think it's actually raining … not yet, anyhow. But I'm not putting up my brolly … too many people milling around.*"

"Tourists heading to or coming from the Pompidou Centre, I reckon. It's just around the corner. Look, there's no hurry to eat. What about taking a quick look at that mad industrial tangle of steel and glass … for old time's sake?"

"*If you really want to … go on then, cross the road. And be careful with the traffic.*"

"Funny you know, but there's an art gallery near to my flat back home. It sometimes exhibits oil canvasses by a young and talented local artist who seems to specialise in portraying Paris in the rain … brightly lit yet indistinct café interiors, fuzzy yellow streetlamp globes and car headlights refracted and reflected in glistening wet boulevards. They're very attractive pieces of artwork, really. But I've often wondered about contacting the painter and telling him that the heavens don't always open up and flood down onto this beautiful city. What's the point? Artists, even people generally, see what they want to see. And in the end, that's fine. I can't do anything about that anyway, even if it affects me in however insignificant a way."

*"Forget about the rain. Here we are, the Pompidou Centre. Had enough?"*

"We've only just arrived here. Give me a moment, eh? It was opened as an arts and culture venue in 1977, about five years before the restaurant atrocity. I recall the year, because … because … You know, I can't remember why I can remember the year. Anyhow, there we are. I suppose it was quite avant-garde, architecturally speaking, at the time. But in my view, it's a glitch … a carbuncle on a sublime Art Nouveau Paris! Like that kitsch glass pyramid at the Louvre. I think the Pompidou construction may've also had a practical significance, though. Maybe it was something to do with the plumbing or air conditioning, I can't recollect exactly. The idea could've been to expand the interior space available by erecting or attaching the tedious utility stuff onto the outside of the building … like wearing your heart on your sleeve or not, as the case may be."

*"You're quite the amusing little tourist guide, aren't you?"*

"Did you see that girl who was staring at me on the Métro train? Maybe she found me attractive, what do you think?"

*"You do change the subject, don't you? But no, I didn't notice her or any other of the women in our carriage staring at you. And although I personally consider that you do look substantially fine for your age, I really don't believe a young girl would fancy you. It was probably that old and odd trilby you wear that may've gotten you some incredulous attention. I've been meaning to enquire, adopting the lyrics of an ancient tune … Where did you get that hat?"*

"You know I've cherished it for a long time. I can't remember where I acquired it. And as for your personal opinion regarding the girl, well …"

"*Look, can we move on now?*"

"Okay, let's go. Sometimes, I can't recall what I had for breakfast. But I can remember walking past the jolly old Pompidou on my way to the restaurant thirty years ago, as if it were yesterday. In cosmic dimensions, I suppose it was."

"*A few minutes back, I asked how you were feeling. You said you felt wet, but you knew what I meant. How do you feel on the inside, not on the outside?*"

"I'm okay. It's proceeding slowly but surely. That's best, I think. But forget Zeno, we'll definitely reach our destination in the end."

"*In which direction do we head now?*"

"As I recollect, but quite precisely now mind you, we'll need to return back over Rue du Renard and walk along Rue Rambuteau, cross over Rue des Archives and proceed down Rue des Francs Bourgeois to the intersection with Rue Vieille du Témple, turn right then third left into Rue des Rosiers. That's the route I took from the Pompidou Centre on Monday the ninth of August nineteen eighty-two, you know that."

"*Your memory feats never fail to amaze me. Right, let's walk the walk whilst we talk the talk …*"

"It was terrorism, you know that."

"*What, architectural terrorism?*"

"Beg pardon?"

"*The Pompidou Centre, of course. I know the building represents an aggressive tendency in modern construction technique, and therefore it's artistic anathema to you.*"

"That's where you're wrong. I can't abide extreme views …"

"*What was I just saying?*"

"What are you going on about? It's not a joking matter. I'm

talking about the bloody attack on the restaurant in Rue des Rosiers, not the dubious ramifications of the Beaubourg. It was terrorism … there was a lot of it about at the time. Plane hijackings, hostage taking, bombings, shootings … you name it."

"*Plus ça change, plus c'est la même chose, eh?*"

"Watch out for that car … bloody French drivers! You okay?"

"*Yes, I'm okay.*"

"Good. But you're right, of course. It's still going on … terrorism, I mean. Old groups have disappeared to be replaced by new ones. And so it continues. This was the birthplace of human rights, the Rights of Man. What human rights have the innocent victims of terrorism enjoyed? And what have the extremists achieved, aside from evil notoriety? Wanton destruction and the untimely deaths of innocents … I could so easily have been one of them. I was just moments away from entering the restaurant …"

"*Weren't there some innocent bystanders involved, too … people just going about their everyday business on the pavement outside?*"

"That's correct. I seem to recall reading in the newspapers that some pedestrians, not all of them Jewish, were hit in the line of fire. I suppose I could've easily been one of them. I would just need to have been walking a little faster on my final, unsuspecting approach. It's that baffling, mind-boggling juxtaposition of life and death … being in the wrong or the right place at the wrong or the right time. Like the prospective airline passenger or the survivor of, say, Babi Yar that I mentioned earlier. Remember that scene in Spielberg's *Schindler's List?*"

"*Which one was that?*"

"You know ... the one in the concentration camp. A terrified Jewish man in a striped tunic is frogmarched, by two grim-faced SS officers, out of the widget workshop for deliberately labouring too slowly. The saboteur is forced to a kneeling position on the ground as one of the two Nazis draws his Lüger, aims it at the Jew's head and squeezes the trigger. Nothing happens. He squeezes and squeezes with increasing vehemence. But, again and again, the pistol fails to discharge. The SS man realises with disgust that the gun has jammed, leaves the Jew cowering with shock and fear on the ground and storms off in a sulk with his equally dismayed colleague. The Jew, of course, can't believe his miraculous salvation ... the beginning of his second lifetime. I'm sure that must've occurred many times during the Shoah. Was it just random luck, a practical display of chaos theory or inexplicably particular Divine intervention ...? Maybe survival affected their lives afterwards, just like it has impinged itself so deeply on my life."

"*Perhaps you should've gone along to a Holocaust survivors' group and talked to some of the members about* their *experiences ...*"

"This is Rue Rambuteau, isn't it?"

"*Yes, I checked out the street sign.*"

"They're not always easy to locate in this area. Believe it or not, I used to get lost quite often seeking to negotiate the maze of twisting and turning streets and alleyways criss-crossing the venerable yet fashionable milieu of the Marais."

"*I know what you mean.*"

"We continue straight down here. Still lots of cafés and bars I see, but so many more trendy clothes boutiques, arty shops and picture galleries. Look at the piece of abstract artwork in that window. I'm not a Philistine, but what's it all about? Can you explain it to me? Can you explain anything to me?"

*"The appeal, if any, lies in the eye of the beholder."*

"That's just a cop out. To me it's transient, opaque, incomprehensible, meaningless …"

*"But not to the artist, at least … and it may just reflect his or her suffering. Sometimes it's all about suffering … pain, anguish, torment. We need to spend time just trying to understand. It's not always easy, I know that much."*

"I'm not an artist, but you don't have to tell me. Just ask the medical advisers for the records of my mental and physical history, and I hereby waive data protection."

*"But you're still feeling okay … right now, I mean?"*

"Don't concern yourself on my behalf. I'm taking it easily, slowly and reflectively. It will be good for me at last … I think I realise that now. Look, can you see the Tricolour fluttering from the roof of the Archive National? I haven't been here for thirty years, but seeing the French flag flying aloft has made me come over all patriotic suddenly. I haven't got a clue as to why that should be the case. I've not been resident in this country for three decades. Anyway, the red, white and blue pennant indicates that we're getting nearer to des Rosiers. Why aren't you using your umbrella?"

*"It's only spitting … and it's only water, after all. It can't hurt me. And isn't the street a gleaming reminiscence of the paintings of Paris in that local art gallery of yours?"*

"You know, I really don't need reminding."

*"I recall you said that we cross the road at this junction, and then turn right along Vieille de Témple. The road's clear, thank heaven. Here we go. Yes, check the street sign up there. Excellent, we're on course. What are you thinking now we haven't got that much further to walk?"*

"First that you should definitely be inflating your brolly ..."

"*And what do you think next?*"

"It's something I know rather than think. My heart is fluttering and my breathing is not quite as smooth as it should be ..."

"*You told me you felt alright. Shall we just retrace our steps, find some enchanting Belle Époque and lusciously mirrored restaurant to sink into for a long leisurely French lunch, and forget about all this?*"

"Never ... the *all this* is my raison d'être for being here, for returning to Paris. I appreciate that now. I told you I'm okay, and I am. The symptoms I mentioned are purely superficial, like your own thinking sometimes. Sorry, I didn't mean that. My heart's okay now. It has calmed down. And I hope it's in the right place. I expect it's only natural to experience a trace of hyperventilation ... and I remember those brown paper bags of long ago very well. Wouldn't you agree?"

"*Yes, I would agree. Might you prefer to rest for a while and just have a coffee before we go on? There are plenty of rather chic cafés to choose from around here?*"

"No, let's go on. Hey, look at those two young men across the street. Have you ever seen such bizarre hairstyles and clothes, assuming that's what they are?"

"*In fact, I have ... But so what, anyway? This is the post-modern Marais you understand.*"

"See that, they're not even French!"

"*Japanese, maybe ... and they're probably students, possibly at the Sorbonne. But why do you say they're not French? They could be, for all you know. Contradictions ...?*"

"We've now passed two streets on the left ... the next one will be Rue des Rosiers. It's quite a lengthy narrow street. The restaurant was about a third of the way down, standing on a corner at the right hand side as we'll be approaching it."

"*Okay, ignore my question. But we're almost at our objective and you still haven't told me properly how you're feeling ... emotionally, to make myself clearer.*"

"Emotionally ...? I'll tell you how I'm feeling emotionally. I should close my eyelids so that they can act as a dam, to prevent the deluge of tears that are building up behind them from cascading down my cheeks. But I'll not allow myself to enter Rosiers unseeingly ... unaware and without consciousness. I do have the strength of will, don't you think?"

"*I believe you do.*"

"My life hasn't been quite what I'd hoped for since I walked around the next corner into a world of Judaica shops, kosher bakeries, delis and restaurants some thirty years ago. You ask how I'm feeling emotionally. Maybe I was an overly sensitive individual. Perhaps someone else, with a different persona, might've carried on with life regardless and thankfully. But what happened, or didn't happen, to me ruined whatever chance I might've had for happiness in this life, in this world. How can you explain the inexplicable? What more can I say?"

"*You're right. There's nothing more to say. Shall we turn the corner now?*"

"Yes, I'm ready. So let's just do it."

"*Here we are then ... Rue des Rosiers. Ah, there's that kosher bakery over on the right. The rabbinical certificate displayed on the window confirms it. Do you want me to get a couple of their salmon baguettes?*"

"On reflection, and there is certainly an abundance of expanding rain puddles around here to reflect on, I don't think so. I really don't fancy sitting and munching away on a damp bench in the Place des Vosges right now. We'll eat later, if that's okay. I'd just like to slowly saunter along and look at …"

"*I've got no problem with that, provided you haven't.*"

"No problem … But I'm begging you to put up that umbrella now. You don't want to catch the flu on top of everything else, do you?"

"*You know I don't like umbrellas. Once they're up, you don't know what's transpiring in your vicinity.*"

"Don't be a paranoid Jew!"

"*And don't you speak so loudly! Look, that young woman queuing at the kosher falafel café across the street is staring at you …*"

"I would say she's an American Jew, and likely to be from the Big Apple. Maybe she fancies me … like that girl on the Métro."

"*If it makes you happy to say so … Okay, let's move a little further on.*"

"It's just a few more steps … to the restaurant, that is. It'll be visible soon …"

"*Don't worry. Be strong. I'm right here alongside you …*"

"Aaaah …!"

"*Aaaah …!*"

★ ★ ★

"I'm an American … I don't speak any French."

"That's not a problem, mademoiselle. I'm with the tourist police section. I do speak English. Did you observe what took place across the street a little while ago?"

"I sure did, officer."

"What was it you witnessed exactly?"

"Well, I was waiting here in line for some falafel to go. I just happened to notice on the sidewalk over there this old guy in a peculiar-looking hat holding a long, furled black umbrella. It was very strange. He appeared to be talking to himself, and real loud if you know what I mean. Maybe there was something wrong with him."

"He was talking to himself, mademoiselle?"

"Yes, officer ..."

"Did you hear what he was saying to himself?"

"No, I'm afraid not. He was just that little bit too far away to catch any words. I can see the paramedics over there now. You all arrived so quickly ... and in this monsoon downpour, too."

"Yes, we received an emergency call from a mobile phone a short time back, mademoiselle."

"Is the guy okay?"

"No, I regret that he's dead. But please continue with your account, mademoiselle."

"Oh, my God ... Well, all I can say is that there was this sudden and booming roar of thunder. I've never heard anything like it ... and I live in New York! It was the loudest, most intimidating crack of thunder I've ever heard ... and real frightening it was, too. We've got some atrocious weather sometimes back home ... but I've never experienced this kind of storm."

"And what happened next, mademoiselle?"

"I heard the old guy scream. He cried out only once, raised his hands to his chest then sort of crumpled to the sidewalk. It was dreadful, and like in slow motion. And that was it. I'm so sorry to hear that he died, that's just awful ... I didn't see any lightning, so he couldn't have been struck by an electric bolt. Do you know why the guy died?"

"We don't know for certain yet, mademoiselle. He would need to be thoroughly examined when he's taken away to the mortuary. It's possible he may've had a weak heart, and the shock of that abrupt and terrible clap of thunder that you've described to me caused him to have a fatal attack."

"What do they say, officer? Ya gotta go when ya gotta go! It's destiny."

"Perhaps, mademoiselle …"

# *Déjà vu*

"W-WE SHOULDN'T be here, Isaac."

"Why should we not be here, Hannah? And why are you looking around so furtively, like a thief in the market place? We're just two young Jews in love taking an afternoon promenade along the riverbank. What can be wrong with that?"

"You can be too confident, too stubborn and too radical sometimes, Isaac …"

"Am I anything else, Hannah?"

"You know I love you Isaac, despite …"

"And I love you too, Hannah."

"But you know very well why we shouldn't be here."

"So you tell me, my sweetheart."

"Very well, I shall remind you. There are two reasons. First, our respective parents would be very disappointed and dismayed, to say the least, that we're meeting together all alone like this …"

"But we're engaged to be married. We've been promised to each other ever since our childhoods, maybe from even before we were born. We were meant, if not made for each other. Why should our parents be so concerned ... we're not going to *do anything*, are we now?"

"I don't know what you're talking about. But don't you dare say anything like that again, Isaac. You should wash your mouth out in the water over there!"

"The water's too murky. Anyway, why are you getting so excited, Hannah?"

"It's because you know the rules, Isaac. We shouldn't ... no, we *can't* see each other like this now ... not until we've been under the chupah. You know that."

"But we *are* seeing each other *like this*, aren't we? It's a fait accomplis, Hannah."

"But I'm telling you we *mustn't*! You know full well how our families had lived their Torah-loving Jewish lives for centuries in France. Now we have had to make the best we can of it here, in another country ... But whatever is happening around us, though we know it's definitely not beneficial for the Jews, we must still strive our utmost to respect the rules, customs and traditions that have held our people together through both joyful and malevolent times. And also we must continue to abide by our beloved parents' wishes and requirements, as they were always obedient to their parents and so on down through the ages. The ancient rules, customs and traditions and our parents' wishes go hand-in-hand, Isaac. I don't know why I ever let you persuade me to come out here with you. If anyone we know sees us ..."

"That's extremely unlikely in this place, as you doubtless know. So ... what's the second reason Hannah, as if I didn't know it?"

"Your blind hubris could be our downfall Isaac, may the Almighty forbid it."

"I'm sorry, Hannah … truly I am. You're absolutely correct, of course. I shouldn't have asked you to come here with me. It is a little way from our homes, though not really too far … but I do know that being in this locale, although it's very beautiful, could be perilous. My dearest Hannah, my nice sweet partner for life to be, I wouldn't want anything to happen to you, to *us* … may the Almighty forgive me. You know, I'm not really thinking straight these days. How can anyone have a clear mind in the frustrating and unpredictable circumstances in which we have to exist? Sometimes I feel the walls bearing in on me … even c-crushing me … g-grounding my bones … and t-tugging me apart … l-like I want to pull those walls apart!"

"Isaac … *Isaac*! What's the matter, as if *I* didn't know?"

"It's just that I had to escape those dark and sombre narrow streets and menacing alleys for a while, to breath in deeply some fresh air for a change … here, on the open lush meadows beside the river and under a big blue sky. I want to gaze from between the weeping willows on the rippling sun-dappled water, flowing tranquilly to the world far beyond our reach. I needed to be here, Hannah … I thought you would understand … and I wanted you to be with me. I yearned to sense close by the warmth of your love for me. But I know that I'm being selfish, self-seeking and, yes … maybe even foolhardy. But I love you so much, Hannah. A-And I-I'm so sorry for putting you in the path of danger. I-I d-don't know what I would do if anything … if-if you weren't …"

"Don't aggravate yourself Isaac, my dearest one. And I do comprehend your feelings … I know that I'm just a young girl, but I really do follow what you're trying to tell me. Don't you think I harbour the same kind of emotions as you do? You must realise that your feelings aren't unique in our situation here. I'm sure that the members of our families, and our friends, are also burdened by these fearful and volatile times. You can see it every day ... in their dull baleful eyes, in their nervous manner of speaking to one another, in their joyless mode of eating and even in their way of moving, so hesitantly, so cautiously and with so much anxious trepidation ... just like hunted animals. You can almost smell, even taste the anxiety if not the terror beneath the surface, the distressing apprehension for what the future may bring hurtling down upon us. It pains me to witness these things, and that hurt adds itself to the icy ache I have in my own Jewish heart and soul. I often cry myself to sleep at night ... softly, quietly so as not to alarm my even more fragile younger sisters. And when I fall asleep, I dream ... every night I dream."

"Never stop dreaming, Hannah. You are indeed a sensitive and gentle poetess. Yes, you *are* very young ... and I'm not that much older. But you have a veritable clarity of thought, and an appealing way of expressing it that makes me envious of you."

"Please don't envy me, Isaac my love. In any case, the way you were talking about the walls informs me you can be just as lyrical, if that's what you think I am. I'm merely telling you about what I see all around me. But I believe we really have to thank our parents for the education we've been given. Our tutors have inspired us to use words wisely, meaningfully and genuinely. Words are so much abused today, and deliberately misused all the time ... especially when it comes to us Jews."

"Can I hold your hands in mine, Hannah ... I just want to

clasp your small tender hands, so that at least they will be warmed in the cold and unfeeling world that envelops us like an unfathomable fog. And it seems to be getting colder with every day that passes, even on a day like this when the warm sun is shining in the wide blue heavens."

"It's strange …"

"What is, Hannah?"

"What you just remarked. It's precisely what my father says …"

"Pardon me?"

"My father often reflects that the world is becoming nightmarishly colder every day. Like you, I think he means for the Jewish people of course."

"Yes, we know that. Incidentally, how's his business getting on these days? I've heard in the minyan the mumblings and grumblings of the community's elders. My own father is having real problems holding his trade together. It's a great worry to him and one that rests heavily on his shoulders."

"Business does seem to be going downhill, so far as I'm able to hear and grasp what's going on. From what I can gather, my father has lost many customers. And I'm sure you know that his partner Samuel was thrown into prison. My father asserts it was for a crime that he never committed … that it's what we Jews, as useful scapegoats, have to put up with these days. There appears little we can do about it. And as he continually laments, anti-Semitism is always with us, or rather *against* us … though on occasions he smiles, albeit sardonically. But I do know that, in truth, he's terrified for us. Sometimes, he adds, the age-old hatred can have a terrible outcome, as seems to be happening now. It's like an evil and merciless bird of prey that swoops down relentlessly on us from time to time … Doesn't the old castle look pretty from this distance?"

"I beg your pardon?"

"Look beyond the bridge to the castle on the hill, Isaac. See the battlements and their little turrets, and the pennants fluttering from the tall towers of the citadel. From here it has the appearance of a mysterious palace floating high on a green cloud …"

"You're very imaginative, Hannah! But I thought we were talking just now about the clawing talons of anti-Semitism … Anyhow, have you ever seen the castle up close? It's not quite as pretty a picture as it looks from this downstream viewpoint! Its huge stones are dour, forbidding, menacing … and dripping with damp moss."

"No, Isaac. I haven't ventured anywhere near the castle … even though, as you know, it's not far along the road from where we live. It's much too dangerous, we think. From a distance I've seen the dark-uniformed soldiers garrisoned there. And I'd really like to keep them that way … at a distance. Some people say that the troops are present to protect us from rampaging mobs, but I don't believe that for one tiny moment. And I'm told there are always troublemakers in the castle's vicinity, that's troublemakers for the Jews, naturally … and especially for Jews needing to cross the bridge. And it doesn't seem to matter whether you're a Jew or a Jewess. I've heard some terrible stories …"

"So have I, Hannah … really dreadful incidents."

"And it doesn't help that we Jews stand out like sore thumbs, because of what we look like … and wearing this standard mark, this symbol we're compelled by law to display in public, stitched onto our outer apparel to identify us as Jews. Why do they discriminate against us, persecute us, oppress us,

terrify and kill us, Isaac? I constantly ask myself the question …
as I suppose every Jew does. I don't understand the rationale for
such hate … and that's because it's without reason!"

"It's in their blood now, Hannah … handed down from
generation to generation. It's effortless for them to tell lies and
concoct terrible, extravagant tales about us, our faith and our
religious practices. How could any human being believe the vile
and wicked falsehood that we bake the unleavened bread for
our Passover observance with the blood of Christian boys?
We're just a vulnerable and handy minority to scapegoat for the
trials and tribulations of their world, and they're not ills of our
making. And that anti-Semitic tyrant takes advantage of all this
to stir up the people against us … not that they need much
rousing to further the miscreant's nefarious objectives. We must
continue to have hope and faith in the Almighty, Hannah …
and the coming of Moshiach, speedily in our days. But there's
one thing that we must *not* do. And that's to allow the actual
wearing on our garments of this symbol, even though in
appearance it represents the fundamental basis of our national
identity, to characterise and delineate us. We shouldn't permit
our prosecutors and persecutors to dictate our distinctiveness as
a people by means of a mere visible sign. But rather we should
preserve and sustain our identity by virtue only of our belief in
the Almighty. That's *our* rationale … for *our* survival."

"Well said, my dearest Isaac. If I'm a poetess, then you're an
orator. I do love you so much."

"You know what I would really like to do now, Hannah?"

"No, what …?

"I would very much like to hold you close and kiss your
pure sweet lips."

"What are you saying, Isaac? It's forbidden! My lips must remain pure … I-I shouldn't even be out here with you."

"I know, Hannah. I'm sorry … again. It's just that …"

"Our beloved parents will decide when it's the right time for our nuptials and wedding feast. It may not be that long to wait … we must be patient, Isaac."

"I know. I know. If only things could be different, and by that I mean *every thing*!"

"What are you saying …? What was that, Isaac?"

"What was what?"

"That noise …"

"I never heard anything, Hannah."

"It sounded like something hitting the water over there. Look, do you see that little water spout in the river? And there's another … and another! What is it? I-I'm scared, Isaac."

"See! See! … It's those youths on the other side of the river. They're hurling stones, and the little rocks are getting closer. I've no doubt that they're aimed at us! Can you hear the louts shouting abuse? They know we're Jews. They're screaming at us, and calling us those offensive names. We'd better run … and right now, Hannah! Look, the foul-mouthed boors are racing towards the bridge. If they cross the river and catch us, we've had it. Come, we've got to get out of here. Hurry my love, hurry …"

"Ouch! Ouch! Don't pull my arm like that, Isaac. It will pop out of its socket!"

"Never mind about that, Hannah … I'd rather you lost your arm than your life. We can't hang around else we'll finish up as minced mutton!"

"Oh, oh … I'm afraid I can't go any faster, Isaac! The riverbank's too slippery wet from yesterday's rainstorm."

"You've just got to try harder, Hannah … I can see those yobs have made it to the bridge."

"I'm sorry, Isaac. I really don't know if I can run any further … you know I've got this little breathing problem when I exert myself too much …"

"Let me carry you across the meadow, Hannah."

"No, Isaac! You know that's impossible …"

"But what if it would be necessary to save your life? Oh never mind, it's not that far now to the edge of the wood …"

"Thank the Almighty! I'm exhausted …"

"Come … only a few more yards, Hannah. We can conceal ourselves amongst the trees. You can rest for a short while, and catch your breath. Then it's got to be quickly through to the other end of the forest and on to the edge of town … No, we need to move forward quickly *now*! I can't make out our pursuers on the bridge. That must mean they're on this side of the river …"

"Oh no, Isaac …"

"I'm really so sorry, Hannah. All this is my fault and mine alone. I'm stupid and unthinking, my own worst foe! But please don't worry. I'll make sure you get back safely."

"I do hope so. I'm panting like a dog … and my arm's killing me, even if our enemies aren't … yet!"

"When we get you home, I'll bring my uncle the doctor to look at your arm and give you some ointment for the soreness. I'm desolate, Hannah. But I have to drag you to some cover, so that we can hide ourselves from the sight of those hateful brutes …"

"Oh thank heaven, Isaac … we've reached the tree-line. I didn't think I could make it in time. I've just got to sit on the ground and take a rest."

"Not yet, Hannah … Let's go a bit deeper into the wood, then we'll find a large tree behind which we can seek to make ourselves invisible …"

"And against which I can have some respite for a while, yes?"

"Yes … but not for too long, Hannah. We would need to get moving again very soon, you understand what I'm saying?"

"Yes I understand you well enough, Isaac …"

"Here, this seems like a suitable spot. Let's disappear into the undergrowth behind that sturdy old oak over there, and scatter some of the leaves and stuff from the forest floor over our clothes. That's right, Hannah. Keep as low down as possible. And scoop up as much of the leafy and twiggy bits and pieces as you can. Cover yourself like this … yes, that's very good. We've got to be properly camouflaged, so that we look as greenish and brownish as our woody surroundings."

"I–I'm very frightened, Isaac … about what they might do to me if we're trapped here."

"Don't concern yourself, Hannah. I'll protect you …"

"How many of them are chasing us?"

"Three, I think."

"And you believe you can protect me, Isaac?"

"I'll safeguard you with my life, Hannah. I'll never let them harm you in any way. I'm strong … they would have a real combat on their hands. Believe me, they're cowards if you fight back …"

"Let's hope they don't discover us. But I think that I'd better start praying to the Almighty for our salvation."

"Quiet now, Hannah. I think I can hear something or rather someone approaching …"

"*Where are those Jews?*"

"*I can't see the Jews anywhere. Can anyone see the Jews?*"

"*The Jews have vanished into thin air. Trust the Jews.*"

"*No, but did you see the Jew boy pulling his bit of Jew skirt?*"

"*Ha, ha … that's a good one! The she Jew couldn't run so fast.*"

"*The little Jew girl looked good. Pity we didn't catch the Jews. We could've had some Jew sport.*"

"*The little Jew girl looked good? Idiot! What* are *you talking about?*"

"*Come on … let's go and drink a huge amount of beer at the inn.*"

"*We're with* you, *mate!*"

"H-Have they gone now, Isaac?"

"Yes, Hannah. But you're right to be whispering. We were fortunate, I suppose."

"I-It wasn't luck. T-The Almighty saved us, you know that."

"Well, I …"

"I-I was terrified … L-Look, I-I can't stop myself from trembling … all the leafy stuff is falling off me. I-I look like the personification of autumn …"

"Didn't I say you were a poetess? Do you want me to hold you?"

"Can you take me home now please, Isaac … *please?*"

"Not yet, Hannah …"

"Why not, if those boys have run off? And why did you say that I'm right to be whispering? You're scaring me …"

"I think we should be cautious and remain here, just for a

brief time longer. You never know. The louts could've been pretending about racing away to get themselves inebriated. They might be lying in wait a little way off, watching for any tell-tale movement … just to see whether we're still around and if we are, as we are, hoping we'll break cover and reveal ourselves."

"You're petrifying me to death now, Isaac."

"Please don't be frightened, Hannah. It's only a precaution. I'm sure we'll be safe now. When we're ready to leave, I think we'll make a detour and hasten home by a slightly different route."

"You're still chilling me. Not that you need to … I think I'm more anxious about being away from home for so long. I don't know what my parents would say if they knew about this … yes, I do know. And it could definitely affect us. I'll need to think up something plausible to say, if necessary … without actually telling an outright lie. I-I'd never do that. I-It's not right. N-No, wait … I-I can't think of anything I'm able to say. I-I'm getting quite upset about it all …"

"I'm truly regretful that I'm the author of this afternoon's stupidity. Please forgive me, Hannah. I wouldn't want your father to withdraw his consent to … I don't know what I would do. I don't know what to think or to say anymore …"

"You don't have to *say* anything. I'm equally to blame for us being in this plight. You didn't force me to accompany you to the river. But you have to *do* something, Isaac."

"What's that?"

"Get me home, please … and quickly. Oh, no! W-What was that rustling sound?"

"Ha, ha, look over there … it's only a squirrel."

"Thank the Almighty. I'm feeling so jittery …"

"We'll go very soon. I promise you, Hannah. You know what … I sometimes go to the cemetery."

"You do what?"

"I walk to the cemetery, occasionally at night … and I sit there amongst the gravestones."

"You shouldn't go to a cemetery, not so long as your parents are still alive anyway. You know our customs well enough."

"No one knows that I go there. If my father and mother don't know, they can't be offended."

"I really don't understand what you and the world are coming to …"

"But Hannah, it's so quiet and peaceful there. It's curious really. That's how life should be … filled with quietude and peace. But its death that enjoys these things I crave … for me, for us, for every Jew. You know the Jewish people traditionally refer to a cemetery as a *Beis Chayim*, a House of Life. It's all so … so mystical and so confusing."

"What do you do there, Isaac?"

"I just sit there in calm solitude and serenity, away from everything that causes me heartache."

"My dearest, that's so sorrowful and melancholy. You're far too young to have to suffer any heartache … But what about me?"

"What do you mean, Hannah?"

"Do I cause you heartache too, Isaac?"

"Never … at least not in the sense I was speaking of just before."

"In what sense then do I cause you heartache?"

"I think you're fishing for some compliments now, Hannah."

"I suppose …"

"You're smiling, Hannah … May you always have reasons to smile."

"From your mouth to His ears …"

"Come my sweetheart, I think it's time for us to go now."

"Thank the Almighty"

"You know what, Hannah?"

"What?"

"I like it when you smile. It's a lovely winsome smile."

"You smiled when you saw the squirrel. You have a lovely winsome smile, too."

"Let's hope that we can smile winsomely together through all eternity."

"That's a really long time, Isaac. And it involves another place far away. Right now we're here in England, and it's only the year 1285 …"

*Note: The symbol, mark or sign referred to in this story is not the* Star of David, *generally yellow in colour, which Jewish people (for identification purposes) were forced by the Nazis to wear in public; but it is the so-called* Tabula, *which was a representation of the tablets of the Ten Commandments and which Jews in medieval England were compelled by the authorities to stitch prominently onto their outer garments.*

## Stand-up

"GOOD EVENING, ladies and gentlemen … and many thanks for inviting me to entertain you at this wonderful Melava Malka. My name's Clint. Yeah, I know … it doesn't sound very Jewish, does it? It's just that my parents loved that *Rawhide* series with Clint Eastwood on the old telly."

*Ha-ha-ha …*

"You've got a really magnificent hall here at the synagogue. I was absolutely gob-smacked but delighted when the rabbi called me up to ask if I could do this gig tonight. You know the last time I was called up by a rabbi was at my barmitzvah …"

*Ha-ha-ha …*

"… and that was twenty years ago! It's entirely my own fault that I don't come to shul with the family that often. I think the minister at my barmitzvah fairly quickly twigged my lack of enthusiasm for religion. After he'd made his address from the pulpit, instead of presenting me with the usual inscribed Siddur he handed over an umbrella. Yeah, I was just as puzzled as you look right now. That's until the rabbi said to me: 'At least this is something you're likely to open, Clint.'"

*Ha-ha-ha ...*

"Okay, so I won't be allowed into Heaven. But I'll definitely be happy with the next best thing ... yeah, my wife Angie's chicken soup with kneidlach!"

*Ha-ha-ha ...*

I have to say that I'm unconcerned about not going to Heaven ... really. Look, I've never been to the South Pole. So what? It's not the end of the world!"

*Ha-ha-ha ...*

"As it happens, I've travelled quite extensively. I actually met Angie in a travel agency. Yeah ... she was the last resort! No, I shouldn't make jokes at my wife's expense. Mind you, who else would've paid for the petrol to get me here this evening?"

*Ha-ha-ha ...*

"Actually my wife's a very beautiful person, inside and out. She's very good-natured and really trim. Does she work out? Of course she does. She works out of the office most days. How much do you think I get for these performances?"

*Ha-ha-ha ...*

"Unfortunately, she couldn't be here tonight. Our younger son's not very well. He's got rabies ... What did I say? I'm an idiot! I mean rabbits ..."

*Ha-ha-ha ...*

"No, it's not a laughing matter. He's passionate about the bunny pets, which incidentally brings to mind some of my passions before I got married ..."

*Ha-ha-ha ...*

"I should say our boy has only got a bad cold. But we have

to look after our children. One day, they're going to be selecting our care home for us."

*Ha-ha-ha ...*

Now what was I saying about my wife? Ah yes, she's a great gal with a really neat figure. I wish I could say the same thing about myself ... no, not that I'm a great gal!"

*Ha-ha-ha ...*

"In fact, I'm on a seafood diet ... yeah, whenever I see food I've just got to eat it!"

*Ha-ha-ha ...*

"Everyone seems to be on a diet these days. My brother's wife eats only coconuts, mangoes, dates and bananas. I don't think it's doing much for her looks, though. But boy, can she climb a tree!"

*Ha-ha-ha ...*

"What can you say these days? Look ... if a pizza can get to your home quicker than an ambulance, what can you do?"

*Ha-ha-ha ...*

"I love pizza, but I've got to watch the weight. I ordered a thin-base Romano in an Italian restaurant last week. The waiter asked whether I wanted it cut into six or twelve slices. I told him, you'd better make it six ... I don't think I should eat twelve!"

*Ha-ha-ha ...*

"And there are loads of calories in alcohol. I know that most Jewish people of a certain age would get dizzy after just a single cherry brandy. Unlike them, I can really hold my liquor. But I can honestly state that I don't drink any more. Mind you, I don't drink any less ..."

*Ha-ha-ha ...*

"I accept that I should reduce my whisky intake, I really do. You know, I was in this bar at a swanky West End hotel the other evening. And I asked the barman to give me a treble Scotch. 'I shouldn't be doing this,' I said as the guy was pouring my order from a bottle. 'Why?' he asked, and I said: 'Well, I've only got fifty pence and no plastic on me!'"

*Ha-ha-ha …*

"So tell me, what did you have to eat here tonight? What? Chopped liver, salt beef and tongue? A vegetarian's nightmare … but who cares? I don't. I'm a carnivore, like you lot. I didn't evolve my way through millions of years to the top of the food chain to become a vegetarian, I can tell you!"

*Ha-ha-ha …*

"I seem to be talking a lot about food. But then it's a traditional Jewish thing, isn't it? Eating, I mean … and let's face it, Jewish food, bless it, as I should but never do, isn't that healthy. You've really got to admit it. And obesity looks like it's going to be the curse of the twenty-first century. But my wife's a great cook … exquisitely fine. You should taste her cholent and chips …"

*Ha-ha-ha …*

"And Angie loves cooking with wine. Sometimes she even puts it in the food!"

*Ha-ha-ha …*

"And I have to confess … I like my grub. Well you can't miss me, can you? You know, I was in a pub with my friend Dave last weekend. After we'd downed a couple of beers, he said to me: 'Your round … I looked daggers at him and commented, I believe justifiably, 'Well so are you, you fat lump!'"

*Ha-ha-ha …*

"Maybe the Jews' love affair with food is a kind of

psychological safety valve that makes us forget about, or at least sublimate, the whole anti-Semitism thing. I realise this isn't the occasion for a serious discussion. So let's just say it's unlikely we'll be starving ourselves to death for a while yet, eh?"

*Ha-ha-ha* …

"You see, we even have the capacity to laugh off our own misfortunes. Anyway, on a lighter topic … Angie and I have just got back from the Caribbean. I love cruising … What? Excuse me for pointing. But that guy, third table on the left … go wash your mouth out!"

*Ha-ha-ha* …

"I'm talking about sailing the ocean blue … in a cruise liner. And we've sailed on some wonderful ships … Who just shouted out, '*including the Bounty*'? Get out of here!"

*Ha-ha-ha* …

"I know that cruising isn't everyone's cup of tea … being incarcerated for two weeks on a mammoth hulk alongside five thousand other passengers and one thousand crew. But the food's fantastic. That's why many thousands of Jewish people adore cruise ships. You can eat 24/7 … until you get giddy and fall overboard, and that's even without a single cherry brandy!

*Ha-ha-ha* …

"Coincidentally, a friend of ours won first prize in a prestigious charity raffle last month … it was a week's cruise around the Mediterranean. The second prize was a two-week cruise in the Med!"

*Ha-ha-ha* …

"I know some people can't swim and are really scared of boats and the sea. I say, just hang loose. The chances of a cruise ship sinking are remote. Look, the hundreds of fat people onboard make the vessel really buoyant! It's never going to sink, is it? Though I'll never forget what that passenger supposedly remarked to a barman on the Titanic after it had hit the berg … 'I know I ordered ice,' he said, 'but this is ridiculous!'"

*Ha-ha-ha* …

"I try not to sail with any over-confident, big-headed captain. That'll be a skipper with a large cap size … Capsize? Okay, I'll try to make them easier."

*Ha-ha-ha* …

"What I'm saying, I guess, is that you should always expect the unexpected. I'll give you an example. Last Chanucah, I asked my wife what she would like as a present. Every year it gets harder to get her a gift, or to do something different for her. 'Surprise me,' she said once again. So this time I phoned her from Tenerife …"

*Ha-ha-ha* …

"No, I'm joking of course. I actually got a diamond eternity ring for Angie. Not a bad swap, really …"

*Ha-ha-ha*

"Sometimes, I do actually go abroad by myself. I generally stay in business class hotels … nothing too fancy. But one time recently I had to go a bit downmarket. I was checking in at this one-star budget hotel's tiny desk. The receptionist handed over the key and asked me, 'Do you have a good memory for faces?' I was really puzzled by the question. 'Why?' I enquired. 'Well,' she said, 'I'm afraid there isn't a mirror in your bathroom'."

*Ha-ha-ha* …

"And the hotel's room service was dreadful. You know, I phoned down for a hot chocolate, and you know what they sent up? ... a chipped white mug, a bar of Cadbury's and a book of matches!"

*Ha-ha-ha ...*

"But we love holidaying in Israel. I can't wait to hear the airplane's captain announce, 'We'll be landing at Ben Gurion in ten minutes ... but to you, five minutes.'"

*Ha-ha-ha ...*

"I know what you're thinking. Why did he ever decide to become a stand-up comedian ... if such he is? Well, to tell you the truth, this wasn't a career that I'd planned originally. My parents were eager for me to enter one of the professions. Dad wanted me to become a lawyer, and Mum would've liked me to work as a chartered accountant. My bubbeh asked why I couldn't be a chiropodist ... I wonder why ... Ugh!"

*Ha-ha-ha ...*

"I'll have you know that I did go up to university. I read Philosophy. Actually, I came out with a 2.2 ... And no, I wasn't intending to be a gay transsexual ballet dancer!"

*Ha-ha-ha ...*

"My first job was as a quality controller in a battery factory. Not really a job for a Jewish boy. But I did use to sit by the assembly line whispering, 'I wish you long life ... I wish you long life ...'"

*Ha-ha-ha ...*

"After being dismissed for gross misconduct, I managed to find work in an equine hospital near Newmarket. I used to answer queries on the phone about the sick horses. It was easy really. Generally, all I needed to say was, 'It's in a stable condition.'"

*Ha-ha-ha ...*

"Someone then suggested I should do the Knowledge and

be a taxi driver. They said a philosophy degree was a perfect qualification. I don't know about that, but I'm aware that lots of Jewish guys are in the trade. I couldn't be a cabbie, though … I really can't stand people talking behind my back!"

*Ha-ha-ha …*

"Then I took up photography professionally. You know the kind of thing, wedding and barmitzvah DVDs. I used to sing to the bride, *Someday your prints will come*!"

*Ha-ha-ha …*

"Incidentally, I used to do photography at the Jewish youth club I attended as a lad. But I was always being naughty in the classes. The instructor often used to hit me round the head with a camera … I still get flashbacks!"

*Ha-ha-ha …*

"Then at a mate's stag night in a comedy club, I stood up and told a few select jokes. I haven't looked back since … I daren't!"

*Ha-ha-ha …*

"No, actually it's all going very well … lots of bookings around the London area. And you know what? My wife is my number one fan. Yeah, she is … Whilst I'm performing on stage, she's doing rapid, on-the-spot cartwheels in the wings … it creates a fantastic breeze. Angie keeps me really cool in a hot theatre!"

*Ha-ha-ha …*

"And my Mum believes I'm mustard, too. I'm not sure about Dad. I don't feel he has a very high opinion of laughter-makers … In fact, he thinks that anyone who's been to university is soft, yellow and wet … so looking on the bright side, same view as my Mum then."

*Ha-ha-ha ...*

"My wife, bless her, really wants me to make something of myself. I'm well lousy at DIY, so it couldn't be a bookcase, a sideboard or anything like that. So I thought, what about a barrel of laughs? But I'm no Tommy Cooper ... Geddit? ... Cooper? ... A barrel ... of laughs ...? Oh please yourself, I'm getting paid whatever happens here tonight ..."

*Ha-ha-ha ...*

"Personally, I consider my material's fairly good. In fact, my agent Harry has just booked me in provisionally for an entire summer season on the south coast. He says it all depends on my initial performance at the pier theatre. I think he's reasonably confident about my ability, if not talent for sharp and biting humour ... Well he did tell me that after the first night, and if I offended enough of the audience, I'd probably have a long run ..."

*Ha-ha-ha ...*

"I suppose if it doesn't work out for me, I could always join the army. I wanted to be a soldier when I was a kid ... ever since my skinflint Uncle Morris surprisingly bought me an Action Man as a Chanucah gift. Well, I say that ... but when I opened the box, there was nothing inside it. When I asked my uncle where Action Man was, he said the soldier had deserted ..."

*Ha-ha-ha ...*

"Well it's been really lovely being here with you. You've been a great audience. Enjoy the rest of the evening ..."

\* \* \*

"So Angie darling, as my audience of one what do you think of my trial run as a stand-up in this our through-lounge, dining room doubling as a synagogue hall?"

"I'm trying *not* to think about it, Gavin … or should I say, Clint?"

"But you were laughing, honey …"

"I'd hardly call it laughing … anyway, it was only in pity. And I'm not very keen on wife jokes …"

"So you don't believe I could make it as a stand-up comic then, Angie?"

"I believe that to be about right, Gavin. So I wouldn't give up your day job quite yet."

"Did you think *any* of the jokes were good?"

"Gavin, I have to tell you honey … the jokes weren't good full stop. But perhaps it's just my imagination!"

# Glossary

Barmitzvah *A Jewish boy's coming of age on reaching thirteen*
Batmitzvah *A Jewish girl's coming of age on reaching twelve*
Beis Chayim *Literally, House of Life; a Jewish cemetery*
Bubbeh *Grandmother*

Challah *Plaited loaf of bread eaten on the Jewish Sabbath and festivals*
Chanucah *Jewish festival of lights celebrating an ancient miracle at the
    Temple in Jerusalem*
Charedi *Ultra-Orthodox Jews*
Cholent *Jewish stew originating in Eastern Europe, eaten on
    Shabbos/Shabbat*
Chumash *Volume containing the Five Books of Moses*
Chupah *Canopy under which a marriage ceremony is conducted,
    generally in a synagogue; the actual marriage ceremony itself*

Davening *Praying*
Drosha *Sermon*

Dybbuk *In Jewish folklore, a devilish spirit capable of occupying a human body*

Frum *Very Orthodox (Jew)*

Gelt *Money*

Gezunt *Health*

Golem *In Jewish legend, a figure made from clay and given life by magic means*

Haggadah *Book relating the story of the Children of Israel's Exodus from Egypt*

Halachah *The body of Jewish laws*

Haman *A wicked character in Megillah Esther, which relates the story of Purim*

Hamantaschen *A tri-cornered cake representing Haman's hat*

Hashem *Almighty*

High Holydays *Rosh Hashanah and Yom Kippur*

Kashrut *Jewish dietary laws that prescribe whether particular food or drink is Kosher*

Kiddush *Blessing recited over wine and challah on the Jewish Sabbath and festivals*

Kneidlach *Matzah balls served in chicken soup, often alongside lokshen*

Kosher *Food and drink that can be consumed under Kashrut*

Krenker *Literally, a person who is ill; an individual who complains or moans continually about personal ailments*

Kugel *Savoury pudding, served hot and usually made with potatoes or possibly other vegetables*

Lokshen *Thin noodles, usually served in chicken soup*

Leyning *Reading aloud from the Torah (scroll), generally but not necessarily by a rabbi*

Ma'ariv *Evening service*

Mazel *Luck*

Megillah *A scroll relating to one of five ancient Jewish stories*

Melava Malka *Literally, saying farewell to the Shabbos/Shabbat "Queen"; a communal celebration, usually held annually with a meal and entertainment*

Minchah *Afternoon service*

Minyan *The quorum of ten Jewish men required for prayer*

Moshiach *Messiah*

Mutti *Mummy*

Niddah *Deceased*

Noch *Also*

Pesach/Passover *Jewish festival commemorating the Children of Israel's Exodus from Egypt*

Pikuach Nefesh *Rule whereby the safeguarding or preservation of human life may be implemented in circumstances that would otherwise contravene Halachah, including the laws relating to Shabbos/Shabbat*

Purim *Jewish festival celebrating the rescue of the Jews in ancient Persia*

Rabbi *Jewish religious leader and teacher*

Rosh Hashanah *Jewish New Year*

Rosh Yeshivah *The head of an advanced religion college for Jewish men*

Schmoozing *Chit-chatting and gossiping*

Seder *Literally, order; the traditional Pesach service, generally held in the home*

Semichah *The qualification required to become a rabbi*

Shabbos/Shabbat *Jewish Sabbath*

Shacharis *Morning service*

Shema *Prayer acknowledging the sovereignty and Oneness of the Almighty*

Shiva *The period of mourning for a deceased close relative*

Shul *Synagogue*

Siddur *Jewish daily prayer book*

Sifrei Torah *Two or more Torah scrolls*

Simcha *Joyous celebration, such as a wedding, barmitzvah or batmizvah*

Shteibl *Small shul*

Synagogue *Building or part of a building used specifically for Jewish worship*

Tephilin *Small black boxes containing a Jewish prayer, and which are strapped onto the forehead and around the left arm*

Torah *Five Books of Moses (scroll): Genesis, Exodus, Leviticus, Numbers and Deuteronomy*

Treif *Non-Kosher food*

Yahrzeit *Literally, time of year; anniversary of the death of a close relative*

Yiddish *A language (basically German with words added mainly from Hebrew) originated by Central and East European Jews*

Yom Kippur *Day of Atonement, the holiest day of the Jewish calendar*

Yeshivah *An advanced religion college for Jewish men*

Yeshivah bocha *Student at a yeshivah*

*Praise for The Shtetl and other Jewish stories*

"Humorous, sad, thought-provoking and relevant to each of us and our life-style today ... I enjoyed this book more than I could ever have thought possible."

Reggie Ross, *Belfast Jewish Recorder*

"Mark Harris follows brilliantly in the tradition of a writer with a gift for descriptive narrative and the ability to paint his characters so accurately that you can see them in your mind's eye... The author senses he is building a pipeline for the thoughts and emotions of the characters that walk through the pages. And he does it with style and feeling."

Manny Robinson, *Essex Jewish News*

*Praise for The Chorister and other Jewish stories*

"Mark Harris' style makes for easy reading and comprehension. He paints the background to each story with a delicate, gentle and at times humorous touch. The subjects of his stories are seldom light-hearted, dealing with sensitive issues ... but they are all worth reading."

D L Coppel, *BJR*

"The author meticulously outlines the theme of love, an emotion that weaves like a piece of tapestry through the pages ... In many of the stories there is a twist in the tale. And that, perhaps, is Mark Harris' greatest strength ... having the ability to describe a seemingly everyday scenario and make the reader sit up at the surprise ending."

M Robinson, *EJN*